131818

PR
6005
A486
S28
1980

Canning

The Satan sampler

DATE DUE		
DEC 3 '80		
MAY 10 '82		
WITHDRAWN		

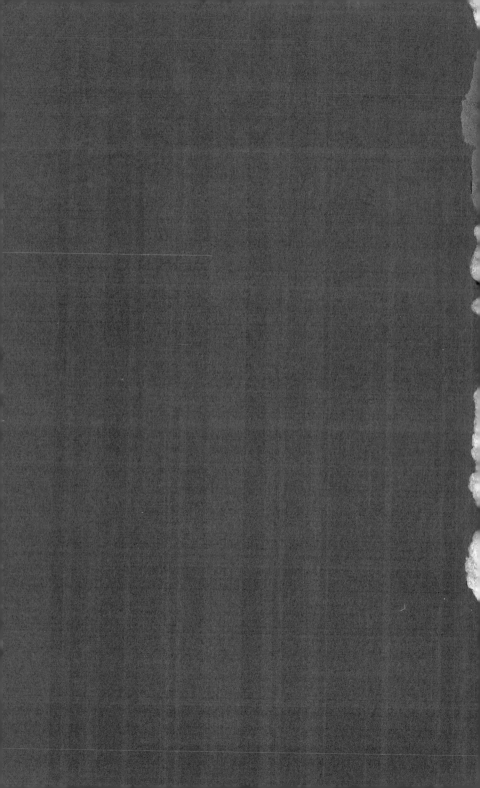

The Satan Sampler

The Satan Sampler

VICTOR CANNING

WILLIAM MORROW AND COMPANY, INC.
New York *1980*

Library of Congress Cataloging in Publication Data

Canning, Victor.
  The Satan sampler.

  I. Title.
PZ3.C1636 Sat 1980   [PR6005.A486]   823'.912   79-27310
  ISBN 0-688-03612-0

Printed in the United States of America

First U.S. Edition

1 2 3 4 5 6 7 8 9 10

CHAPTER ONE

RICHARD SEYTON CAME out of Customs and looked along the top hall to the spot where Manard, his chauffeur, always waited for him. There was no sign of Manard and he frowned, more from surprise than irritation, at the breakdown of a familiar routine. For a moment or two he contemplated calling his office, then rejected the idea and decided to go outside and get a cab.

From thirty yards away, shielded by the moving crowd, Kerslake watched him. He had never seen him before except in photographs—and that only very recently—but there was no mistaking the man; tall, slim-built with broad shoulders, dark-haired, sun-tanned, self-contained, expensive light-weight suit, hatless and a well-worn leather brief-case in one hand, severe good looks, and still a few years to run before he hit forty. Fairly easy-going, he guessed, unless you pushed him unwarrantably. Only a guess, though, this last. But in his, Kerslake's, world guessing was a fine art in which he did not often indulge. From himself the Department wanted only facts. The guessing, if there had to be any, was done at a higher level.

Ignorant of the fact that he was being watched, Seyton was about to turn away to go out and find himself a cab when someone touched his right elbow from behind and said, "Hullo, Richard."

He turned, recognizing the voice, and smiled.

"Nancy. Now I get it. What have you done with Manard?"

"Nice, warm loving greeting. Just what I expected."

He grinned, then brushed her cheek with his lips, and said, "Nancy, I am pleased to see you. You're looking marvellous."

"That's better. And to answer you—I phoned your office and said that you'd called me from New York and said that Manard needn't meet you—I was doing that."

"How did you know that I was in New York?"

"You had dinner there with Max Beaton. He phoned me and told me your Concorde flight."

"And why would he do that?"

She shook her head in brief exasperation and taking his arm began to lead him away. He caught the breath of a scent new to him and the pressure of her hand on his arm waked briefly a stir in his nerves which surprised him as she said solemnly, "Because of Punch and your not being able to be here for the funeral—and generally the whole rotten business. Oh, Richard . . . I'm so sorry about it all. Not making a big thing of it. You know that. Or capital—you know that, too. We know where we stand. But I thought . . . well, that it might be the time for a little mild cherishing."

He put his hand on hers. From her he had always had and welcomed cherishing. Neither of them had ever called it love openly—maybe it was not. "I'm glad you came. Punch would have approved. Oh, it's all right. I'm long over the bad part— and the muck-up which stopped me from coming for the funeral. Now—what do you propose to do with me? You've something in mind I'm sure."

"Oh, just the usual coddling and fussing. No arguments. You're not going to your hotel suite. Until tomorrow morning you're in my hands. Have you much luggage? I've only got the Mini Clubman."

"No luggage. Just this." He indicated the brief-case. "All my London stuff is at the hotel."

"Not all. I got your office to pack a case for you and bring it round to my place. Miss Figgins was short about it—so I got short with her. A battle of the Amazons. I can't think why you keep the woman."

"Because she's efficient and has a heart of gold. I'd be lost without her."

"There's no woman you'd be lost without—or if there is she's

2

a long time turning up. And when she does I'll retire to a nunnery. What are you going to do about the Hall?"

He said casually, "I'll work something out. I'm seeing Bellamy tomorrow. But that's tomorrow and can wait until then."

They were outside now and, as he took her arm and they began to work their ways through the crowd and the traffic to the car park, she was undeceived. By now he would have long known what he was going to do. Punch, his elder brother, was over three weeks dead. He would by now have it all settled in his mind. Quick and solid decisions had put him where he was. She knew the Seyton feeling about the Hall. He would know and have already accepted that his brother's death, so unexpected, demanded one thing only from him. But, whatever he had decided, she knew that there would be no place for her . . . no real, permanent place. She was just Nancy. Nancy Hope. Always around. Always hopeful. Always would be.

*　　*　　*　　*

Kerslake called Quint from an outside Heathrow telephone booth. He had no idea of the reasons for the interest in Richard Seyton. That was far from unusual. Sometimes you could spend months marking a man so that you knew things about him that not even his wife or girl friend suspected—and still have no idea why *they* at Birdcage Walk were interested. Odd, too. Just give it time and more often than not you ended up with some intangible bond between you. Give it enough time and it would happen with this one as with others. This was the first time he had seen him in the flesh and some things stood out at once. Just as an experienced trainer could run his eye over a new horse and read more than would ever be apparent to the uninitiated, so he, too, was adroit at assessing human blood stock. Seyton had breeding, arrogance, and charm when he chose to display it. Watching from a distance as he had met Nancy Hope all these had manifested themselves like cloud shadow and sunlight over his face. Curiosity about Quint's interest he kept submerged. It was not his business unless and until Quint made it so.

At the other end of the line Quint said in a near asthmatic voice, "Well, young Kerslake?"

He said, "He travelled hatless, coatless and carrying a well-stuffed tan brief-case—old-fashioned sort. He was met—to his surprise, I think—by a tallish, very good looking blonde, early thirties. Old flame. No guess, it's on file. Embers still hot though. There's a photo of her on page three of the file. Nancy Hope. They drove off in a Mini Clubman. Hers. Registration number on file."

Following a little rasping cough, Quint said, "Embers still hot? How do you know?"

"Something in their manner."

"Stick to facts. When I want your intuitions I'll ask for them."

"Yes, sir." He heard Quint chuckle at the other end of the line. Now that he had been baptized and had proved Quint's unholy faith and confidence in him he had slowly been granted occasional liberties. One dark, proving act had given him, too, the right of an occasional mild levity. He added, "But I'd bet on it. She lives in Cadogan Place. Do you want me to check there?"

"No. I don't care where or with whom he sleeps. Your time's your own until tomorrow morning."

"Thank you, sir."

In a front office overlooking Birdcage Walk and St James's Park—to which he had only recently been moved from dingier and darker quarters in the rear of the building—Quint turned to page three of the Her Majesty's Stationery Office file and studied the photograph, head and shoulders, in colour, of Miss Nancy Hope, the youngest daughter of Captain Phillip Hope, Royal Navy—retired—of Fardsley in the County of Worcester and Herefordshire. Good looking woman. High cheek bones. Blue eyes. No vapid looking blue-eyed blonde. Unmarried. Why? Why not? Plenty of time. At a guess—bad habit—her sights had probably long been set on Richard Seyton who was still shy of going into the starting stall.

4

He closed the file and made a wry mouth as he looked at the cover which was plain except for the name—Richard Seyton. No official index number. Well, a lot started like that but only a few stayed like it for good. He lit a cigarette and coughed gently as he played a tattoo on the file cover. Tall, dark hair greying, worn, he was suddenly conscious of feeling far more than his forty and few years. Something about this he did not like. Funny how you got the feeling. He sat brooding. Outside it started to rain. A pigeon flew on to the window sill, ruffled itself to free its plumage of rain, and then methodically began to preen in its meagre shelter. Uncharacteristically, out of his present mood, Quint picked up a paper clip and flicked it at the window. The pigeon turned and stared at him like an offended duchess over its heavy grey-white wattles. From a sudden irritation which had nothing to do with the bird Quint waved his arm at it crossly and watched it move out over the park and its lake and then through the fine rain squalls turn south and disappear from view towards the river and the Houses of Parliament. If there was one thing he did not like it was undocketed files. And neither did Warboys, his immediate superior.

He picked up the telephone and rang Warboys on the floor above. He said, "Kerslake just called. Your Richard Seyton came in some time ago. Was met by Nancy Hope and could well be staying the night with her in Cadogan Place."

Warboys, always elegant in his phrasing, always sounding as though he had just awakened from a refreshing and pleasant sleep in the best of humours, said, "Not my Richard Seyton. But I hope he had a good flight, and how nice to be met and cherished by a constant, I understand, flame."

"Do you want me to follow up on him?"

"I don't think so. Leave him in comfort. Eros undenied. And——" the pause was filled with a gentle chuckle, "——to give you a happy night as well, dear Quint—I'll be a little indiscreet and say that I am as curious as you are."

"That's companionable. Thank you."

"And to anticipate your next question—I don't want the file

5

indexed or numbered. Keep it in your private safe. I think we've both been here before a few times, haven't we?"

"Of course. But I've never liked it. A remark I would only make to you, naturally."

"I should hope so. But to comfort you I'll be equally indiscreet and say that I've never liked it either. So with that happy interchange of sentiments I wish you a pleasant evening whatever you are going to do."

As Warboys hung up Quint smiled. Warboys hated it and he hated it. Thank God it did not happen often, but once or twice when it had there had been real trouble—and heads had rolled. As for his pleasant evening he was going home to his bachelor flat in Dolphin Square, cook his own dinner out of choice not necessity, then go to bed with Jane Austen and forget his dislike of unmarked files in his milder dislike of Miss Emma Woodhouse.

* * * *

Seyton awoke to hear some nearby church clock strike three. The curtains had been partly drawn back from the windows. Nancy must have done that while he slept after they had made love. The March sky was frost clear. At his side she slept now with her back to him. The first time they had slept together had been in her father's house after a hunt ball, both in their twenties. Everyone had marked them down for marriage, but with so many years waiting ahead they had been in no hurry—and then Ruth had come along, and that had been that. Ruth had gone when Roger was only three, and that was when he had taken off. The Hall and the estate would never be his anyway, he had thought. Punch was always in love with someone and it was only a matter of time before he settled, married and had children. Ruth's death had changed everything. From country boy to whizz-kid. That's what they had called him. New York and the South Americas. Instinct or luck had gone with him. Over eight years had passed with the memory of Ruth fading gently and Roger growing up, living with Punch—and Punch still somehow not marrying. *Plenty of time, old boy.* But time was a factor no man could depend on. All it had needed was a frosty evening, a touch of rain to turn at once to black ice, a deer coming across the road to make Punch go heavy on the brakes of the old estate car, a skid and Punch going right through the windscreen to break his neck. And old Shipley beside him sitting untouched through it all. And then himself away on a shooting trip in Brazil after three weeks' hard dealing and no one able to get in touch with him until it was all over. Maybe luck was running out for the Seytons . . . just as it eventually had done for that far off Owen Glendower in the fourteenth century from whom they claimed bastard descent. First Ruth, then Punch taken from him. Punch after a good market day, with a few, but not too many he was sure, drinks inside him, laughing and joking right up to the last minute probably. And Ruth, out hunting, taking a fence she had taken a hundred times before, catching the top rail, only the smallest mark on her forehead where she had hit one of the few stones lining the far ditch, and gone before he could get to her.

At his side Nancy stirred slightly and in a voice which was too fresh to have just come from sleep, said, "I can listen or talk—whichever you like. Or neither."

He put out a hand and let it rest on the top of her bare arm. "I don't know. This is the time of bloody night when things get to you."

"Will you see Roger on the way down?"

"Yes. I've already arranged to have him out."

She was silent for a while, and then said, "Did I do the wrong thing?"

"In what way?"

"Coming out and snatching you. Bringing you here."

"No. I'm glad you did."

"Pushy Nancy."

He gave a little laugh and put his arm around her. "There's nothing wrong with that except . . . well, I wish I could be really co-operative."

"The last thing I want is any make believe. And, anyway, I'm grateful for——"

"I don't want to hear anything like that from you. But you wouldn't want me to be less than honest, would you?"

"No. Make believe is fine. Just for now and again—but not for good." She moved her head and kissed his hand on her shoulder, but she was thinking that it wasn't true, of course. She would settle any day for make believe with him. Plenty of people did—and found it quite satisfactory. But he wouldn't. For all his hard, stubborn nature, he was an idealist. No, perhaps romantic. Hard to believe because when he wanted something he could be quite ruthless and push the limits of truth and desire wider than most. Her father had once said 'They carry the Glendower blood. Robber barons. Sword in one hand and the priest in the palm of the other. They've only one true love. Their land, their broad acres. They live in the twentieth century—and are still fighting the battles that began in the fourteenth.'

He said, "You'll come down for the memorial service?"

"Of course. And after that—what will you do?"

He was silent for a while and then said calmly, "Do what I offered to make possible for Punch, only the stubborn bastard wouldn't take it. Move into the Hall. Make it what it was."

"But what about the people there?"

"I'll get rid of them. Buy them out. Kick them out. It's our place, not theirs."

Ours, not *mine*. The Seytons. Not any particular Seyton, but the Seytons stretching right back to the first who had come riding down the river valley with a sword in one hand and a land grant in the other. She held down a sigh. How could he be like that? Punch had had a lot of it, but nothing like the measure of his arrogant dreaming . . . and the difference in them had, she knew, caused a breach between them which had been slow to heal. The one and only time they had really truly differed. And that, too, not because Punch didn't share his feelings but because his Seyton pride forbade him to take help from his younger brother. It suddenly struck her for the first

8

time that there was a fanaticism in him which would take him without a qualm into devices and deeds as arbitrary and violent as any that had marked the life of that far distant Glendower—if the need arose. Fleetingly but forcefully she felt in that moment that if he did ever ask her to marry him she would be hard put to know her answer . . . No, no, that wasn't true—she'd go into it gladly and with her eyes wide open.

He said, "Tell me about the last time you saw Roger."

"Yes . . . well, I drove him back after the funeral. He was fussed and embarrassed because he had a black eye. Some dormitory fight. I think he felt Punch might have been upset."

"Not likely. Suitable mourning colour. Nice to think Punch might have known about it. What's he crazy about this time?"

"Motor scooters. He had a pocket full of brochures. Things with strange Japanese names. He reckons that though he's under age he could drive one around the estate."

"Well, I was doing it with an old bull-nosed Morris at his age. Punch wrecked it eventually trying to jump the ha-ha for a bet."

She laughed. "You were a wild pair."

Later, after they had breakfasted and he had gone she went up to her bedroom to find a parcel marked with her name on the dressing table. In it was a small brooch set with a cluster of Brazilian topazes, and a note which said—*I didn't know you would be waiting, but I was bringing this for you anyway. Love—Richard.*

*   *   *   *

Arthur Bellamy of Bellamy and Franks was a fresh-faced, white-haired man in his sixties and the last of a line of Bellamys who had been solicitors for the Seyton family for over a hundred years. When he went, as Richard Seyton well knew, his place would be taken by a nephew on the distaff side. Franks and his line had long died out. Bellamy was sole master in this office high above Trafalgar Square whose turgid traffic Seyton half-watched as the man slowly and with a precise diction read

9

Punch's will to him. At his side was a glass of dry sherry and another stood on the large Chippendale pie-crust table at Seyton's elbow. Bellamy's sherry was traditional.

The will was much as he had expected. The Hall, Dower House—with all contents—came to him and the farmlands on lease and tenure. There were various bequests to tenants and friends and a Trust Fund for Roger. He had sat here with Punch and heard his father's will read and had then been requested to leave them while Bellamy had a few private words with Punch. He had never asked Punch what the few private words were about and Punch had never enlightened him and he had known better than to show his curiosity. He sat, quite content to listen without interruption. He already knew the real state of affairs. Punch had been a bad manager. Not spendthrift, but just inept . . . too easy-going, thinking he had all the time in the world to pull things together.

When Bellamy had finished reading he looked up and said, "Well, Richard?"

"It's much as I expected. Gooch, Hill and Fairton are trying to make sense of the financial side, I presume?"

"Yes."

"I'd like to put someone in from my office to work with them."

"Uum . . . they mightn't take kindly to that."

"Maybe not—but that's what I want. So I'll be very glad if you will arrange it. But I can guess what the final situation will be."

"Yes, I'm afraid it's not going to be very good. Harry was rather casual about that side."

Seyton smiled. He had never heard Bellamy refer to his brother as Punch. He said, "I can handle it. But I just want to know the real position as soon as possible."

"I'm glad to hear that. All right, I'll arrange it. Now there's just one other thing . . ." He paused and then chuckled. "You won't know why, but I imagine you remember that when your father died and you and Harry came here you were requested to leave the room after the will had been read because I wanted to be alone with Harry?"

"Yes. Of course."

"It was to give him this." He picked up a long envelope at his side and handed it across the desk. It was an old worn envelope, foxed and stained with age and thick at the back with the remains of broken wax seals. There was no inscription on the plain side. "I would like you to open it and read the contents—of which I must know nothing—and then I must reseal it before you and it remains here in safe custody. My father did this a few times for your family and I have done it twice before. I may say that the envelope and its contents have been renewed over the years. The last occasion was in my grandfather's time. This will help you." He handed over a sharp-bladed steel paper knife. "Don't worry if you ruin the envelope. I'll give you another to replace it."

Partly amused, partly curious, Seyton began to work the seals free. Punch had done this once and his father before. Just now and again, no matter his feeling for tradition and family, he found his Seyton temperament no proof against an element of the ridiculous and arcane which had been and was common to them all. What had once been kept secret in the family for the sake of their own security was now no more than ritual. No member of the family ever went to the Hall chapel on Easter Sunday without wearing or carrying a bunch of white violets because once the carrying of the flowers by a member of the family had signalled to one of their kin hidden there that as darkness fell on the Holy Day he must be ready to leave that night since from treachery his hiding place was no longer secure.

He freed the envelope flap and from within drew a single folded sheet of thick paper covered with writing faded to the colour of dead oak leaves. On it were a few lines in a thin, elegant script. Victorian. He read with difficulty.

> *He who would leave the Hall unseen must*
> *take the old Squire's way.*
> *He who would enter the Hall unseen must*
> *pass by long silent Sarah.*

Bellamy said quietly, "You seem amused, Richard. So was Harry."

"I'm sure he was. Small boys sometimes ferret out the secrets of their elders. It's a nice tradition, but of no importance."

"Well, anyway, let us remain faithful to tradition. It's a good habit which is dying fast in this country."

"I'll say Amen to that."

Seyton slipped the note back into the envelope and Bellamy passed him wax and a box of matches so that he could reseal it. As he did this, he said, "Before I go there's one thing I want done. How long has the lease on the Hall got to run? Two or three years, is it? I want them out and I'm prepared to buy them out generously."

Bellamy was silent for a while, watching the slow drip of the red wax on to the envelope, then he said, "Did Harry never tell you? The lease was given for five years in the first place. That was three years ago. But two years ago at their instigation he renegotiated the lease—at a very handsome figure—for twenty years."

"For what?" Seyton was on his feet.

"For twenty years."

Angrily he said, "Well, I can't have that! The Hall's mine now and I want it! It's the Seyton home! Sorry . . . I didn't mean to blow my top. But I can't have it. I don't want those people there. No matter how worthy they are, and no matter what help they were to Punch. The damn fool. Why did he do that without saying a word to me?"

Quietly Bellamy said, "Because, Richard, like all of us, he wasn't able to foresee the future. He did what he thought was best to keep the place together. However, if it is your wish, I'll approach them and see what they say. But it will be an expensive business."

"I realize that. But I don't care what it costs. I want them out. They'll agree if the price is made right."

"I wonder?"

"I don't. There isn't anything of that kind which can't be

bought if the price is right. And I can afford it. Have you got the lease—or a copy?"

"The original is at the Dower House. Harry had it. But yes, I've a copy. Would you like it?"

"Please."

He waited while Bellamy telephoned to his main office for the copy to be sent up. Listening to Bellamy and waiting for him, he realized that close though he and Punch were there had been—and this perhaps exaggerated since his own financial successes—a growing stubbornness and arrogance in his brother which had slowly begun to impair the relationship between them. Where Punch had always turned to him for advice—particularly over money and the running of the estate and the Hall—he had more and more acted on his own. What a damn fool thing to have extended the Hall lease for twenty years. Well, it was done—and now he would have to undo it. The Hall and the estate were going to be what they had once been.

A clerk brought in the lease document and, when he had gone, Bellamy said, "Shall I read it to you?"

"No, thank you. I'll take it with me. On second thoughts, too—I'll handle it direct myself." Glancing at the document, he went on, "Who's the top man of this Foundation?"

"You'll see his signature at the end. Charles Bernard Felbeck. An old Yorkshire family. Rags to riches."

"Then he'll be a sensible man and know the value of money."

"Maybe . . . I certainly hope so. But don't rush him."

Seyton smiled. "I can't imagine that I'll have to. Brass talks. Every man has a price."

Bellamy shook his head. "You don't believe that."

Seyton grinned. "No. Let's say most men."

At his office suite in Curzon Street some time later, Seyton called in Miss Figgins, his private secretary. Tall, angular, with mild brown eyes, around his own age, hailing from the Welsh side of the Wye beyond Hay-on-Wye, her birth and blood clear in her voice, known to him since the day she had first come to work in the Estate Office as a girl of sixteen, often saving himself and Punch from many a strapping, she was beyond price and spoke her mind without fear or favour.

"Welcome back, Mr Richard."

"Thank you, Figgy. And don't say anything about Punch. We both feel the same."

She nodded and then said, a little too briskly, "There's a fair bit of stuff waiting for you to clear up."

"Let me have it and I'll do it today. Max Beaton is coming over soon. He'll hold the fort here for a while. Be nice to him. He's frightened of you."

She smiled. "Pretends to be."

He handed her the lease document. "I want you to read this and tell me if you can see any way of breaking it. Also I want you to get what you can about the man who is the principal signatory—Charles Felbeck."

"You want to upset it?"

"Mind reader."

"No, clear on your face. And, anyway, I could have guessed it. Inscrutable is one thing you've never been. Or devious. Always a straight line across country. You handle a fish the same way, too. That's why they break you so often. You'll be wanting an appointment with him, I imagine?"

"Yes. But I want what you can get on him first. You've met him?"

"Once or twice."

"Like him?"

"He seems a nice enough gentleman. You'll see for yourself. Are you back at the hotel now?"

"Yes."

"You should marry her, you know, Mr Richard."

Seyton laughed. "I thought you didn't like her?"

"Then you thought wrong. I don't like the situation. The Hall's yours now and it needs a mistress."

"I agree. But unless we can do something about Mr Felbeck it won't be really mine for twenty years."

Figgins nodded, then, her brown eyes steady on him, said,

"Mister Harry—God rest his dear soul—did what he thought was for the best. There was no way he could keep things going on his own——"

"But twenty years! That was a long time to tie the Hall up."

"At his age? What's the point of living if you're always thinking you may be dead tomorrow?"

"True, Figgy. I'd probably have done the same in his place."

"Maybe. Anyway—I'll get this stuff for you."

An hour later Figgins brought him the information she had gathered about Charles Felbeck. Charles Bernard Felbeck had been born in 1921, and had been educated at Hanley High School and St John's College, Oxford. He was the son of the late Thomas Race Felbeck and Anne Felbeck, both now dead. Felbeck had been married in 1946 and had two sons and one daughter. His principal residence was Felbeck Grange in Yorkshire, not far from Ripon. His clubs were the United Oxford and Cambridge and the Athenaeum. He came from an old family of woollen mill owners. Over the years the family concern had grown into a small business empire with varied interests . . . cellulose acetate yarn producers, mail order clothing, jewellers and multiple stores. He was the chairman of Felbeck Textiles Ltd, Parkway Stores Ltd, and Felbeck (Holdings) Ltd, all of whose head offices were located at Bradford House, Gracechurch Street, London. His grandfather had created and endowed the Felbeck Christian Heritage Foundation which had originally given aid for the repair and maintenance of the fabric of cathedrals and churches (irrespective of denomination) and, in addition, had collected religious works of art and ancient ecclesiastical sculptures and artefacts. Over the years—as the Foundation had grown wealthier from donations, legacies and the shrewd management of its own funds—the organization had branched out to support various charities, welfare projects, old people's homes and the relief world-wide of famine and the ravages of natural disasters. Figgins had made a note—*They are no soft touch for woolly-minded do-gooders. So far as breaking the agreement is concerned—unless Felbeck succumbs to your charms—then you have only clause seven which, considering the nature of the Foundation, is a hope remoter than remote.*

And clause seven, he had already considered and dismissed. All that was left to him was charm. Well, Felbeck came from an old family—one that had never cared a jot about titles and honours clearly—like his own—so he might, if the compensation were right, have a soft spot for ancestral feeling. Beyond that, at the moment, he did not care to speculate in any detail. All he knew was that he was not going to wait twenty years for the lease to fall in.

CHAPTER TWO

SEYTON SAW CHARLES FELBECK that evening. He was a little surprised at the promptness with which the man had given him the appointment until almost the first thing the man said after their formal greetings was that he was travelling to Yorkshire the next day. The flat overlooked Park Lane and was plainly but solidly furnished. Over the fireplace of the sitting room was a large pen-and-ink drawing of Ripon Cathedral. Seeing Seyton's eyes on it, Felbeck said as he handed him a whisky and soda, "Do you like it?"

"Yes, I do. It's a very fine drawing."

"Its appeal is also sentimental to me. I was christened and confirmed there. Lovely, isn't it? The west front and twin towers are fine specimens of Early English architecture. It was founded on the ruins of St Wilfred's Abbey of the seventh century." He nodded across the room to another drawing clearly of the same hand, and went on, "That's Felbeck Grange. Nothing like as old—that was built with money that came from the Felbeck mills, but on the site of the farmhouse which was the home of the family until it went into wool. I'm sorry my wife isn't here—she would like to have met you. By the way, in case you don't know, we both went to the funeral of your brother. We'd met him quite a few times and were very fond of him."

"I appreciate that."

As the man had been speaking Seyton had been studying him. He was a short, hard little nut of a man, his fair hair thin over his scalp and sporting a crisp, well-trimmed military moustache. His face was lined, squarish, almost pugnacious in repose, and the nose was squashed back as though it had taken a lot of punishment in the ring during its time—which later Seyton learned was true for Felbeck had been a well-known amateur boxer.

"May I say, too, that we got on very well. In a way the same kind of family—though yours of course can trace a longer recorded history. But springing from one place and holding on to it. And no titles, no honours. Not worth a damn these days, anyway. The only honour a man needs lies in the cultivation of his own character and abilities and a dedication to the spirit of self-enterprise and self-discipline. Oh, dear——" he made a sudden boyish grimace half of reproach and half of apology, "——I do apologize. Riding the hobby horse."

Seyton laughed, suddenly liking the man where he had half expected to be opposed to him since he stood in the way of his own hard intentions. "No apology is needed. I agree with you. Unfortunately, however, I come riding my own hobby horse to ask a favour of you which I am sure you will appreciate."

"I can guess what you want. Oh, yes, that's not difficult. I'd feel the same were I in your place." He sat down and Seyton noticed that he was drinking plain soda water.

"Then I'll be frank. My brother would never take any help from me—and anyway until fairly recently I had none to offer. But we both shared one desire. To keep Seyton Hall and its lands in the family——"

"My dear Seyton, you don't have to say any more. I know how you feel and I can guess what you want. And I have the greatest sympathy with your desire. But you must see that over the years while the Foundation has had its headquarters at Seyton Hall we have spent a lot of money, not merely on the building and the adjacent grounds, but also in recruiting staff and housing them in the Hall and the district and, in fact, and I say it with pride, establishing one of the finest collections of Christian ecclesiastical treasures in the world to be housed in a secular building." He suddenly grinned impishly. "And now you want us to up sticks and away. Is that it?"

"Broadly speaking, yes. Naturally there must be a reasonable time allowed to you—and, equally, adequate compensation to be made to you for your expenses and for waiving the lease."

"That could cost you a lot of money."

"I know—and I'm prepared to meet the cost which, of course, would include a reasonable amount for the inconvenience which the Foundation would temporarily suffer."

Felbeck fingered his short moustache for a moment and then, an impish light in his eyes, asked, "You could afford all this? Pardon my directness."

Seyton laughed. "If I couldn't, Mr Felbeck, I wouldn't be here wasting your time. Yes, I can afford it. It's the one thing I want and——"

"And," interrupted Felbeck with a pout of his under lip, "you're a very determined man when you want something. Saints and soldiers and merchant princes. Men with ideas and visions and ambition—their logic and spirit aren't found loitering on street corners. The Church, the Army and the Yeomanry. No country can abuse them except at its own peril." With a sudden harshness in his voice he went on, "I mean that! And it is just that peril we face today!"

"I agree. But of the three neither the Church nor the Army is anything without the land. Man springs from the land and lives by it—nobody in this country can deny the hunger for land all men have. Walk through any town or village and look at the gardens. Look at the Park out there. Where there's no greenness the eyes of man grow dull . . ." He broke off, embarrassed more for himself than Felbeck, and then added, "I'm sorry—but that's how I feel."

"There's no need for apologies. I feel exactly the same. I say more, too. If the matter were entirely in my hands I would agree at once that you should have what you want and at a fair valuation. But, unfortunately, the decision is not in my hands. You see, Seyton, the Felbeck Foundation is run by a Board of Governors—a body of eminent men and women from many walks of life. I am, it's true, the Chairman of the Foundation and have considerable influence over them, but in fact I can take part only indirectly in their decisions. There are eight Governors, all with votes. But as Chairman I only have a casting vote in the event of an equal number of votes for and against a proposition." He smiled and shrugged his shoulders. "I wish it were otherwise—but that is the way my grandfather had the constitution framed. So you see, I can't speak for the other Governors. But I can say that they are a body of very reasonable people."

"Would I be in order to approach them individually before a vote is taken?"

"I don't think it would be necessary—or do you any good. But, of course, they would all concede you have a perfect right to appear before them to put your case when the matter comes up for decision."

"Well, that's something. May I ask further how you think they will react?"

"I don't think it would be proper for me to guess. But I will tell you this in confidence—were it to come to the point of a decision being made on my casting vote then I would be on your side—much as I should regret the loss of the Hall as our home. In a way, the Foundation really stems from the feeling you have for your place . . . the preservation of our heritage, traditions and culture. Yet ironically, in your case, it is doing just the opposite. But in these days that is a paradox which cannot be avoided. However, leave it with me—and I'll be in touch with you as soon as I can."

Seyton rose. The man was clearly on his side. For the moment he could hope for no more. And he was Felbeck—the grandson of the man who had created the Foundation; the best ally he could have—though that would bring no concessions, he guessed, when the matter of compensation for buying out the lease arose.

He said, "Thank you very much, Mr Felbeck."

"Not at all." He pressed a bell push at the side of the mantelpiece. "You came by taxi?"

"Yes, I did."

"Well . . ." Felbeck smiled. "I'll save you a little pocket money. My car's waiting down below for you. No, no . . . I insist."

When Seyton had gone, Felbeck carried his glass of soda water, now half empty, to the sideboard and filled it to the top with whisky. He sat down by the telephone and lit himself a cigarette. He sat, smoking and drinking, lost in thought, for a long while and then he picked up the telephone and dialled a number.

"Grandison?"

"Yes, my dear Felbeck?" The voice was cultured, weighty and slow.

"Seyton has just left. It was as you expected."

"It had to be." The other's voice was faintly tinged with amusement.

"I told him I would put it to the Foundation Governors."

"Very proper."

"He's not the type to be put off."

"If he were we'd have no problem."

"I don't see that we have one anyway. The Foundation members will vote against selling back the lease—and that will be that."

"Either you're an innocent or an optimist. Six centuries ago Owen Glendower, the last independent Prince of Wales, fathered a bastard girl on a farmer's daughter at Pilleth in Radnorshire. She grew up to marry a Seyton—only they were named Satan then——"

"Grandison, spare me."

"All right. Is he a sticker or a non-sticker?"

"He's a sticker. The kind I like in fact."

"Let's avoid sympathies. There's no way of leaving the Hall. We all agree about that. But you can have a meeting and a vote and make it look close. Thereafter there's nothing he can do."

"There's clause seven."

"Yes, yes, dear old clause seven. But, I don't think you need worry about that. In the very unlikely event of its ever arising . . . well, I think you will agree that that's my province. To save you worry I promise you that I will start doing something about it right away. And when I say *doing* I'm not talking about extreme measures. Just a few discreet moves against a possibility which is very, very remote. Am I soothing you?"

"No, damn you. You're just having fun at my expense."

"No, Felbeck. I'm quite serious."

"Well . . ."

"Well, what?"

"Oh, nothing . . . no, that's not true. Talking to him he struck me as just the type we could take in. Just the type."

"So he may be. But it's too late for that, isn't it, in the circumstances?"

"Yes, I suppose so."

"Then forget him. He's my worry from now on. Goodnight."

Felbeck put the receiver back, drank some more whisky and then lay back and stared at the pen drawing of Felbeck Grange. Just the type. Just the type that this damned muddle and mess of an age needed. Yes, that was Seyton.

*   *   *   *

Quint was on the point of leaving for home when Warboys came into his room. That he entered without knocking was no surprise. Warboys only knocked at the doors of those few who exceeded him in rank. He was an elegant man, tall, spare of flesh, the long, pale face deeply cleft below the cheek bones, the hazel eyes large-lidded, the pink of his scalp showing warmly through his thinning white hair. Without a word he walked to the window and stared out at the distant lights of the Mall.

Knowing the game . . . perhaps ritual would be the better word he sometimes felt, Quint got up and moved towards his small wall cupboard and said, "It will be a glass of Tio Pépé, I presume?"

"Half a glass—just to observe rare custom."

Quint brought a tray with glasses and a decanter to the old green leather-topped table in the centre of the room. As Quint poured sherry into the two glasses, he said, "The last time I had this pleasure was four months ago."

Warboys turned. "Do you wish it happened oftener?"

"Frankly, no."

"True. I come as no harbinger of spring. Something moves in the air around us and it is not the first mild touch of the reviving year. Something . . . but what?"

"Give me a clue and I'll break a firm rule and make a guess. Your sherry."

Warboys took the glass and sipped, and then said, "Put together the Felbeck Foundation for the Preservation of the Christian Heritage and Grandison, and then stir in Richard Seyton and one Georgina Collet. What kind of mixture is that? Unpalatable?"

Surprised, Quint said bluntly, "What on earth has Georgina Collet got to do with it?"

"Nothing yet—but she's going to be required to. *Faire des agaceries*, perhaps?"

"On whom?"

"Richard Seyton. Is she capable of that?"

"She's capable. If the inducement is right—and I can only think of one."

"Quite. Her fool of a father gets a far earlier parole than he could ever have expected. But that's not the point. You know her. Is she capable of handling someone like Seyton right up to the limit?"

"She might be. Yes, I think she could—and would if it were for her father. She dotes on him—though God knows why. He was a useless type."

"No, not useless. He served us well—up to the time where he decided to listen to the call of conscience. Does she still use the name Collet?"

"Yes. People's memories are short. Anyway, she doesn't run away from that sort of thing. But what is all this interest in the Christian Heritage people?" Quint waved a mollifying hand. "I'm sorry, I shouldn't have asked that."

"Forget it. And between ourselves I wish I knew." Warboys smiled. "Perhaps they're shipping too much rice in famine relief to countries of doubtful political colour. Perhaps, on the other hand, someone in the higher regions has decided that they are an organization we could use if only we could compromise them discreetly and then turn the screws. I don't know, dear Quint. And when I really, *really* don't know, it upsets me to the point of coming to drink sherry with you. And to unburden myself further—an act I would normally deprecate—I don't like it when our organization thinks less and less of using ways and means which smack more of the Inquisition than Intelligence. Oh, dear, oh dear—I am really quite upset . . ." He smiled suddenly and held out his glass. "On reflection, a little more, I think."

As he poured from the decanter Quint made a wry face.

"In the good old days this used to be a profession for gentlemen—gentlemen adventurers and officers who chivalrously served the Empire."

Warboys shook his head. "No, Quint. It never was like that. And you know it. But at least there was some kind of ethos. Some limits. Oh, dear—this is the kind of discussion I deprecate. It can lead to a stirring of conscience and that's fatal."

Quint laughed, but beneath his true humour there was disquiet. Warboys had spoken, although lightly, more freely to him now than ever in his whole service before. If something were deeply troubling the man then it had to be abnormally serious to unsettle him to this point. Briefly the unworthy thought occurred to him that Warboys was getting beyond it—letting imagination distort reality, a common enough development among lesser men in the Department at times. He brought the conversation down to a practical level by saying, "Tell me what you want done about Georgina Collett."

"Not what *I* want done."

Quint was not deceived, nor, he guessed, meant to be. The answer was not meant to be evasive. It was an invitation—and of a very rare kind from Warboys. "Who then?" he asked gently.

"I don't know. The interest comes either through or immediately from Grandison. Sir Manfred Grandison."

To himself Quint reflected—*Knight Commander of the Most Excellent Order of the British Empire. The* éminence grise *of this establishment in Birdcage Walk. But to the outside world the only note of any public service was in a listing of the members of the Agricultural Research Council under the Ministry of Agriculture, Fisheries and Food—which was only part of the truth, the tip of the iceberg.*

Looking at Warboys who had turned his back and was staring out of the window, Quint said, "Grandison—above whom there stand very few. Originator? Or passer-on?" He spoke knowing the bluntness might be rebuked.

Warboys was silent for a while, and then turned and with a mild smile, said, "The latter would be an unusual role. But far from an exception."

"But," said Quint, uncertain of his own boldness, "you have doubts?"

Warboys laughed. "Who serves here who doesn't live all day with doubts? They are the essence of our being. What is truth or reality? Fire-thrown shadows on a cave wall. And honour— what is that? Here, admittedly, we have to and *have* made our own kind. Tarnished though it would be if exposed to the public eye, it is all we have. We both would have it stay that way. You are, I know, possessed with thoughts to which, at the moment, I have no wish to become privy. Out of an uneasiness of instinct perhaps too much has already been said. So let us be practical. Georgina Collet."

Quint shrugged his shoulders and knowing now that the almost dialectical play of dialogue was to cease, though he had drawn pleasure from the rare display of oblique confidence, said, "She has done one small thing for us before, as you know. To get her idiot father out of top security into the comparative luxury of an open prison. For an early parole . . . well, there should be no trouble. I'm still in touch. But I would, of course, need to know her role. And, of course, she can't step out of her true character and profession."

"It's because of just that that she has been chosen. She is to be herself. No more. And she is, to use a vulgar phrase, to go to the limit with Richard Seyton. A pastoral love affair."

"Marriage?"

"My dear Quint—what an old-fashioned thought."

131818

Quint grinned. "She is in some ways quite old-fashioned. I mean to the point of going to that limit if it could bring her father's release."

"Then make it clear that—unless exceptional circumstances arise—no such development is at all necessary. There's no need for any holy blessing on their pillow talk. Grandison, or whoever, just wants to share any confidences which Seyton may trust her with. You'll see her?"

"Of course. But I can make the firm promise that whether she does or does not turn up anything her father will get his parole?"

"To his credit, Grandison made that point clear. When you've seen her let me know what you've arranged."

"Of course. I'll see her tomorrow. I presume she'll need a stand-off?"

"Of course, again. Choose one of your bright boys."

*   *   *   *

Seyton gave Nancy a lift as far as Oxford on his way to see his son, Roger. They had spent the previous night together, and this Oxford visit, he guessed, she had arranged in order to have more time in his company. To begin with she was unusually silent, but after they were clear of the London suburbs she suddenly said out of the blue, "What did you think of Felbeck?"

"I liked him. Have you met him?"

"Once or twice. He's hunted at times when he has been staying at the Hall. Do you think you'll get what you want from him?"

"I don't see why not. But it all rests with his fellow Governors. He only has a casting vote."

"He struck me as the kind of man who'd screw the neck of any committee which didn't want to go his way."

"I hope that's true." Then, knowing her, sensing that she was not just making conversation, he asked, "What's on your mind?"

"Just a feeling."

"You can do better than that."

She smiled. "I'll try. Punch liked him, you know."

"Punch liked most people. Could have been a failing."

"I know. That's why I thought it was odd. Fair or foul weather—if Punch liked someone he stuck to them. But he suddenly went off Felbeck."

"How do you know?"

"If you mentioned someone to Punch his face told you a lot at once. About three months before his death he came to town for a few days. We had dinner, and I happened to mention Felbeck—in fact I had a feeling that he'd come up to see him."

"So?"

"Well—you know Punch's give-away face. All he felt always on the surface. He usually said what he thought and his face, on the few occasions when he didn't want to say, showed his feelings plainly. He just put on that face."

"So you just shut up."

"I would have done normally. But we'd had a few drinks and I was over-bold and jollied him. Asked him what had changed his opinion—because that's what it was clearly. And then he said that he wished he'd never seen the man and that it was not a subject he wanted to talk about. So that was that."

"Was it?"

"So far as Punch was concerned, yes. But since we were old friends, I pushed a bit. You know—you can tell old Nancy about it. That sort of thing. So he laughed then and was suddenly all nice, the old Punch. And he said—I remember his words clearly—*There's only one person I want to talk about Felbeck to and that's Richard—and God knows where he's globe-trotting at this moment.* And that was the end of that conversation."

"Well, that's that. But Punch could get steamed up over small things. I remember there was hell to pay when he met one of the Foundation staff coming back from the bit of water we leased them carrying two salmon kelts. Christ—you should have heard his language about bloody idiots who couldn't tell a kelt from a fresh-run salmon and so on. Though, to tell the truth, it is sometimes difficult with a well-mended kelt if you haven't been at it for some years. He had the poor sod in tears almost. Then Punch calmed down and was charming in the way he could be and showed the chap the differences."

"Well, maybe I'm exaggerating."

After he had dropped Nancy in Oxford the conversation went from his mind as he drove on to Cheltenham. He had got permission to take Roger out to lunch—the house master was an old friend of his. Roger—almost fourteen—had his leanness of body and the same dark hair, but his face held much of his wife, Ruth; clear, olive skin, the same dark eyes, the same feeling about him of self-possession and then—when touched with a sudden absurdity or moved by a joke or deep emotion—showing all. He took him to Cavendish House for lunch and they talked easily for there had never been any shyness between them. Both he and Ruth had brought the boy up to a frankness of communication, so that he knew if he were in trouble or perplexed over anything he could come to them and get advice or explanation. He had loved Ruth and he loved his boy. And now, out of the blue, it had become a reality that one day the Hall would belong to Roger; should and would.

After lunch, to please him, they went to a couple of places to look at motor cycles and scooters with Roger enthusiastically discussing their merits and drawbacks and—Richard Seyton had to smile to himself—already assuming that there could be no objection to his having one before age so long as he used it on the estate private roads (a promise which Seyton knew at a pinch would not be honoured, but later the breach confessed without prompting).

"Punch said it would be all right—so long as I cleared it with you, dad. And he told me about that old bull-nosed Morris you had before age."

They were driving back to the school at the moment and Seyton said, "Well—we'll see what your end of term report is like."

"Oh, that's fine. Thanks, dad."

And it was fine, for he was a good worker, had a keen

memory and intelligence so that schoolwork came, perhaps, a little too easily to him. But what matter? thought Seyton fondly. You don't have to be ashamed about the gifts the gods honour you with at birth.

As they sat in the car for a few moments in the school driveway before Roger left him, the boy said, "Will the school let me get away for Punch's memorial service? I'd like to come."

"I think it can be arranged."

"Oh, good. You know——" Roger paused, looking away at a quarrel of sparrows squabbling in the branches of a newly-budded thorn tree on the driveside. Then with an unnatural briskness said, "Oh, well, I suppose I must be going."

Seyton was going to let him escape, and then decided against it. He recognized the boy's sudden change of mood and decided to hold him.

He said, "You were going to say something."

For a moment Roger was silent and then, with a little half nod to himself, said, "Well, I was and I will. Though . . . well, dad—do you think Punch could have had a feeling that something was going to happen to him?"

"What makes you fancy that?"

"I don't know. Not really. No, that's not true. I do. You see, I went down to the Hall for half-term. That was a few weeks before it all happened and . . . well, Punch didn't seem quite the same."

"How do you mean?"

"Well, he didn't seem to be his old self. You know . . . laughing and full of jokes and taking me everywhere he went. In fact he stuck to the house most of the time. He didn't ride and he didn't shoot. And mopey. Not like he usually was. They say some people get a feeling of . . . well, things that are going to happen."

"I think that was just your fancy. Something you've read into it afterwards."

To Seyton's surprise the boy said with a sudden surprising firmness, "Oh, no dad. I don't think so. He was different. Well,

29

for instance . . . you know how I always liked to go up to the Hall and look at the things they've got there. He more often than not liked to come with me. Well, I asked him if he'd come up with me one day and I nearly fell over backwards. He suddenly went all funny and told me I wasn't to go up there. Just like that. Flat."

"Did you ask him why?"

"Oh no. Not the way he was. I wasn't going to risk it. But it wasn't Punch, was it?"

"No, it wasn't." Then to ease the boy's feelings, he grinned and said, "But as you get older you'll find that grown-ups can be unpredictable at times. The thing is not to read too much into it. Could be as simple as indigestion or a hangover. We all have moods. I guess you just struck one of Punch's rare ones. Come on now—off with you. Academe calls."

But as he drove off to take the Gloucester road, Seyton knew there was no question of indigestion or hangover. They were things that Punch suffered from all right, but one thing Punch would never do was to issue a flat edict and give no explanation to someone like Roger . . . at least, not normally. Punch was as normal and uncomplicated as rice pudding. And Roger had inherited all his mother's sensitivity. Odd.

*   *   *   *

Though not a Cordon bleu cook, but an enthusiastic one, Quint was careful to keep the meals he served to guests simple. He supposed, he thought, that he could call Georgina Collet a guest in the usual sense of indicating some form of friendliness . . . certainly sympathy. Anyway, her father had been an old friend and his daughter always welcome to his flat. So, there was avocado pear for what some people disgustingly called 'starters', celery rolled in ham with a cheese sauce for the main dish—with a Petit Chablis from the Wine Society and, not unsurprisingly, very good—and then fresh peaches *trempé* in brandy. A simple little meal well within the capabilities of himself and his tiny flat kitchen. The whole costing him—for he was careful of money—less than a third of the amount which would have been charged him at even a normally decent West End restaurant. Vivat home-cooking, good home-cooking, he said to himself as he began to make the roux for the cheese sauce with a kitchen glass of the lunch Chablis at his side.

Because he had that kind of memory, he could recall exactly the details of the meal he had last served to her father in this flat—two days before he was taken up, and knowing perfectly well that it was going to happen and too sensible to try and avoid it. Details hung like sleeping bats in the great vault of his memory. An amber-clear julienne, a fillet steak and fresh peas, and strawberry ice cream with fresh Devonshire cream—this last a concession to his guest who, as well as being very stupid for an intelligent man, had a sweet tooth. No wine—since his guest did not drink it. Just a glass of Perrier water which he drank too out of politeness.

Now came the daughter for the first time to his flat since her father had been put away—though he had met her quite a few times since then . . . used her, that too—just once, out of which had come her father's transfer to an open prison against a great deal of opposition which had been a waste of time and energy since Birdcage always got what it wanted. Well, almost always.

Watching the roux come, the memory banks in his mind clicked gently and faultlessly. Georgina Collet. Georgy, familiarly. Only child. Thirty-two less a very few months at this moment. Because he was a bachelor and quite enjoyed a little mild eroticism, made easy now because he had once inadvertently seen her naked in her father's house where he was a favoured guest, he let her parade in memory. Though, in fact, at the actual time she had never moved, had just been standing like a statue at the side of the family swimming pool while he had been screened by the lattice work of a growth of roses—Gloire de Dijon—growing up over rustic work. He held the memory fondly. Brown-skinned, for she had just come back from a Spanish holiday, middle height, narrow waisted with perhaps the breasts a little too full for the slender figure which was sleeked with watery highlights from her swim, the short-cropped auburn hair, wet too, closely framing the still, pensive face, not beautiful but pleasantly compelling which could move from solemnity to gaiety as though a racing sunbreak were chasing across it firing the grey-green eyes with life . . . Aye, and mischief, for she had suddenly called out, 'You're a dirty old man, Quinney dear.' Embarrassed, he had moved away without a word. *A dirty old man.* Well, in some ways, yes—for he had used her since then without decency but with her consent because she was prepared to do anything for the sake of her stupid father. He remembered her comment when it had all been explained to her. *So what? If it comes to the point of getting into bed—it's a simple enough act. Leaves no mark on the mind like the one on my father's. I want him out of that ghastly security place . . .*

He stirred his sauce. What a dirty world. Full of dirty or dubious arrangements. His world. Birdcage's world. And to be honest he loved it for long ago he had abandoned all other.

When she came, her green beret and green mackintosh soaked and sleeked with a sudden heavy shower, she kissed him with warmth and the dampness of her cheek was cold against his cooking-warm face.

"My lord, Quinney, something smells good."

He made her a martini and sat sipping his Chablis opposite her as she chatted away telling him of her recent life—whose details he already knew—and showing no hint of curiosity for what might lie ahead of her. Nothing mattered except her father. Warm, good looking, all woman, no cares allowed to furrow her brow. Georgina Collet, D.Sc., and Ph.D. of Oxford University and sometime Senior Lecturer in Zoology at Sussex University—but all academic life put aside now in favour of her writing and her painting—talents discovered not in any with-drawal from university life after her father's disgrace, but a growth always there, an ambition slowly dominating all others, which had flowered what . . . in adversity? . . . like some random, misplaced bulb or tuber buried by chance in a compost heap suddenly to thrust its emergent, exotic flower to life . . . He smiled gently at his own unspoken simile and said cheerfully, "It's not very bad—or difficult—and you won't have to make any break in your work. It's sound enough cover."

She laughed. "Don't even half apologize, Quinney. To get father out on parole I'd do Jerusalem on my knees. He was an altruistic fool—still is. But he's my father. So no big speeches to soothe me. Just tell me straight. But I'm glad I can still work. And be frank—I might have to go the limit, yes?"

"Yes—and maybe more than that."

"What is there more than bed?"

"Love and marriage."

Georgina laughed. "Oh, come, Quinney. Not in your world."

"It happens sometimes. I don't mean the true substance—but the shadow."

"Well, that's a relief because nobody can command the other. Love and marriage—if necessary—*à la mode* of Birdcage. And I'm to use my own name?"

"Naturally."

"More people than you imagine remember, you know. 'Collet . . .? Collet . . .? Wasn't that . . .?' And then out it comes."

"No need to be less than honest. Your father was listed at the Ministry of Defence, just that. Birdcage doesn't exist. Just let the apparent truth run. You either get sympathy—invaluable—or, if the cold and uncharitable shoulder, well, we pull you out and put someone else in."

"I see. Well, can we eat? I take this kind of thing better on a full stomach."

"Of course."

He gave her fuller details as they ate, and she said little and—he smiled to himself, though his deep mood was far from cheerful—in no way showed any lack of appetite. There was an earthy naturalness and phlegm about her, now long developed and strengthened by concern for her father. He could give her no line for any direct investigation of Richard Seyton (he scarcely had one himself). Some pointers might be made available to her later.

33

When he had finished, she said calmly, "It doesn't seem much. I'm to make a natural, unexceptional contact with him. Be myself. Go, if things develop, from acquaintance to friendship and then to wherever these lead. To bed. Even to marriage bed?"

"That would be expected. But the prospect is remote."

"And what am I looking for—because there must be something?"

"Oh, yes—there must be something. But I can't tell you what it is. We want you to find that for us."

Georgina shook her head, laughing. "The whole thing sounds just too daft for words."

"That's true. That's why I lack more precise words."

"Dear old Quinney. Either you're deeper than I think or you're all adrift. The former, I think."

He grinned. "I wouldn't hazard a guess myself. But I'm glad you can take it light-heartedly."

She frowned then suddenly and said sharply, "I'm not taking it light-heartedly! Treating it so, yes. What other way is there? I'm in your hands. I think it's disgusting." Her frown went and she smiled and put a hand over one of his across the table. "But I'm happy to do it because of father. But I see now why he kicked over the traces. When is all this supposed to happen?"

"It is happening now. You've started by being here—but I want you up in Herefordshire by the end of this week. He lives in the Dower House, quite close to Seyton Hall. The whole shooting match has fallen into his hands at the death of his brother." He ran on, giving her such information as he could and she sat silently looking into her coffee cup but seeing nothing—which was her remedy for despair; to look at the world and see nothing.

"You must fix it up yourself. As though you were going at your own choice because the area held something for you. His place is on the Wye, not far from Bredwardine. He's hunting, shooting and fishing—so there's a start. Something in common."

"I don't hunt and I don't shoot. Fishing, yes."

34

"You can do all three if you have to. Anyway I've told you that you must play it the way advantage lies. Expense is no consideration. You might even do good work up there."

"I bloody well will!" She was stiff with brief resentment. "I have to have some compensation personally. Oh, God—what sods you people are."

"All in a good cause."

"Oh, I know—you have to believe that, don't you? How would you sleep at night otherwise? Oh, dear Quinney, how could such a nice man as you be so bloody awful? Don't get me wrong. I'm not grumbling. I'm grateful—for my father's sake. It would have been nice though had it only been a question of money being needed to help my father. Then I could have set myself up in Mayfair, earned an honest living on my back and kept most of my self-respect. Damn you, and damn all with you, I say." She shrugged her shoulders, the movement lacing her auburn hair with red gold gleams, and then smiled. "Okay—that's the end, the limit of my personal reaction. So now your Georgy will be a good girl. Pillow talk or marriage bed chatter. And no clue as to what you want?"

Quint fetched the brandy from his sideboard and standing poised with the decanter said, "None at the moment. But with time I might be able to pass you a hint or two. Not personally. You'll have a stand-off. He'll make himself known to you in good time. When he does everything comes and goes through him. I don't exist. Nor those above me. How many studies do you make before you get to the essence of the animal or bird you mean to put on canvas? Many, many? Do the same with Seyton. We want the whole man exposed to us. You go to Herefordshire and by chance you meet a man called Seyton who attracts you. A blank sheet with just his name at the top— the blankness is for you to fill if you can—for us."

As she left she put an envelope into his hands and said, "A little present—in return for your kindness. And I do mean kindness." She leaned forward and kissed him lightly on the cheek.

He opened it when she had gone. It was a very fine woodcut

—which he would have known anywhere as her work—of a grass snake swallowing a frog backwards, the frog's mouth gasping and one small foreleg raised in a gesture that looked like farewell. Not for one moment did he think that any sentiment had been in her mind. She had just marked down a moment she had seen without any personal comment. When she worked, her work claimed her, precluding all sentiment. That was the way he wanted it; the way which would serve Birdcage.

CHAPTER THREE

RICHARD SEYTON WOKE early. Although it had rained hard and consistently through the night the morning was now bathed in sunlight, the cropped grass and smooth lawns glistening like bright enamel. Distantly, below a high wooded bluff, he could see the river running brown with brief spate water. From this room—always his when he stayed at the Dower House—he could see neither the Hall nor the family chapel. In the park sheep cropped below the bare beeches and oaks and, more distantly, on the rising ground there was the red and white movement of the cattle of the home farm. Below him to one side of the gently terraced lawn stood the old black-and-white timbered dovecote which had been built by some long distant Seyton. A handful of white doves rose from the high-pitched dark-slated roof and then dropped to fly low across the grass and swing round the far corner of the house where, he guessed, old Shipley would be throwing out their corn. For years and years Shipley women had house-kept, served and nursed for the Seytons, and Shipley men had farmed, laboured, groomed and kept kennels for the family. Now the Shipleys, childless, served on with Mrs Shipley as housekeeper and cook and old Shipley, devoted to Punch, ready to turn his hand to anything, driver, ghillie, groom, a shadow cast by his master, and a faithful friend.

While he loved this house and had had a room here ever since Ruth had died and he had given up farming, his true love was the Hall. His true room—even after his marriage—had always been the one he had slept in from the time he had outgrown the Hall nursery—a small raftered room, the plaster

37

walls pargeted inside, the leaded, narrow windows facing the buffeting winds and storms which came down from the Welsh hills to the west to howl and whistle around the solid red Tudor brickwork of the high round tower which for generations had always been the quarters of the young Seytons. Now, God-knows-who of the Foundation staff slept in it. He smiled to himself, discounting his bitterness.

Bathed, shaved and dressed in comfortable country clothes, he went along to Punch's room. It was still as it had been while Punch lived, poignantly so. A pile of sporting magazines cluttered the bedside table. In a cut-glass bowl on the dressing table was a bunch of keys and a collection of loose change which each night Punch had emptied from his pockets. The top of the Chippendale mahogany desk in the window was crowded with framed photographs—Punch's first pony, a Welsh; a long dead, favourite Labrador bitch; girl friends; and one of himself with Ruth and Roger, placed between two studio portraits of their father and mother. On the wall to the right was an oil painting of the rose garden at the Hall. Grouped around a sundial were three men—his great-grandfather, then old Sir George Cornewall of nearby Moccas Court, and the third the Reverend Francis Kilvert—the famous diarist— destined to die in his thirties as Punch had done—who had been vicar of nearby Bredwardine and rector of Brobury.

Seeing the wall safe, he smiled to himself and went over and opened it. It was never locked for Punch had used it only as a cupboard. It held now a half full bottle of Haig whisky, a soda syphon, a chipped crystal glass and a half-empty box of cigars. Turning away to leave the room he paused for a moment at the second window. Before him was the full stretch of land running back from the river Wye. Close by was the Shipleys' old black-and-white timber-framed house which lay to one side of the red-bricked kennels and stables, no hounds now but a couple of hunters still kept. There was no view of the Hall, but as he stood there he saw three or four cars come into the park and move up the driveway to the Hall which was hidden by the angle of the house. There was a fairly large staff employed there and nearly all of them lived in the close neighbourhood. It was almost nine o'clock and they were on their way to work.

The sight gave him no pleasure. There was a fast tide of change running now which many found hard or impossible to resist. Estates far larger than the Seyton place had long made a compromise with the times, turning themselves into show pieces, museums, fun fairs and zoos and wild animal parks . . . the public gawping, few realizing or caring that change—and not for the good—was eating into their own lives. The breezes that blew over England's green and pleasant land were soured now by the stink of car exhausts, and that not the only pollution for the spirit of man was being poisoned by the decay of the old virtues. For a moment or two bitterness and anger stirred him. In the long run, perhaps, there would be no standing against the change. But here, as long as he could make it so, things must stay as they always had been. Once he had the Hall back it should be the way it had always been; some small part of the tide of change could be resisted by him. After him? Well, he could only do what he could do. Roger would either be able to carry on or he would have to make some compromise. But that was the future. For the present he meant to have his say. He smiled suddenly, knowing how most people would regard and pity his attitude. Well, let them. The good Lord in His wisdom was over careful with His miracles these days, waiting perhaps for the first true cry of deep anguish from His people.

He went down to breakfast and was served by Mrs Shipley, stout, formidable and loyal, her hair, which as a boy he had known as black as a raven's wing, now iron-grey, wearing on her high-necked blouse the old cameo brooch which his mother had given her for a wedding present. As he ate his kidneys and bacon he went through the few letters which awaited him. Some of them were bills—addressed to him as executor—which had been outstanding at Punch's death. One was from his wine merchant, another from a Ross-on-Wye saddler . . . all of them from tradespeople he had used and knew himself, except for an account rendered from a firm of photographic and high fidelity specialists for quite a large sum. He smiled to himself. From his early days Punch had been mad about radios, cassette-recorders and photography. Well, as executor he would have to get details of the purchase. Punch had probably lit his pipe with the original detailed bill. He leaned back, suddenly touched by the black shade of anguish at the thought that never again would he see Punch come stumping into this wainscoted room, calling to Mrs Shipley for food, but before the mood could fully claim him Mrs Shipley came in to say that Shipley was waiting in the Land Rover.

That morning they drove around the home estate and farm and quite a few of the tenanted farms. The estate itself had about two thousand acres in hand and was run from day to day by an estate manager. Shipley drove and behind them sat Punch's labrador bitch, Honey. At the outset, after their greeting, Shipley, over sixty, lean and sparse as a winter hawthorn, his thin face deeply cleft, his pale blue eyes missing little that moved in the world of man and beast around him, said, "You want me to follow Mr Punch's round, Mr Richard?"

"Yes, Shippy. Do that."

Shipley hesitated a moment and then, before driving off, said, "Best to say it now, Mr Richard. If there'd been a thing I could have done, I'd have done it. But it came like lightning. One minute he was with me, and the next, dear soul, he was gone. I'd rather t'would have been me, dear God, since I've had most of my rightful span."

"I know, Shippy. It was God's will."

"Aye, and that's something no man can read."

They drove off into the sun-warmed, sparkling March morning, and every twist and turn of road and track brought back memories sharply to Seyton. In time he knew that the memories would dim and lose their poignancy, but for now there was no escaping their bite. He had gone through this after Ruth's death and found a new kind of peace for himself, and he knew it would happen now with time. But there was no hurrying the present. It had to be lived at God's pace and endured at His will even though no man could ever read final understanding of His purpose. Punch was dead and all around him the morning was alive with a new awakening. The rooks were building in the thinly greened elms. The hedge bottoms were golden with new coltsfoot blooms. In the long pasture at the western end of the estate three hares were fighting, not in play but courtship earnest while above them the lapwings flew and tumbled through the air in mating display. High up on the wooded hillside the badgers would be clearing out their winter beds from their setts and biting bark from the trees to get at the rising sap. Strings of toad spawn dully pearled the ditches and in the river and sidestreams the gravel beds now abandoned by the trout were being taken over by pike and grayling for their spawning. Birth, mating and death—nothing that fully lived could escape that cycle.

Towards the end of the morning they stopped on their way back upriver to have a drink at the Red Lion at Bredwardine. As they drank their beer Shipley said, "Do you want to call at the Hall on the way back, Mr Richard?"

"I don't think so, Shippy. I'll go up there later." Then on an impulse, he asked, "Did Mr Punch go up there much?"

"Not much." Shipley shook his head. "Oh, no—not much . . . well, that is towards the end. He never said anything to me, of course, but I got the feeling that something must have gone wrong between him and that Mr Shanklin."

"I always thought that they got on well together. I've always liked the look of him."

"Maybe, Mr Richard. But good and bad can't be judged by looks." Shipley chuckled. "You remember old Slinger, the Baptist preacher? Face like an angel and always spouting the good book—but he'd tup anything in skirts that showed willing. Oh, yes, he looked after his flock all right."

Seyton laughed, but decided not to follow the line any farther. Once Shipley knew you were in the mood for gossip he revelled in the dissection of local reputations. But he did find it a bit odd that Punch should have taken against Shanklin who, it had seemed to him, had always been most courteous and, without putting it in so many words, had indicated that he had a sympathetic understanding of their feelings at having to let the Hall go out of their hands. The man had always gone out of his way to make sure that the presence of the Foundation's staff at the Hall gave no trouble to them and had often consulted them over the most trivial matters which he felt might affect their ancestral feelings.

For this reason it was no surprise to him that evening as he was having a drink before dinner that Shanklin called to see him. He was a man in his early fifties, tall and plump where once he must have been muscular and hard. His once fair hair had gone almost white and his round face was as red as a misty autumn moon. Although he had never taken Holy Orders he gave the impression of a jolly, sporting parson. He was a bachelor and precise and particular about his clothes which were always sober and expensive.

He accepted the offer of a drink and while Seyton fixed it for him, expressed his sympathies over Punch's death briefly but sincerely and went on, "I came, too, in order to welcome you back and to ask if you would care to dine at the Hall some time soon?"

"I should like that. Thank you."

"Oh, good. Then we'll arrange it. We've got one or two new things I don't think you've seen yet. A set of particularly fine sketches of the fifteenth-century murals in Eton College Chapel, and there's a good old argument going on as to whether they were made by Baker and Gilbert or just copies of their set by an unknown hand. Probably an argument which will never be resolved but all good cut-throat fun amongst the experts. Then there's a splendid choir banner embroidered with the last words of Mary Queen of Scots—*In manus tuas, Domine, confido spiritum meum* . . . Oh, dear, what am I doing?"

Seyton laughed. "It's all right. I like people with enthusiasm."

"Ah, yes. How good of you to say so." Shanklin put his drink to his lips briefly. "But, to be honest, in this case you are wrong. Embarrassment, I think, is the word, not enthusiasm. On my part, of course, for I have only heard today that you are hoping to get the Hall back into your hands."

"That's true."

"And given the circumstances—very natural. But where should we ever find another home for our work and our treasures to compare with the Hall?"

"The country is full of Seyton Halls going for a song."

"Well, that's undeniable. But, oh dear, the upset and all the arrangements for moving. Still, I have to say that I understand your feeling and sympathize with it."

"You think the Board of Governors will decide in my favour?"

Shanklin gave a slow sigh and hunched the shoulders of his broadcloth jacket. "I'm in no position to answer that. I've worked with committees and boards of governors a great part of my life and I never cease to be amazed at their ways. But for your sake—though it would mean a great upset to me—I sincerely hope they will give you what you want. You look a little surprised, but you have no need to be. Part of our work is the preservation of traditions . . . in all justice we have no right to stand in the way of your family tradition. However, we shall soon know—the meeting is to be arranged for next week, down here. That's another reason why I'm here—to ask you if you would like to come up and meet them all before they go into committee?"

"I certainly would."

"Splendid. I'll let you know the exact time and day. But before that I shall look forward to your coming up to dine with us."

*   *   *   *

Georgina Collet lived in a deep fold of the Cotswolds some miles south of Cirencester. A pot-holed track, leading off a side road, ran along the edge of a small lake surrounded by forestry plantations, to an old gamekeeper's lodge at the far end. Surrounded by a small garden, honeysuckle-hedged, it sat on a little bluff overlooking the water. Picturesque, Kerslake thought . . . just the place for an artist, or whatever she called herself. He was in a bad mood and knew exactly the reasons. He did

43

not like amateurs and—though he was used to it—he was always irritated by being left too long in the complete dark. Oh, her role was easy enough to understand without any explanation from Quint—but the purpose behind it . . . well, he might live to be an octogenarian and never know.

He climbed the stone steps to the front door and was further and irrationally irritated when, in answer to his ring, she came out of a door some way to his left where he had already noticed a row of outhouses converted into a studio. She wore a shabby old green studio long coat, the late morning sun burnished her rust-red hair, and she was a good-looker. All he had to do here could have normally—even in this service—been done by letter or a telephone call, except that Quint had insisted on his driving down and that meant that Quint—though he would never have put it into words—wanted him to make some assessment for himself, which, in turn, meant that since she was not true Birdcage she was not going to be trusted. Assessment as bait . . . to catch what? Long years with Quint and his methods told him that of that, not even Quint might be sure—and that was a situation which made Quint awkward, even petty at times.

He introduced himself and she took him into the studio which was freezing cold and made his toes curl. She boiled an electric kettle and made him instant coffee which he loathed, and then suddenly surprised him as she handed him the drink and said with a momentary wry twist of her mouth, "You look thoroughly fed up, Mr Kerslake."

"I am." He was surprised to hear himself say it.

"With me?"

He was surprised again with the frankness, and said quickly, "No."

She laughed. "That's not true. Oh, I know all about it from my father. Professionals don't like amateurs on their patch. But don't blame me—I had no choice. You must have guessed that, no?"

He gave a dry laugh, conceding her something though he had no words for it right then. "Your situation is your concern

—and I don't deal in guesses. And I don't mean to be rude either."

"That's nice of you. Neither do I. Let's say we're both embarrassed—and then push it behind us since maybe we've got to work together. You because it's your job and me because of my father about whom I imagine you know everything?"

"Yes, I do. I knew him, but only very briefly. He went . . . away soon after I joined."

"Nicely put. His conscience got the better of him. That's a crime at Birdcage. Foolish, isn't it, to join an order and then break your vows?"

"In my book, yes." As he reached down and began to open his brief-case he was aware that he had got it all wrong . . . making the elementary mistake of pre-judging. Birdcage had chosen well. She could match mood for mood without giving offence and with her face and figure she was pleasant on the eyes and there was something about her which, though not easy to put into words, made its impact. A saucy bitch, really, but not one to waste energy trying to be other than she was. Maybe that was another reason why she had been chosen for whatever it was . . . bait? That meant, too, that someone had read this Seyton bloke well. He handed her a thick manilla quarto envelope. "You'll find in this a whole lot of agents' stuff of country cottages and holiday bungalows and lets in the area. There's no pressure on that kind of accommodation at this time of year—you should have no trouble. There's a sheet too with three telephone numbers on it—you can get me on one or the other usually—but if not they've all got message recorders and I'll ring you back."

She took the envelope and without opening it said, "Is that all?"

"Yes, that's all."

"You could have sent this through the post."

"Oh, yes. But I was told to bring it."

She smiled. "So that you could have a good look at me?"

He laughed. "Photographs would have done for that—but they don't tell the whole story, do they?"

"Thank God, no. The human spirit is like running water, constantly changing as it follows its course. That's why, for considerations well known to you, I'm happy to be given the chance to play the whore if necessary for my father's sake. He's a stupid man and a weak one—but I love him. Will you be coming up to Herefordshire?"

"Only if and when it's necessary."

She was silent for a moment or two as she broke open the envelope, glanced briefly at its contents and dropped them on to the table at her side. Then with a sudden smile she said, "I can see that you are hating that coffee. Would you rather have a glass of sherry?"

He smiled, wondering briefly how in a few minutes he could have changed so much in feeling towards her. "Yes, I would. Thank you."

She nodded to a table by the window. "Perhaps you'd like to help yourself. There's dry and medium."

"Thank you." He crossed to the table which held two decanters and some glasses, one of them still half full of dry sherry. He poured himself a medium sherry and then came back to her and handed her the half glass of dry sherry. "I must have interrupted your mid-morning tipple."

She laughed. "Thank you." Then raising the glass, sipped at it and said, "Here's to Birdcage."

"And here's to you."

"Personally or professionally?"

"Personally. You'd never last professionally."

"Why not?"

He reached out to the long table where a portfolio of drawings lay open and picked up the top one. It was a red chalk drawing of two swans fighting . . . probably something she had seen on the lake outside.

"That's your profession. You can hear the water foaming and the great thud of their wings."

"Thank you, Mr Kerslake."

"I used to see the mute cobs fight like that in the spring on the Taw in Devon."

"They do it on the lake in St James's Park, too."

He laughed. "True—but it's not the same. Or doesn't seem to be."

"Perhaps the change is in you?"

He was silent for a moment or two. Against his will she was reaching him, making a mark where he would have thought he was least vulnerable . . . disturbing him emotionally just by being herself. The emotion was one which he only allowed himself on his own terms. To his own surprise he heard himself say, "You do some things in life which change you and automatically put some things out of your reach."

With a change of tone she said in a low voice, "Oh, yes, I know all about that. From my father. Though he never passed into your arcane circle. Or have I guessed wrong?"

Frowning, anger stirring in him, he said, "Somebody has to be capable. Few are. But the garden has to be weeded. Anyway——" he threw off his mood and smiled "——you feel and guess too much. You'd better watch that with Seyton. Also, too, you show too much."

"Only to those with the right kind of eyes—like yours. If they told you tomorrow to go and kill him you would, wouldn't you? Just as you have done before with others."

"I draw my pay—but first I do my work."

"So will I for the sake of my dear, stupid father. But I shall hate it without showing it. Just as you do your work. I don't care how you contain or disguise your self-loathing—you hate yourself. What would you give now to be a man who had recently come through my door to choose a few drawings, a free man, and we discovered we liked one another? And then after a few drinks we both knew we wanted to go to bed with one another. Just ordinary, simple people, moving to their own uncomplicated and innocent emotional tides. You'd like to turn the clock back to that, wouldn't you?"

He laughed gently. He liked her even more now, though he was still sure that Quint had made a mistake; liked her because she felt certain that she had read him correctly and wanted to ease some of her self-disgust by probing bluntly at the heart of

47

his. And he was sorry for her. She would do her job all right, but no one would ever be shown the spiritual bill she would have to pay. He said, "Yes, of course I'd like it, Miss Collet. The idea that is. On the other hand I would just as easily—if Quint had ordered it—pull a gun from my pocket and shoot you dead. That's why your father is in prison and I'm not. I'd even go to bed first with you and then shoot you—if Birdcage wanted it that way."

Pursing her lips and giving a quick, dismissive shrug of her shoulders, Georgina said easily, "What a perfect sod of a man you are. I wonder why I like you?"

"Because you envy me for having settled for what I am while you haven't settled for what you have—a stupid father who has mucked up your life. I'm sorry, but——" he slid the drawing of the swans back on to the table "——since you wanted a chopping-block I was too much of a gentleman not to oblige." He turned towards the door to leave and said, "Thank you for the sherry. Have a nice time in Herefordshire—and don't treat Seyton like me. You'll confuse him which won't do at all. Idyllic is the word, I think, for the relationship we're after."

She laughed then, shaking her head like a man and hugging her elbows, and said, "Bully for you! I just wanted to stamp on someone's face—and you've been so nice about it. Thank you."

Kerslake paused by the door and said, "You'll be all right. It's quite pleasant at times to forget your true self and act a part. Sometimes, like me, you end up opting for acting all the time. Goodbye, and thank you for the sherry. We'll be in touch."

When he was gone Georgina poured herself another sherry and sat at the table staring at the two swans and then after a little while said with quiet passion, "Oh, my dear, dear father—I do really damn, damn you . . ."

*　　*　　*　　*

A few days after Shanklin had called on him Seyton went up to the Hall to dine. He walked up in the near dark, the Hall little more than a formless sprawl of dark bulk against the western sky. Here and there a light showed from an upper floor while the main steps were held in a shadowy amber glow from the great lantern over the wide double oak doors. There was a flicker of pipistrelle bats from gloom to light as they hunted the early moths along the façade. At the top of the steps he hesitated a moment, amused but also knowing the touch of resentment in him that he should have to pull the great bell chain to gain admittance to his own house. Memory transported him to the far gone days when he had been too small even to reach its great wrought-iron pendant at the end of the thick chain.

Before he had even begun to reach for the bell pull the half door opened to show him Shanklin. Was the man so considerate of his feelings that he had set watch for his coming to spare him even a brief moment of bitterness? Probably, he thought. Shanklin beneath the eagerness and slight pomposity was a man of feeling.

A manservant, a hovering shadow, came across the large red and black quarried tiles to take his hat and coat and then Shanklin, enveloping him in small talk and charm, took him into what had once been his own father's library and study. The old faded brown velvet curtains had been replaced at the mullioned windows with a rich, red damask worked with gold thread. Bookshelves lined two of the walls. To one side of the Italian marble fireplace hung the Gainsborough painting of the notorious Sarah Seyton . . . blue gown, a wide white sun bonnet hanging from one idle hand, her other hand resting on the head of her favourite lurcher, a mocking smile on her lips and a taunting, wicked look in her green eyes; wicked she had been and joyful with it, a red-haired enchantress in the true Circe mould.

Standing by the fireplace was—as he soon learned—the only other guest who was introduced to him as Sir Manfred Grandison, a large, bulky pirate of a man—a wooden leg and a black eye-patch all that were missing. In the place of a patch he wore a monocle, its red silk cord looping over the lapel of his dark grey suit. He was black haired and black bearded and his broad red face, time-creased and experience-scarred, wrinkled

49

with a warm friendly smile as he was introduced to Seyton.

As they shook hands Grandison said, "Knew your father a little. Came down once or twice when you were young but you won't remember me."

"I do now, sir."

"Oh . . .?"

"Well, not you so much but your car. It was a nineteen twenty-eight Hispano-Suiza 'Boulogne' with an eight-litre engine with Gurney Nutting coachwork."

"Dead right. Long gone now. God knows where."

Shanklin, who was hovering, took Sir Manfred's empty glass, asked Seyton what he would drink and as he went to serve them, said, "Sir Manfred is the political adviser to our Foundation. With our world-wide operations . . . all so complicated at times with political difficulties we are very lucky to enjoy his services."

"Blah! Blah! Blah!" said Sir Manfred and gave a great laugh.

As Seyton smiled, to his surprise Shanklin laughed as well, and said, "Don't be deceived. We'd be lost without him."

Sir Manfred shook his head. "Plenty of others as good as I am. And anyway, in this world, political advice is child's play. Weigh up the pros and cons intelligently, make a decision—and then advise the opposite. You can't go wrong." He grinned at Seyton as he took his glass from Shanklin, and went on, "Too broad a statement for you, Seyton?"

Seyton shook his head. "I'd call it a smoke screen behind which to hide your talents."

"So you can turn a phrase as well as a furrow?"

"Well, I don't know about that, sir. But since I became a business man, and a successful one, much to my surprise, I've found that political forces mean little. If you want something then you must find the right man to buy or bribe. Not that I care for the condition much, but that's the way you get what you want."

"Oh, I feel that's far too cynical," said Shanklin.

"Not at all," said Sir Manfred. "Never was and never will be. Man is a dirty little pig who just wants to make sure his own trough is always full. Any exceptions, and to be honest there are a few, are very, very rare. Just read your history. As it was in the beginning, is now and always will be."

To Seyton's surprise Shanklin, far from being put out, laughed and said, "Don't be deceived, Seyton. Sir Manfred just enjoys putting a cat among the pigeons. But at heart he knows that there is an undiminishable longing in all men for that which is right, ennobling and virtuous."

"The only thing I know about all men," said Sir Manfred, "is that like sheep they can be led astray by any goat. That's the first principle of all political systems—and the *obiter dicta* of many not so new religions and religious organizations. Always excepting the Foundation, of course, Seyton, since they pay me a very handsome retainer."

Seyton smiled, enjoying the man, yet a little surprised that Shanklin clearly had the same feeling. Nodding at the painting of Sarah Seyton, he said, "I think she would have been on your side."

Sir Manfred nodded. "Oh, yes. I know all about her. At one time I was almost tempted by your father to write a biography. But after a few talks with him about her I realized that—I was young and ambitious then—it would do nothing for my career. So I chose William Wilberforce instead. It sold one thousand and forty-nine copies."

As Sir Manfred was speaking Seyton remembered how as a growing child he had been given modified versions of the notoriety of Sarah Seyton and to them, with further years, had been added the full knowledge of the woman, a hell-raiser, a rebel, a great beauty with the courage of a lioness and the morals of the barn yard; witty, cultured and fearless for her own neck or reputation, never to marry and lucky never to bear love child, and finally to take her own life as her beauty—or zest for life—waned, leaving behind her a defiant farewell note. Glancing up at her now as Sir Manfred spoke, it seemed to him that she looked down on them all with amused contempt.

They had dinner, not in the great dining hall, but in a room which he remembered as being his mother's sitting room, a small octagonal chamber, lofty and elegant, the ceiling painted gold and blue and with a classical design of Venus imploring Vulcan to furnish arms and weapons to aid Aeneas in his fight against the Rutulians; and remembered how when a lad and had sometimes sat here with his mother, enduring some homily for misbehaviour, his eyes would stray when chance permitted to contemplate the half naked beauties of Venus, remembered too with a sudden waywardness the first time his own hand had rested on a breast as firm and round as any this ceiling Venus displayed to tempt Vulcan . . . that of the home farm manager's daughter in one of the lofts over the stables.

They ate and the talk was light and stimulating, a little dominated by Sir Manfred, but amusingly so, and the food was good, so good that it was clear that the distress and want of the world which the Foundation fought did not cause them here to practise any monastic self-denial. Also too—with that instinct for marking the undercurrents in men's designs which, always latent, had ripened tardily in him and contributed largely to his success in business—he realized that this invitation was not made from plain and due courtesy. He was here for a purpose as indeed was Sir Manfred who, clearly, despite his bombastic and amusing projection of himself, was acting in his official role as adviser to the Foundation—a role which, when they retired to the library for port and a servant came to call Shanklin away to answer a telephone call from overseas, the man wisely acknowledged quite openly with a big, bluff sea-captain smile creasing his face.

"We've been left alone. Of design, as you undoubtedly have guessed?"

"Yes, Sir Manfred. Shanklin is too sincere a man to be a good actor."

Sir Manfred laughed. "Aye, but he has one or two invaluable qualities which we won't discuss. But the point at issue is bluntly that you have thrown the cat among the pigeons by wanting the Hall back."

"In my place would you have done differently, sir?"

"No. I happen to have a high regard for tradition and attachment to place. More than that, I regard such a feeling as grossly lacking in the world today—and part reason for the God-awful mess the world struggles in. But for this evening I just have to limit myself to my brief as adviser to the Foundation. You'll appreciate, of course, that I have discussed this with Felbeck?"

"Yes. But I made myself very clear to him. This house is mine and I want it back and I am prepared to pay the price for breaking the lease. That is the very simple situation."

Sir Manfred smiled and began to prepare himself a cigar after Seyton had silently refused one. He said, "Pray God, Seyton, that life always sends you complicated situations—they are so much easier to deal with than simple ones. If you get one girl in trouble that's a simple situation, you think. But it isn't. Get two in trouble at the same time, which seems more complicated, and you have no worries since not being able to do justice to both, you need render justice to neither."

Seyton laughed. The longer he was with this man the more he liked him, but he was not fooled by his manner or his questionable, though amusing, sophistry. "I'll remember that. But as for the Hall—there are no complications on my side. I want it. I've told Felbeck so, and I am prepared to pay the price. Surely all that remains is for the Governors to vote for or against?"

"And if they go against?"

For a moment Seyton made no reply, fingering his port glass, weighing frankness against obliqueness, and then, quickly deciding that no amount of soft talk would conceal his true intentions, said, "Then I'll do my damndest to find some way—though God knows what."

Sir Manfred, pursing his lips, smiled and began to polish his monocle. "You're like your father. We were at Balliol together, did you know that?"

"No, sir."

"What kind of way would you imagine you could find?"

"Well, given my recent successes in business I would say that if they voted against me I would find out the ones who were against my offer and then I would work on them. Every man has his price."

"You're a determined bugger, aren't you?" It was said pleasantly. "How would you fix a bishop?"

"Sir Manfred—are you telling me that in the whole of history there has never been a bishop who was fixed?"

"Alas, no. Too many. In fact the two bishops on our Board . . . no, I mustn't say that. You'll probably get their vote, anyway."

"I'm glad to hear it."

"Don't let it raise your hopes. We've a general and a cabinet minister. You won't get theirs. They both happen to be thoroughly disreputable men who are trying to achieve grace through the Foundation—they've reached that age when they worry about their immortal souls. Never a failing of bishops that. They know they're safe."

Seyton laughed. "I begin to doubt your qualifications as adviser. You give too much to the other side, Sir Manfred."

"Don't be deceived by words or appearances. The devil has many voices and many shapes. Still, there it is."

"You think they'll turn me down?"

"I don't know. They will vote as each decides—aided a little, I trust, by my report of our meeting. You have no objection to that?"

"No."

"But, in fairness, I shall make clear your absolute sincerity and determination to have restored to you what is yours. It's a laudable ambition—rare these days simply because so few people ever find themselves in the position you are to say that cost doesn't mean a damn. The clocks need turning back, and I think the time for this is long overdue and—between ourselves, my dear chap—I also think the world needs far less charity flung around and far more discipline and hardship to stimulate the true virtues which brought man down from the trees to stand on his own two feet. Sweet charity has gone sour. I say this in confidence which you are at liberty to break.

54

Discipline. *Hoc opus, hic labor est.* As the inscription on the ceiling in the room in which we dined says."

Seyton hesitated for a moment or two and then, deciding he stood on safe ground, said, "And you, Sir Manfred—are you worrying about your immortal soul? Or, perhaps like the two bishops, probably on my side already?"

Sir Manfred laughed loudly, the monocle popping from his eye and swinging to reflect the room lights. "Well, I'll be damned! You don't pick the easy fences, do you? A straight line across country. But you forget I haven't got a vote."

"You've got something more powerful than that . . . more persuasive. A voice which is listened to."

"And what would you offer me in return?"

Seyton shrugged his shoulders. "I wouldn't be sure. Not money certainly. You'd need something far more significant than that."

"I might need that as well—but just what can you offer me in the way of temptation?"

"Well . . ." Seyton hesitated, frankly lost and at that moment almost as though she were coming to his help, his eyes were held by those of Sarah Seyton in the painting on the wall. He went on, "Well, Sir Manfred . . . I'd make you free of all the family records, diaries and letters which we've never made public, so that you could write a life of Sarah Seyton and so forget William Wilberforce. And, in addition, I would make you a present of the Gainsborough portrait."

Sir Manfred, face expressionless, put down his port glass deliberately and slipped his monocle back into place and then said heavily, "You are Satan's disciple. Satan and Seyton. Now I really know how you went from country squire to an international business tycoon so easily and quickly. And, God help me, you have tempted me. But sadly, my dear boy, you have come many years too late."

"A pity. You would have sold one hundred thousand and forty-nine copies and had a pretty Gainsborough and a name to rank with whom . . . Boswell?"

"Coarse sod."

"Then Lytton Strachey?"

"Forget him. But, for the pleasure you have given me and would by your offer have given me, I promise you this. I shall present your case with a certain amount of bias your way. But think little of that. The Governors tolerate no canvassing. Until their votes are cast they keep their own counsel. And now, here comes the worthy Shanklin, so our matter is ended. I thank you for the refreshment your talk has given me. God help anyone who really gets in your way." He looked towards Shanklin who had stopped just inside the door and, grinning, said, "You came back just in time. I was near to be taken up to a high place and sorely tempted."

Seyton only stayed for a short while after Shanklin's appearance and when the man returned from seeing his guest away he poured himself a large brandy in silence and then, his eyes on Sir Manfred, studied his face, clearly with concern.

After a while, and clearly unconcerned with Shanklin's interest, almost in fact unaware of him, Grandison said, "I knew his father well at Oxford, but not much after. He was a hellion and a scholar—and what, I think, might be described as of a slow-burning temperament. But, by God, when too far a point had been reached it was like a volcano exploding. So too, I would say, is his son."

"What did he say . . . his manner . . . well, your assessment, Sir Manfred?"

Grandison nodded to a small display cabinet for coins near the window and said, "Play the tape back and hear for yourself. The cheeky, clever sod."

The tape was replayed and when it was finished Sir Manfred Grandison said, "What do you think of that?"

"He certainly handles himself well, as I said he could. But there is nothing he can do if he loses the vote."

"He's not the kind of man who accepts that he can do nothing. His mania is hard set. If he loses the vote he will try to find a way——"

"But what way?"

"None, you think, to be found? Have you forgotten clause

seven in the lease? No Seyton property or tenancy ever let without it."

"But that's ridic——" Shanklin broke off for a moment or two, and then went on, "That's unthinkable."

"So was landing on the moon once. But it happened."

"I know, Sir Manfred. But anything that could be raised under that clause . . . well, all that has now ceased."

"My dear Shanklin—time is not a straight line. It is a lake without limits where the ripples of every human act spread but never die. We only think they do because we have not God's eye to capture their everlasting diminishment. And do not forget the Devil. He has a malign sense of humour." He smiled suddenly, shrugging concern away, and raising his glass said, "I think we might in propitiation drink a small health to him with the plea that he stays on our side. No?"

Grinning boyishly, Shanklin said, "Certainly, if you think it will help."

"Well, it's a small gesture, but sincere." He raised his glass and before touching it to his lips said, "To Satan, not Seyton."

*   *   *   *

Warboys, forgetful of the time, which was near midnight, was seated at his fly-tying desk in a corner of his bedroom— which overlooked the Embankment not far from the Tate Gallery and gave him a view of the river—when the telephone rang. For a moment or two he ignored it, not hoping it would go away and leave him in peace, but reluctant to come back from what in sentimental and rare moments he would have described as the haunt of coot and hern. The nearing month of April would bring trout fishing and his occasional days on the Test. With the high-powered angle-poise lamp low over his vice and looking like an eighteenth-century bibliophile with a pair of high magnification Bishop Harman spectacles perched on the tip of his nose, he was tying the last of a new batch of flies for the coming season. It was a blue dun which was a

57

pattern supposed to imitate the dark olive and iron blue duns, though he knew perfectly well that, since Charles Cotton first mentioned it in 1676, it had never been satisfactorily decided as to which natural species he had intended the name to refer, there being no such insect as a natural blue dun. However, he did not care a tinker's curse about that because he frequently caught fish with it. Breaking away from dubbing yellow silk with mole fur for the body he reached absently for the telephone and said, "Warboys."

Grandison's voice at the other end said pleasantly, "I had a bet with myself that you would be doing one of three things. Either listening to Bach and drinking whisky, or warm in bed with one of your Knightsbridge matrons, or with feet up, nodding gently over one of Milton's sonnets . . . 'Avenge, O Lord, thy slaughtered saints'."

"None of them. I was tying a fly."

"Ah, yes. April cometh. And——" the tone of voice changed on the last word "——I want to know when this damned girl Collet cometh. Is she in the field yet?"

"She moved into a bungalow up there yesterday, sir."

"You can forget the *sir*. I want her to get off her undoubtedly neat little bottom and get operating."

"You would like it expressed to her in those terms?" Only late at night—and not then at the Birdcage Walk offices— would he have been so mildly flippant, but with Grandison he had long established that after midnight he was his own man and could choose his own moods and, if he wished, show them openly.

"I do not at this time of night propose to instruct you as to the exact style in which your directive to her should be set. Tell her to get up off her arse and start working—that is the content. The phrasing can be elegant or menacing . . . which-ever you wish. Also . . ." the voice at the other end of the telephone broke off and in the silence that followed Warboys idly speculated whether Grandison was taking a long and refreshing pull at the whisky which would be undoubtedly to his hand or was merely pausing undecided of the wisdom of opening some line which had suddenly struck him as perhaps likely to be fruitful.

Enjoying himself, Warboys broke the silence by saying, "I think you said 'Also'? Or was it perhaps just a long sigh?"

"It was 'Also' underlined by a sigh because—unusual for me—I am not relishing crossing swords with our Herefordshire squire. However, it must be if I read him right. So, get someone to investigate his meteoric—as the papers would say—rise to eminence in the business world. Dig for dirt? Yes. Has he crossed the line which so hazily divides right from wrong at any time? Bribery. Currency regulations. Somewhere it could have happened. High success allied to purity of thought, word and deed is as mythical as the unicorn."

"I will do what I can while at the same time correctly schooling my own curiosity about all this."

"And so you bloody better had!" Grandison gave a great bellow of laughter and rang off.

Warboys shrugged his shoulders and went back to his fly-tying. He had no intention now of disturbing any duty officer or of hauling from bed or dalliance those of his people now in their homes who had earned the right to an honest night's respite from professional concern; a sentiment, he knew, which sprung from his own frustration at not knowing what the hell all this was about.

CHAPTER FOUR

SHE HAD FOUND a solidly built and comfortable bungalow some way to the west of Leominster, standing on a small bluff which overlooked the river Arrow, and not more than a half an hour's drive to Seyton Hall. Sliding doors at the end of the lounge opened to a semi-circular sun room which would serve quite well as a small studio. Not far away was a woman who kept an eye on things for the owners when they let the place and, additionally, was happy to come in and cook and clean when required and also prepared to do a certain amount of shopping for her. The bungalow was called Arrowbank. It had a small garden and a thin strip of neglected orchard which ran down to the river. On the morning of her second day there the telephone rang as she was breakfasting. Answering it she had no difficulty in at once recognizing the voice.

"Good morning, Miss Collet."

"Good morning to you, Mr Kerslake."

"Settled in?"

"More or less." He was being brisk, just as he had been when she had telephoned his number the previous day to give him her address. She matched his mood, for ever since her first meeting with him she had slightly regretted her attack on him, knowing that, no matter what comfort it had given her, she had been unfair to him. Personal feelings and private emotions were from now on to be banished in their exchanges.

"Good . . ." He let the word hang for a moment or two longer than he need, and then went on flatly, "There seems to be a certain amount of urgency about all this which has only just been made clear to me. I was under the impression that you could choose your own style of approach and with such timing as you felt wise. But now it seems not so."

"You want me to get cracking."

"Those above me do."

"Like knocking him down with my car and then carrying him back here to put his bloody broken leg in splints and gain his confidence, love and adoration, while playing Florence Nightingale?" She paused, waiting at least for a chuckle or a cross clearing of his throat. "Is that it?"

"That's exactly it in essence."

"Well then, you'll be pleased to hear that I've already been down to the Hall and seen him. I drove down yesterday afternoon to check the times the Hall was open to the public and he came riding by—not on a coal black stallion snorting flames through its nostrils, but on a nice chestnut mare—and, since I'd slowed for him to pass, he courteously tipped his cap to me. I wrote him down as a very nice chap. The kind which, if I've got at some time to go to bed with, I'd not necessarily find turning my stomach." As she spoke she felt the edge of resentment rising in her and already her vow of no emotion slipping.

To her surprise he said, without any change of tone, "The nurse-patient relationship is a very effective one—but we would prefer him on his feet and active."

"I'm going there today. Out of the tourist season this is the one day in the week when the Hall is open to the public. Afterwards I shall call on him at the Dower House."

"On what pretext?"

"I don't have to tell you, but I will. Reversing a very old gambit, I propose to show him my etchings. I'll let you know how I get on. Goodbye, Mr Kershaw." She put down the receiver.

She was at Seyton Hall just after eleven o'clock when it opened to visitors until three-thirty and joined a party of six other visitors. The Hall itself outside she had seen the previous day and had not been over impressed by it, though she did not discount the inevitable feeling of affection—leading to the assumption that it was beautiful—a family would feel for the place if they had owned it and enlarged and embellished it ever since the fourteenth century, though the earliest structure had now almost disappeared to give way to later additions. The oldest part was an abbreviated wing roofed with stone tiles and faced with an intricate patterning of black timbering to form white plastered quatrefoil panels. The main façade was red-bricked Tudor, holding the great entrance doorway, and was broken along its front and on the west corner with high round towers rising from ground level. The east wing was late Restoration, built of stone, with tall, elegant windows, and seemed to be turning its back politely but firmly on the rest of the house, content to overlook the yew-hedged rose garden and a distant view of the river Wye.

They were taken around by an official guide, neatly dressed in a dark green uniform, with brass buttons on his jacket carrying the monogram FF of the Felbeck Foundation. One day, she thought as she trailed around with the party, if things progressed as Birdcage clearly wanted them to progress, she would like to make the tour by herself and at her own pace and with freedom to linger. The Ballroom—originally the Great Chamber of the Tudor part of the house—had a fine Jacobean ceiling with a richly carved frieze of country pursuits and crafts, the walls hung with a collection of Seyton family portraits. In glass cases arranged down the sides and middle of the room were religious books and bibles with mediaeval bindings, eucharist veils, copes, chasubles, altar fronts and choir banners and—standing alone—a fine set of sixteenth-century Rood screen paintings and triptychs. In the Long Gallery on the first floor of the main building were hung paintings of famous English divines from the fifteenth century onwards and an impressively arranged exhibition of early English sanctuary knockers, and silver chalices, crucifixes, and processional crosses. In a saloon of the late Restoration wing, French brocade curtains drawn up in thick flounces at its windows, the walls ivory coloured and these, with the doors and windows, spangled in dull gold with straying tendrils of gilded wood, a Grinling Gibbons carved choir stall had been set up, together with a display of ecclesiastical needlework and needle-point lace, old and modern, all of it featuring the temptation of Adam and Eve.

It was twelve o'clock before Georgina—as she put it to herself—escaped. Going round even in a small party was inhibiting, the rhythm of one's own natural pace broken, for the guide had allowed no lingering, shepherding his sheep firmly but politely. She went into the car park and sat in her car and smoked a quiet cigarette before tackling Richard Seyton, and wishing she had brought a flask of whisky or sherry with her for purely reviving purposes.

Eventually she drove down the main exit road and pulled up outside the Dower House. Carrying a small portfolio of her work under her arm she walked up the terraced steps to the front door where she rang the bell. *Notice*, she said to herself, echoing the mood of the late guide, *the very fine vine and cable carving round the framework. This was purely domestic work well within the scope of local craftsmen in those——*

Mrs Shipley opened the door to her. Georgina gave her good morning and handed a private card to her saying, "I wonder— if Mr Seyton is in—whether he would kindly spare me a few minutes?" She smiled and added, "I am in no way selling or canvassing anything."

"I see." Mrs Shipley looked at the card and then at her and then during a brief glance again at the card while she was deciding whether to ask her in to wait, decided not and said, "I'll go and see, miss."

"Thank you."

Mrs Shipley gone, Georgina turned and looked across the garden to the black-and-white dovecot and watched a cockbird, gorge bubbling with love talk, bully a hen across the roof. Sex, she thought, made the world go round, and then had a bet with herself that her simple ploy would fail. Mr Richard Seyton would be too damned busy or just bloody-mindedly disinclined to see her.

At that moment in the small sitting room which was used

63

normally only by the family, Richard Seyton, card in hand, was saying, "What's she like?"

Mrs Shipley, who could be sometimes surprisingly uncharacteristic, said, "Well, Mr Richard . . . all I would say is if I were a single man just thinking of having a glass of sherry before lunch on his own, and had been brooding around all morning like a moulting cockerel, I'd say she was not the sort to make any mood worse and worth the trouble of pouring a second glass of sherry to find out what she wants."

Seyton laughed. "All right. Show her in. But there's no need to set a second place at table."

A little while later Georgina was sitting in a comfortable chair by the fire with a glass of sherry at her side and her portfolio on her lap while Seyton stood at the far end of the fireplace and, because he had been bored and out of mood with himself, said affably, "Well, Miss Collet, what can I do for you?"

Georgina handed her portfolio to him and said, "I wonder if you would be kind enough to look through these?"

Seyton sat down, rested the portfolio on his knees, slipped the tape bows free on the portfolio, and began to look through the few pen and colour wash drawings it held.

"I assure you that I am not here to try and sell any of them."

Seyton made no answer and began to go slowly through the collection. Although he did not show it, he was at once impressed. Music—with a very few exceptions—made little appeal to him, and his kind of literature was chiefly that which beguiled a train journey or the cramped tedium of intercontinental air travel. But art did touch him sharply, just as his eye delighted in its subjects. He knew at once that he was not dealing with any enthusiastic amateur or art teacher come to make some request for a subscription for some worthy society or body eager to promulgate . . . well, whatever it might be. He paused for a while over a drawing of a winter hare being coursed by two greyhounds across bare stubble, and then did the same over another of a nightjar on its ground nest giving a threat display—a thing which he had only seen once in his life. With care he went through the whole portfolio and knew that this girl . . . woman . . . had an eye and a talent given to few.

He carefully retied the bows of the portfolio and then handed it back to her with a smile. Then he stood up, noticing her sherry glass was almost empty, and carried the decanter to her and refilled it without any protest from her and was impressed by her calm and silence.

He said, for he could already see them framed and hung in one of the smaller rooms of the Hall when he should get it back, "I'll buy the lot at your own price, Miss Collet. Though something tells me that you are not here to sell—right?"

Georgina smiled and shook her head. "No, Mr Seyton, I'm not here to sell. But I like the compliment. As a matter of fact they've all been commissioned. But if you would like something similar of mine I'll gladly do it for you—in return for a small favour."

"Name it."

"Your permission, Mr Seyton, for a few weeks to walk over your land and estate to make sketches to complete this commission. I need roe deer and water fowl and a few other subjects which I know I shall find here."

"I see." He paused for a while. Not entirely irrationally—but certainly strongly—you see something, you like it, and you must have it: that was an old echo from his mother—he knew that he wanted the portfolio of drawings. He went on, "For whom are these drawings?"

"A London publisher. It's a commission." She smiled apologetically, giving a little shrug of her shoulders. "And I've already spent the advance he paid me."

"Will they belong to him?"

Momentarily, though not showing it, she was slightly annoyed at his persistence, no matter what it told her of his character. "Yes, they will."

"That's all right then. You've got my permission to go where you want and when you want—in return for his name and address."

65

"Yes, of course you shall have it. And thank you very much."

"It's a pleasure." He sipped at his sherry, and then went on, "I saw you yesterday, didn't I? Up by the Hall. A small Renault. I was riding."

"Yes, you did." Oddly, she felt a sudden twinge of uneasiness. Anyone fooling with this man was not going to find an easy adversary. "You must have a good memory for faces. I drove over to find out when the Hall was open. I've been round this morning."

"Like it?"

"To some extent. I don't get a great deal of pleasure at being shepherded around in a party."

"Nor me. If you wished I could arrange for you to go round privately sometime."

"That's very kind of you. I should like that." Georgina took a pencil from her handbag, reached for her visiting card which he had put on a nearby table and wrote on the back of it the name and address of her London publisher. Handing it to him, she said, "That's the name and address you need—if you are serious about having them."

His tone in no way offensive, he said, "Of course I'm serious." Then turning the card over, looking at her old address which she had crossed out to substitute her new one, he went on, "Is Arrowbank just a temporary address while you work on this commission?"

"Yes. The Cotswold one is my permanent address."

"It's a nice part of the country. I've hunted over there quite a lot." He slipped the card into a pocket of his waistcoat and then, politely but clearly dismissive, he said, "Well, there you are, Miss Collet. You're free to go where you want. If you have any problems—just let me know."

"Thank you."

He went to the main door with her and saw her out, and as she went back to her car Georgina had a sudden mood of depression. What the hell was she doing? Playing this stupid Birdcage game. This man was his own man, clearly. Not the kind, she felt sure, to fall for a pretty face or to be fooled by such an age old ploy as Kerslake and his superiors envisaged. There were times when—from the limited confidences of her father and later the more exact instructions of Quint on her first assignment—she had felt that she had walked into an unreal existence, an Alice-in-Wonderland dream world where appearances and meanings were topsy-turvy and all clouded with nightmare shadows. Her father had lived in that nightmare most of his adult life—and reality had only returned when he was sent to prison. Feeling suddenly bloody-minded she drove downriver to Bredwardine and had lunch at the Red Lion, a lunch preceded by two large dry sherries and accompanied by a half bottle of Mersault and rounded off with a brandy to keep her coffee company. She drove back to Arrowbank, feeling murderously bad-tempered, took a Mogadon and went to bed, preferring a few hours oblivion to the harassment of her own thoughts and self-disgust.

That afternoon Seyton spent mostly at his desk going through Punch's papers and accounts to get them into shape for handing over to Figgins so that they could be passed to Bellamy in order to get the estate affairs moving. More than once he groaned affectionately to himself at the muddle Punch had left and was relieved when Mrs Shipley came to call him for tea and to announce that the Rector was here to discuss the arrangements for the memorial service for Punch. And after the Rector had gone, Shanklin telephoned from the Hall to say that the meeting of the Governors to vote on the business of the Hall lease had been arranged for the coming Saturday—two days ahead—and would he care to come up and meet them all for drinks before dinner, but—naturally he would understand—not to stay to dinner since that would be when they would be discussing his offer among themselves prior to the taking of the vote after dinner. He said he would be there.

He then—since it had started to drizzle—put on cap and mackintosh and went for a walk through the fading daylight by the river. Coming back he went into the family chapel which stood isolated in a grove of ancient yews on a hillock in the middle of the park, well away from the Hall and the Dower

House. A barn owl ghosted low under the yews as he went up the path to the main door which was never kept locked. Inside he switched on a couple of nave lights and then went and sat in the family pew where as a boy he had wriggled his backside with boredom so often and as a man—though outwardly a conformist—he had often struggled with doubts until he had learned to lock them away in a secure compartment of his mind where they gave him no trouble at all. He said a prayer for Punch and a remembrance for Ruth and then—since Bellamy and Punch's will had been in his mind so recently he smiled—remembering the ritual of the sealed envelope he returned to the main door and threw its two bolts over so that no one could enter the chapel.

He went to the south transept, under which was the Seyton family vault, on its walls a crowded collection of memorial tablets. Part of the wall close to the entry to the bell tower was covered with old linenfold oak panelling. Above it close to the bell tower door was the memorial stone for Sarah Seyton who had lived joyfully and wickedly and who had written her own memorial which from the time his father had first translated it had touched and still did touch him with sharp sympathy, *Quantae sunt tenebrae! vae mihi, vae mihi, vae!* Crying out against the great darkness into which she must pass without faith or hope, leaving her beloved life behind. Beneath it was a secret entry which ran from the chapel to the Hall itself; its placing leading to the latter-day doggerel ending . . . *He who would enter the Hall unseen must pass by long silent Sarah.*

He turned the two centres of a pair of carved Tudor roses on the panelling which with a slight touch pivoted on its own longitudinal axis to show the beginning of stone steps descending sharply underground, a secret he and Punch had discovered as boys when they had gone up to the old choir gallery at the end of the chapel for a quiet and forbidden smoke one afternoon and had seen their father come in and operate the panel and—since he was that kind of man, hating neglect and disrepair—oil the inner central pivot on which the door swung. Going out he smiled to himself at the long-distant fear which had possessed him that his father might smell their cigarette smoke and find them, and realizing too with present affection how much of his father had been in Punch for the panel this day had swung easily on well-oiled pivots.

*   *   *   *

It was a lovely morning, less late March than anticipating April. In the park outside the lawns were polished green enamel and the lake blue from the reflection of the cloudless sky. Young leaf was hazing shrubs and trees and daffodil clumps lay like scattered golden largesse. God was in His heaven, thought Quint, and saying nothing but undoubtedly pondering with some uncertainty about the future of the human race. The railway train drivers had called a three-day strike, road transport drivers were still on strike unofficially but effectively so that petrol—the life blood of a decadent age—was running short at most pumps and had been exhausted at many others. Foodstuffs for man and beast stayed in store and Trade Union leaders in a variety of accents made belligerent or falsely comforting statements which made one wonder at the debasement universal education had brought to the language of Cranmer and Shakespeare—not without help from the Church. God was in His heaven all right, sighed Quint—and why not because he was damned sure that things were run quite differently there.

Kerslake, earlier summoned, came into the room and put a report before him. It was a report from Georgina detailing how she had made contact with Seyton. It was brief but needed little imagination to see that it might be a fruitful seeding.

"She got moving quickly," said Quint.

"She's that kind," answered Kerslake.

"Do I detect almost a note of admiration?"

"A little, I suppose, sir."

"Generous, considering your abomination of amateurs."

"Any of our other girls could have done it."

"Oh? I didn't know they were all artists of talent and plus."

"They would have found other ways in, sir."

"Which side of the bed did you get out this morning, my dear Kerslake?"

Kerslake smiled. "Sorry, sir. It's just that I've been thinking professionally and a bit beyond. Which you encourage me to do from time to time."

"And it has the same effect as getting out of bed the wrong side? Interesting. Perhaps you'd care to enlarge? And while you do you have my permission to sit down. But not on the window seat. I am enjoying the morning and pretending that God's in His heaven and all's well with the world. A rare fantasy."

"In the past," said Kerslake, sitting himself on an uncomfortable bentwood chair by the filing cabinet, "you have allowed me some liberties. Even encouraged them from time to time."

"True. And interesting, too, that whenever they come you always fall into a very stilted style of speaking. Just relax and be the Kerslake I know. I am more comfortable surrounded by well-known and familiar things—a shade tautological, but it will serve. It is a pity that it is too early for a glass of sherry, but coffee will be along soon. Now then, let me have the benefit of this professional-and-a-bit-beyond thinking."

"Well, Miss Collet, at the end of telephoning her report to me of her visit to Seyton Hall, said that after seeing Seyton she had lunch at a local hotel and had a friendly chat with the waitress who served her about Seyton Hall."

"Naturally. There's no restraining a woman's curiosity and she wasn't exceeding her brief."

"It's let on a long lease to something called the Felbeck Foundation for——"

"I know all about that," interrupted Quint. "Come to the essence."

"Local feeling is that now that Richard Seyton has inherited the estate from his brother and isn't short of a bob or two he will want to have the place back in his own hands, and there's local talk that he wants to buy out the rest of the lease from the Foundation."

"What a wonderful thing is local gossip. It spreads like ground elder. So he wants to buy out the lease?"

"Presumably. And——" Kerslake paused, knowing that he stood on the lip of over-reaching himself, but then, gambling on Quint's present mood and rarely spoken respect for him, he went on, "——and local opinion is that the Foundation won't play ball with that. It's a long lease. They've spent a lot of money setting up their show there. The betting is they will say it's a no deal to Seyton."

"Well, that would be logical and human. They've made their little nest there and, presumably, it's a perfectly valid lease. Seyton will just have to wait until it runs out."

Kerslake shook his head. "That's not what the locals think. Crudely, the feeling up there is that there'll be bloody fireworks if Seyton doesn't get what he wants. He's that kind. In fact all the Seytons have been that kind. One way or another he will get his way—is the local feeling."

"You can't break a perfectly valid lease. You can only buy it back."

"Yes, sir."

Quint shrugged his shoulders. "So that's that."

"One would assume so. But in that case—that he must just sit and wait for the lease to run out—I don't quite see how we can have any interest in him. Or am I being naïve?"

For a moment or two Quint was silent, remembering the time years before when he had first met Kerslake, then a raw young police officer in his native town of Barnstaple, and with an eye for raw potential to feed the Birdcage service had—with little trouble for Kerslake knew his own worth and ambitions—seduced, enticed or with only the slightest of pushes steered him Londonwards to join the happy family whose history—could it ever have been written and exposed—would have, not paralleled, but overtopped that of the Borgias. He said, "If I stated that you were well beyond naïvety—what conclusion would you draw? No guff—give it to me straight."

"I think, sir, that—no matter which way our interest is—there is a way to break the lease, and that either we want it to remain hidden or—not yet knowing what it is—would like to know so that we have a card in hand which we shall be able to play either way."

Quint shook his head, and chuckled. "Oh dear! Oh dear! Kerslake—you have grown up. I think we'll disregard the coming of the coffee and have a glass of sherry. Perhaps you would do the honours?"

Kerslake stood and went to the cupboard and, for the little while that his back was to him, Quint's face sagged to a momentary premature ageing. You picked and trained them, saw them through their first real crisis—when they were Kerslake's mettle—doubtful (because all human nature was unpredictable) whether the finger trigger would work or not. And then, blooded, intelligent, aye, and ambitious for that followed as the day the night, their mettle first matched and then, God help us, over-matched your own.

Taking the sherry glass which Kerslake brought to him, he sipped, sighed and then leaned back and considered the ceiling towards which, after a little pause, he addressed himself aloud.

"This, Kerslake, is between us. I brought you from the leafy lanes of Devon and simple pastoral delights like nicking shoplifters and the tedium of common rapes and burglaries into this rare haven of loftier iniquities. I am father and you are son, absolute loyalty and love binding us. Understood? Just you and me. No one else."

"Yes, sir."

"I am as much in the dark as you, but I share your views. There probably is a way that lease can be broken. Various things suggest themselves. Probably have already suggested themselves to Seyton. Beyond that I must say that I do not know why there is this interest in the air. But I would like to know. And you, of course, understand that, if you step out of line and are caught, you will go to the wolves without saying a word of what has passed in this room this morning. Naturally?"

"Yes, sir. Naturally."

"Think hard on it. Above me stand Warboys and others, and beyond them—though that is not generally known—Sir

Manfred Grandison. You would be a sparrow falling by the wayside, the incident noted, no doubt, by God but not to be averted by any act of His."

"Yes, sir."

"All right. Now drink up your sherry and go and leave me alone to brood upon my possible indiscretion."

But, when Kerslake had gone, Quint helped himself to another glass of sherry and sipped at it with an easy mind. What there was of honour in this organization was precious to him, possibly because there was so little, a tender, struggling growth, but there and comforting. Without that on what would he exercise his love?

*   *   *   *

On the morning of the day when Seyton was invited to meet the Governors of the Felbeck Foundation for drinks, he received from his London office a list of the eight people who would be voting about the lease on the Hall with some brief notes—made by Figgins from sources which so far in his business life had never let him down. Miss Figgins had come a long way since the day she had arrived at the Hall fresh-faced from the winds and weathers of the Black Mountains, capable and resourceful from being the eldest of a family of seven whose head—a widower—wrung, without bitterness, a living for his brood from his small sheep farm in the stubborn hill lands where his sister, a spinster, worked side by side with him with the worth of any man.

There were two bishops on the list. The first, coloured, was the Right Reverend C. P. Oflapi who was bishop of one of the sees of the Province of West Africa. Figgins had noted— *Cheerful, fuddy-duddy on the surface, but politically active and ambitious.* The other was a bishop suffragan from a South of England diocese, the Right Reverend Auguste Miller, M.A., of whom Figgins commented—*A bit mad, but never misses a chance to get in the news. I guess the madness is put on, but the self-publicity is natural. Feels lonely if he's ignored.*

Then came two Armed Forces men. The first was Major-

General V. Stripert, C.B., M.C., recently retired from NATO, who was designated by Figgins as—*Cheerful, smack-you-on-the-backy type, hunting, fishing. Widower which gives him scope for his favourite foible. Not to be treated lightly. Razor sharp professionally. Author of best-seller,* Some Generals Who Shouldn't Have Been. The other warrior was a Rear-Admiral Croft, C.B.E., a one-time Assistant Chief of Naval Staff, now retired, but very active as a fund-raiser on several national charities. Figgins noted—*Dishy. Popular. Specializes in youth organizations. Sailed Atlantic single-handed. Stood for Parliament twice—no luck.*

Then came Alfred Stowe, a big-wig in one of the largest industrial unions, a prominent member of the Trades Union Congress, and a member of the Manpower Services Commission. *Built like a bull*—said Figgins—*and acts like one when thwarted. Nest featherer. Would like to end up as a Life Peer—probably will. Skilled at running with hare and hunting with hounds. Clever bugger.*

After Stowe came a John Kingman, O.B.E., who was an Advertising and Public Relations executive. Figgins noted—*Kingman you know—top firm in the advertising agency world, and holding the accounts of some of the biggest oil companies going. Loves nothing but horses, and would sell his soul to be owner of a Grand National winner.*

The next was a Sir Arthur Pinke, the Chairman of an international electronics firm, and a member of the Council of the Confederation of British Industries. Figgins was brief—*Lives for his job and position, would like a thirty hour day.*

And last of all came a Mrs Delia Parmat, a wealthy widow with a large estate in Hampshire who, according to Figgins—*Is fifty, looks years younger. Lives for causes. You name one she's on it. Blood sports. Women's rights. Conservation. Keep Britain Tidy. Save the Whale. Widowed at thirty-three. Stayed that way since. I wonder why?*

At the end of all this Figgins had added—*The dirt—not much but thought provoking—comes from Helder who billed us a hundred which was ridiculous since he had it all on file. I sent him a cheque for fifty. He can sue for the rest if he feels like it. You won't be able to win them all but, I hope, enough to get your vote. Put on a clean shirt and turn on the charm.*

After lunch he took Punch's labrador for a walk along the river. Where a small brook ran into the main stream he came across Georgina Collet sitting on a log sketching. She half turned her head and with a nod and a smile greeted him. The far bank of the brook was heavily undercut by flood and overhung with a tangle of alders and hawthorns, the lattice work of their lower roots exposed.

She said, "I've been watching a pair of dippers. They're thinking of setting up house somewhere in the roots. But I think she's being a bit choosy."

"Well, it's a woman's privilege." He looked down at the open sketch pad on her knees and was again impressed by her talent. The page was alive with five or six vividly captured impressions of the dippers.

Unable to see his face, more than normally aware of him, and equally so aware that here was an opportunity to lay perhaps the beginnings of some rapprochement which would serve her well with Birdcage, Georgina suddenly felt lost and momentarily angry with her role. Almost as though she were listening to some stranger speaking she heard herself say, "I wonder? Perhaps he just humours her for a while, but makes the final decision."

"Could be."

He was standing almost behind her, his face hidden, the labrador at his feet, and she knew that she was lost for she had no idea how to take the opportunity further. She felt suddenly like an embarrassed schoolgirl in the presence of someone for whom she had a secret yen. Snatching at straws she said, with, it seemed to her, little conviction in her voice, "May I say again, Mr Seyton, how grateful I am to you for being so kind to me?"

"It was nothing. Anyway, there are plenty of places up and down the river free to the public where you could have gone. Though I suppose you'd have had people looking over your shoulder as I'm doing now."

Speaking quite truthfully, telling herself for God's sake to be natural, she said, feelingly, without thinking, "It isn't people looking over my shoulder that I mind. It's the fact of their noisy coming and going and fidgeting around which gives trouble. They just scare my subjects . . ." And then, knowing she had put her foot in it, she added quickly, "Oh dear—that wasn't a very tactful thing to say, was it? I apologize."

"Nevertheless, it's true." It was impossible for Seyton at that moment to keep curtness from his voice. This was his land and she was here on sufferance. Normally he knew that he would have been more than broadminded enough to have taken her gaffe with good humour, but today was different . . . all those bloody Governors waiting to sit like a jury to decide whether he got his own house back had got him into a state where his hackles rose easily. He went on almost sharply, "I'll be on my way."

She turned and looked up at him. "I'm sorry, I was very clumsy in what I said. I feel awful when you have been so kind." She indicated the sketches of the dippers. "Would you like these as a peace offering?"

"There's no need for that." He smiled thinly at her. "I apologize for my touchiness. Between ourselves I'm not quite with things at the moment."

He moved away with the labrador before she could reply. Watching him go, she thought—Oh Lord, what could have been more badly handled when she was supposed to be a bloody siren under instructions to captivate him? Still . . . she consoled herself with the thought that after such a bad beginning he could not possibly imagine that she was here for any other purpose than the one she had stated. She had acted like a self-centred artist . . . perhaps a bad beginning was the best kind to build on.

*   *   *   *

Some time before he was due to go up to the Hall that evening Nancy called him. She had just arrived down to stay with her father.

After a little talk she said, "This is the evening, isn't it, Richard?"

"Yes. How did you know?"

"I hadn't realized it, but I know one of the Governors—a General Stripert. I met him at a party yesterday, before I came down. He mentioned it. Asked some questions about you too."

"Did he? I hope you gave some nice answers so that he'll vote for me."

She laughed. "Not quite. There's only one way I could get his vote for you—and I knew you wouldn't approve of it. Anyway, I don't go for scalp collectors. Though, Dicky, you know if I felt that his were going to be the vital vote I'd do it for you—and tell you about it, maybe, afterwards. But from, perhaps, his manner more than his words, I don't think it will be a matter of one vital vote. That's one of the reasons I'm calling. I think you should be prepared for a *No*, and to say that, if it is that way and you feel you'd like company, I'll come right over. Ma Shipley's used to me turning up at all hours and there's always a guest bedroom. Promise me that you'll at least consider it."

"I promise."

Two hours later he walked up to the Hall. Not unexpectedly the main door opened as he went up the steps and he was greeted by Shanklin and the bizarre thought occurred to him that this over-extension of consideration could only be achieved by having some shivering wretch posted on one of the Tudor towers to signal important arrivals.

Shanklin, in evening dress—he himself was wearing a plain navy-blue suit since he had not been invited to dinner—took him into the first-floor main gallery where all the others were already assembled, and where Shanklin handed him over to Felbeck, who took him in tow—not, Seyton thought, inappropriately because the man fussed before him to the bar to get him a drink like a little tug and where, when he had a drink in his hand and had taken one sip, the man surprised him by taking the attention of the company and making a general introduction of him to the others present, a roll call clearly for his benefit alone. But if this was competent and considerate organization for his benefit, so was the stage-managing that followed, for although it would have been hard to detect any signs of the advance and then withdrawal of the others after a reasonable interval of conversation, he was soon aware of what was happening.

One by one he found himself alone, sometimes briefly and sometimes lengthily, with each of the Governors. The first was Sir Arthur Pinke, chalk-faced, thin and brittle looking, jockey weight and with a set to his mouth which made Seyton feel that whatever horse he rode in trade and commerce didn't just have to give its best but was damned well going to have its all forced out by the rider. Their main talk was largely about the use of artificial and natural manures, their merits and demerits ecologically. Seyton, soon slightly resenting what he could see was a coming inquisition, polite but unavoidable all round, from the Governors, made himself remain affable and said, in effect, that there was a time and place for each and finished, ". . . so if you just think of crop values and nothing else, Mother Nature will soon land you a backhander from some unexpected quarter". Which, to his surprise, made Sir Arthur chuckle and, unexpectedly, pat him approvingly on his arm. Whereupon— and he recognized Shanklin, working smoothly, and enjoying it, as the *deus ex machina*—he found himself in the company of the Right Reverend Oflapi of West Africa.

The Right Reverend was very fat and big and very black, and very soon talking about the Brazilian diamond industry of which Seyton knew more than he was prepared to make public but, knowing that the Bishop came by birth from Sierra Leone, he could well understand his past and present interest. The Bishop was given to laughter and before they were parted told Seyton a very funny, but decidedly risqué story about mixed adult baptism in his native land.

The next visitant was Mrs Delia Parmat who surprised him, first by her appearance—a tall, handsomely figured blonde in a close-fitting, low-cut gown, wearing a diamond necklace which he quickly valued within a few hundred pounds either way of its worth, while his eye also appraised the sun-tanned shoulders and a generous exposure of the smooth upper slopes of her breasts—and then by her first words. "You look amused, Mr Seyton. That terrible Oflapi must have been telling you one of his wicked stories." She then went on to fascinate him by the glib way in which she moved from one subject to another—the cruelty of keeping hens in batteries, women the first to suffer when men went on strike, the appalling failure of comprehensive school education and the even more appalling moral degeneration being caused by the exposure of the young and not so young to the exhibition of pornographic films, literature and sex shows. As she spoke of this last subject she stood before him the living symbol and dream-figure of all those timid adolescents and lonely mature males who went willingly to the brink, and sometimes beyond, of that immoral abyss which from time immemorial had attracted the lonely and the timid and the sick at heart. Her husband, he knew, had been a wealthy Persian and he wondered if he had found her in some Beirut night club—shipped there from where? Certainly from some part of this country, for she was clearly an English rose, a Peace, lusty and exuberant, a rich feeder and prolific bloomer. But no fool. She said, "Why waste your money buying us out? You have everything except the Hall itself, and we are ideal caretakers. Traditionalist you may be, but also, I know, a very successful business man. Just sit out the lease and make your money work for you elsewhere. No? No, I see not—you are a romantic as well then. But, whichever way it goes, may I say that I have been charmed to meet you and if you find yourself in Hampshire I shall be most disappointed if you don't . . ." Her left hand just lightly squeezed his arm as she went on extending an invitation for him to visit her, and the touch sent a trickle current through him which, surprisingly, made him want to laugh. He liked her. She was, as Punch would have said, a great handful of a girl.

The Bishop Suffragan from the South of England, the Right Reverend Auguste Miller, took her place and watched her go over Seyton's shoulder as he began to talk to him. When his eyes came back to Seyton he at once got the impression that there would be no vote for him from this man. The current of dislike was unmistakable. Seyton had met the phenomenon before in his business life. There was no rhyme or reason for it; just quick-born animosity and a display of threat mannerisms thinly masked which could have arisen from so simple a situation that at this moment the assembled company were all far more interested in himself than in Auguste Miller—and Mrs Delia Parmat particularly so.

"So the wanderer returns to take up his inheritance. A quiet life after the fleshpots. And for this you would have us turn out? Go a-wandering to find fresh lodgings?"

"That's absolutely right. I want what's mine—but I am offering adequate—perhaps rather more—compensation. That seems very reasonable and fair."

"Your late brother entered freely into the lease. What would he have said about your now wanting to break it?"

"He would have been all for it. Necessity made him give you the lease. In my place he would be doing what I am doing."

Suddenly the Bishop smiled, but there was no comfort in it, and said, "Well, let me say, I understand perfectly your attitude—but against it, as you will have appreciated, we have to think of the Foundation. No matter the compensation—leaving here would be a tremendous upheaval. But I am a fair man and I shall give your offer the most careful consideration, and in my prayers ask for true guidance."

"I ask for no more, Bishop," said Seyton, though it occurred to him that since the vote was to be taken after dinner which was imminent, the worthy divine was not leaving himself much time for prayer.

After a few more civilities—if they could be called such—the Bishop left him, and left him, too, wondering what maggot of discontent was eating him and guessing that perhaps it was one which ate at the flesh rather than the spirit, for he saw him make his way towards a little group at the centre of which was Mrs Parmat.

A voice at his side said broadly, with a Midlands accent, "I'll bet you get no joy from him, lad."

It was Alfred Stowe, short, plump, bull-necked and with a jolly face that was smooth, unlined and polished with a faint lick of perspiration. He wore a red velvet dinner jacket with a white carnation in his buttonhole. On seeing Seyton's eyes run slowly over him, he smiled, and went on, "A bit eccentric, you think, lad? In this company? Maybe, but it's my style. Probably springs from havin' to wear my father's cut downs as a lad, all flap and no fit. And if I asked you confidentially whether you'd give me a couple of thousand for me vote—what would you say?"

"Make it fifteen hundred and you have a deal, Mr Stowe."

Alfred Stowe chuckled. "Good lad. Still—not that I'm going to pretend that I never took a bribe in my life—I got to keep my nose clean now. One thing I'd like to know is—no matter how much money you've got—what the hell do you want to take on the bother of all this place for? You've got the land and a good house to live in. Where's the sense when we are looking after the Hall and paying you for the privilege?"

"Financially it's a fair deal, yes. But Seytons have lived here ever since the first stones and timbers were raised. That's how I want it to be again."

"Aye, family an' all. I understand that. My old father still lives in the Birmingham back street where I was born. Won't move—though I've offered to set him up anywhere he chooses. Says he'd miss his mates. He's damned near eighty now and his mates get thinner on the ground each winter. Now, I'll surprise you—but you just keep it to yourself—I'll give you my vote for free. You know why?"

"No, I don't."

"Then you should. You want what my old man's got. His place. So . . . there it is."

"Well, thank you very much."

"No need. And anyway, you'll need every damned vote you can get."

After Alfred Stowe, John Kingman came up to him, grinned

81

and said, "Hullo, Richard—no need for us to waste time—unless you can guarantee me a dead cert for the Cheltenham Gold Cup this month—and then you get my vote. But anyway, I'll keep my fingers crossed for you."

General Stripert next approached him and no mention was made of his reason for being in this company. They talked of hunting and fishing and—soon discovered—of friends they had in common. Seyton soon felt—though at the moment he was counting no chickens—that he was on his side. And then, last of all, came Rear-Admiral Croft. He was in his early sixties, a quietly spoken wraith of a man, his pale, lined face seldom changing expression, and with a habit of nodding gently as he was spoken to so that a lock of his greying hair fell forward over his brow which he kept brushing back with a nervous flick of one hand. His eyes were extraordinary—dark and bright with a lemur-like roundness and seldom blinking as though in any moment of obscured vision he feared he might miss the first shadow of a threat. Although he made Seyton feel uncomfortable he took pleasure in the sound of his voice for it was full, controlled, and modulated itself with an actor's skill to the content of everything he said.

He put out a long, thin hand and just lightly touched Seyton's arm as he said, "Remarkable, truly remarkable, my dear Seyton. This house is full of the paintings of various Seytons and here you are so full of the family resemblance on the male side that—ignoring the change of period clothes—you might have just stepped down from one of the frames. I have in mind at this moment a particular one. Could you guess which, I wonder?"

Seyton smiled. "Not very difficult—because I've been so often told. Would it be the one of George Seyton by Sir Peter Lely in the Great Chamber?"

"Exactly. Now tell me, why did your family never accept any honours? The offers must have been made and yet no Seyton was ever tempted?"

"I'm not sure. But maybe because in the early days they had no high opinion of those with them and this became slowly a point of family pride. It may not be logical—but it has held good. And, anyway, these days, the coinage has become debased."

"You talk of family pride—that's why you want this place back?"

"Pride and tradition, yes."

"I don't denigrate either. But we live in a bad season for their proper flowering. There is a sickness over this land of ours—and over the world—which unless checked will lead to the death of all virtues and ultimately to chaos or helotage. And between ourselves, I sometimes wonder if the charity and good works we cultivate and dispense from here are only hastening the black days of mourning to come for the moral death of mankind. Then, when the lights begin to flicker down, we shall need all the Seyton kinds we can find to take a stand against the misrules of disorder and slavery." He smiled, flicked a lock of hair back and added with a charming smile, "Too pessimistic, you think?"

Touched by the man's sincerity, while far from being entirely sympathetic towards his diagnosis of human ill, Seyton said, "God, I'm sure, created us for a better end and higher purposes so——" he grinned, "——we must put our trust in Him and keep our powder dry."

"True, true. Well, we shall see. We shall see." A hand lightly tapped Seyton's arm, and he went on, "Do not take this little ordeal too personally. I may add I was against it. But we have much to forfeit in time and reorganization if we lose this place—no matter what compensation you offer." With a friendly shake of his head, he left.

But a little later when Seyton was accompanied to the great door overlooking the drive by Felbeck, Rear-Admiral Croft went with them. As Seyton disappeared into the gloom of the driveway and the sound of the fall of his feet died away, Felbeck turned and said to him, "Well?"

Croft was silent for a while and then said, "He is what we want. He belongs with us."

Felbeck nodded. "I think so. But Grandison says *no*. It is too late."

From across the park a little owl screeched loudly and as the night swallowed the sound, Croft said, "Sometimes I wonder about Grandison. I, too, sometimes wonder that where there is a great mission and the disciples gather, whether it is not a law—of Nature if not God—that amongst them will be a Judas?"

CHAPTER FIVE

AFTER DINNER, WHEN Mrs Shipley had left, Seyton went into Punch's study—his now, and knowing that he would never substantially change anything in it—and sat at the desk to write a letter to Roger to tell him that he had obtained permission for him to come down for Punch's memorial service which was to be held on the Tuesday of the following week and that Figgins would pick him up on the Monday afternoon as she was driving down from London.

Before he had finished the front door bell rang. When he opened the door it was to find—without surprise—Charles Felbeck standing in the shelter of the porch, a light mackintosh over his evening clothes, and a thin drizzle falling.

He took him into the study, sat him down and offered him a drink.

"A whisky and soda, if I may." Momentarily a rueful smile wrinkled the man's battered face and he fingered his fair, well-trimmed moustache a little nervously. "Usually I'm almost teetotal—but tonight . . ." He shrugged his shoulders.

Although Seyton could guess what was coming, he felt an odd sympathy for the man for he sensed that there was something they shared in spirit . . . both of them came from the same kind of families and knew the meaning of old loyalties and their importance.

Handing the man his drink, Seyton said, "It was good of you to come down. You could have telephoned."

Felbeck shook his head. "No, I couldn't have done that." He grinned with a sudden boyish ruefulness. "You know what I'm going to say, don't you?"

85

Holding down his slight stir of emotion—the real impact would come later—Seyton said, "I think I have known since the day I first went to see you in London. So it's a big, fat *No*."

"Yes, sadly for you, it is No. But—no consolation, I presume —not a big fat one. I didn't—I'm personally thankful to say— have to give a casting vote. The Governors voted five to three against accepting your offer."

"No names, no pack drills?"

"Yes. I'm sorry, Seyton. But there it is . . . the upheaval would have been just too much for us to take." Felbeck ran a hand nervously over his thin, fair hair.

"Well, that's the end of all that then."

"It is. There's one thing I can offer in . . . well, personal amelioration if it would be acceptable by you . . . to give you some—not consolation—but future involvement, a sense of regaining something of your own so far as the Hall is concerned."

"Yes?"

"Every four years two Governors retire in rotation and new ones are appointed—appointed, not elected, and that dispensation is entirely in my hands. This happens next year. I wondered if you would be interested?"

"Did you ever make such an offer to Punch?"

"As a matter of fact, yes. Four months before his accident."

"And what did he say?"

Felbeck smiled. "No, thanks—but not quite as politely as that."

"Well . . . as for me—I thank you for the offer. But—no, thanks."

"I'm not surprised. All or nothing. That's it, isn't it?"

Seyton nodded, and then on the spur of the moment, following a sudden impulse—rare for him—he asked, "Why did you make such an offer to Punch? I always felt that he was well content with the arrangement."

"So did we all. But latterly he now and then showed resentment at our presence. I could never understand why. We have always been most punctilious in our obligations under the lease, and certainly there never seemed to be any cause for personal disturbances. As a matter of fact, if he ever gave you any hint of the dissatisfaction he clearly began to feel, I would—if it is not breaking any confidence—be glad to know about it."

"No. He said nothing to me. But then neither of us was the kind to keep in touch much, and for almost five months before his death I was in South America." Seyton smiled. "Punch was no letter-writer."

"Well, there it is. Perhaps it was just his ancestral feeling. I could understand that. Having to have us here to keep the place going. In fact, the more I think about it, the more I begin to believe that it was as simple as that. He kept away from the Hall completely. Wouldn't come up to dinner. I do hope, Seyton, it is not going to be like that with you."

"Oh, no. Of course, I'm disappointed—very much so. I like getting my own way as much as the next man. But there's nothing to be gained by rudeness or spiky resentment."

"It's exactly what I would have expected you to say. Well, there it is." Felbeck rose. "I must be getting back. But give my offer some more thought. Apart from everything else, you really would be welcomed as a Governor . . . very much so."

After Felbeck had gone, Seyton finished his letter to Roger and was on the point of going to bed when he heard a car pull into the side drive, heard the horn go in three well-known notes and went to the door to let Nancy in.

In the study she came to him and kissed him and then said, "I knew you would never telephone—but when I heard it was a *no-go* I decided to come—to play the role of comforter, if that's what you'd like. Anyway, just to be here."

He put an arm around her and kissed her and then— following a familiar impulse—held her close to him for a while before turning away to get her a drink.

When he brought it to her, she said, "To answer the question you haven't asked—I telephoned the Hall to find out what had happened."

"General Stripert?"

"Yes. He told me. What did you think of him?"

87

"Nice chap, I thought."

"So he is in many ways. Oh, Richard, I am sorry but . . . Well, even you must have known that it was a wild hope."

"It had to be tried first."

"First—what is there to come second?"

"I don't know."

With a slow, but clearly nervous movement, she put up a hand, absently smoothed her fair hair, and said, "Don't look at me like that . . . as though . . . well, weighing up pros and cons. You heard what I said. What is there to come second? What's working in you?"

"Just a few thoughts."

"About?"

"Punch."

"Go on. My God, I do have to drag things out of you. It's me sitting here. Not some crooked old diamond merchant trying to do you down."

"I'm sorry. You're dead right. It just is that I've got a bloody funny feeling about things—things to do with the Hall, that is—and Punch. Particularly Punch—you said yourself that he was changed towards the end. I've got a feeling that something was eating him and—if I'm right—then whatever it was had something to do with the Hall. Not only you noticed it. But so did Roger. And old Shipley."

"So?"

"So—just that."

"No. I mean—what is there to come second still? You've done all you can do—and they've turned you down. Surely that's the end of it?"

"Not necessarily. There are certain conditions in the lease and if they break any of them I could get them out."

She shook her head, faintly exasperated. "Richard, I know you. Conditions, yes. But not some. You're thinking of a particular one. Come clean."

"All right. There is one. I can't quote it verbatim, but generally it is to the effect that the Foundation should not do or permit to be done on the premises any act or thing to the

88

damage or annoyance of the lessor or any illegal or immoral act which would tend to injure the character——"

"Richard!" Nancy laughed. "You're talking about a charitable organization!"

"I know all about that. But people are people—and think of some of the people who are Governors! If General Stripert pops into bed up there from time to time with Mrs Parmat and some servant finds out and the talk spreads and when I go to Hereford market some kind friend of mine asks how the brothel business is going—do you think that wouldn't constitute damage or annoyance to me?"

"And you'd make a case over that?"

"That or whatever else it might be—yes, you're damned right if I could get proof."

"But you've no grounds whatsoever for thinking——"

"I know I haven't. Not firm ground. Except that something began lately to rile Punch so that Felbeck offered him a place on the Board and Punch said No. Punch, who'd sit on anything from a vestry committee to a parish council! He loved that kind of thing. Damn it—if it had been possible he would have sat on a Mothers' Union committee—and I'm surprised you think I'm talking rot. You told me yourself that he went off Felbeck and when you asked him why he just closed up. Or rather, said he only wanted to talk about him to me."

"Yes, that's true. But I think that was just something personal—like the poor chap who took the salmon kelts." She stood up and came to him and held his arm. "Richard . . . I know how you feel just now. That's why I came over. Felbeck's not the kind of man to let anything happen which might lose him his lease. You'll accept that when you've slept on it. And talking of sleeping—that was in my mind too when I came over. But I know you well enough not to want you to start making polite noises about a busy day ahead and——"

"No," he interrupted her. "You've got it wrong. You go on up. I'll be with you soon. I promised to give Figgins a ring."

"At this hour?"

"There's a phone by her bed and she'd slaughter me if I didn't call tonight."

At the end of his talk with Figgins, she said, "And what are you going to do now?"

"I don't know."

"Liar."

"So?"

"You're thinking of clause seven?"

"Could be—but it seems a bit wild."

"I didn't tell you before because I wanted to hear how the vote went, but some fair time before he had his accident Punch came to town and saw—or so I imagine—Helder. Anyway he asked for his phone number. Do you want it?"

"I'll sleep on it, Figgy." He paused, and then added, "Is that why you would only pay Helder fifty instead of a hundred?"

"That's it—though I'm quite sure we didn't get all he found for Punch. That could still be waiting for you—at a price."

*　　*　　*　　*

Warboys was having an early working breakfast with Sir Manfred Grandison, and hating it. Breakfast was a meal he preferred strongly to take alone, and work was not something you mucked up with all the paraphernalia of cutlery and plates and mustard pots and toast. A file sticky on one corner from spilled marmalade was an abomination to him. In addition, he wished to God he knew just what Grandison was playing at, or thinking of playing at, or had long ceased playing at. Availing himself of an established, but seldom exercised, privilege he made no effort to conceal his feelings. While waiting until they had cleared quite a few matters of minor importance to them but of major interest to the people concerned and, since Regent's Park and its Zoo lay immediately to the south of their window, remembering intermittently his mother's odd passion for the reptile house and his own delight in its warmth when she dragged him into it in winter, he said eventually, "I think,

Sir Manfred, before we take the last file——" he tapped the folder which carried the name of Richard Seyton that lay to the side of his plate, "it would be of some help to me administratively—if not realistically—if I could have a little of the truth or a scrap of convincing fiction to feed to those lower mortals who are now working in an irritating darkness on Seyton."

Grandison, in a green dressing gown worn over primrose coloured pyjamas, lit a cheroot to smoke with his last cup of coffee and said flatly, " 'A moment's insight is sometimes worth a life's experience'. I quote back to you what you have so often—and always aptly—quoted to me."

Warboys inwardly groaned, hating the smell of the cheroot wafting towards him, but responded to a well-known ritual— or perhaps, less that than, a boring intellectual game which always gave Grandison a near childish delight—by back quoting, " 'It is the province of knowledge to speak, and it is the privilege of wisdom to listen.' Your province and, with all modesty, my wisdom. And now that we have played out our little game—what can I have to throw to my starving hounds? Principally Quint who will see that some of the scraps from his portion reach the others."

"Let them go hungry. No, perhaps not. Give them this part fiction. Felbeck Foundation. World wide. Immaculate in behaviour. No scandal. Worthy, worthy, beyond the wideness of the heavens. So it would seem, but—the sweetest apple must have a maggot at its core. That's what I want. The maggot. Given that—then we can use the Foundation for our own purposes. Discreetly, but effectively. Remember, my dear Warboys, that at heart all religious institutions are political. That's one of the main reasons why Christ was crucified. It would be nice for us to have in our hands even the smallest of whips to crack now and then over the plump quarters of the Foundation."

Sourly, because doubt still inhabited him, Warboys said, "Why not go for the Church of England or the Holy Roman Catholic Church? Or is someone ahead of us there?"

"You jest, of course."

"Of course, Sir Manfred. But as a placebo your fiction is too thin for me and will be for the others because your target is Richard Seyton. The question will be stirring in their minds— Where does he figure in all this?"

"Naturally. And the answer is clear. He wants the Hall back and—for your information—has just been denied it. But he is not the sort of man to take denial lying down."

"What can he do?"

Sir Manfred Grandison rose and went to the window, trailing a blue swirl of cheroot smoke, an airy serpent. Surveying the green grass of the park, lightly touched with a mild hoar frost, he said, "That is just what I want to know. Perhaps mine is an extreme precaution, remote . . . maybe never to materialize. But I do not want any outsider frightening off our game as it peacefully grazes."

Although he was not going to put it in words, Warboys knew that the inference was clear that *there was* something which Seyton—know it or not at this moment—could do. And Grandison, moreover, might know or guess what it was. But *if* Grandison knew, then why the devil put up this charade, because he would have in his hands already the knowledge which he would deny Seyton, and having that made everything he had already said a nonsense? With a momentary sensation of helplessness and confusion, he said, "I see."

Grandison turned, grinned and tugged at his beard and then, slowly adjusting his monocle, said sadly, "No, you do not see, dear Warboys. And you are entertaining unworthy thoughts. I strongly suspect that there is something rotten in the heart of the Foundation—but I do not know its nature. I shall be very happy if Seyton uncovers the canker for us. Though it will be a sad day for him because—and this I would rather not be saying since it may never arise, but you have clumsily dragged it from me—he must be then neutralized . . . disposed of so that we alone have a free hand to play the advantage which he will have made available to us if Miss Georgina Collet conducts her part well."

"The poor bugger."

"Not necessarily. He may fail—or there may not be anything for him to uncover. On such small arrangements of time and chance and facts or no facts are destinies dependent."

"He may succeed—but Georgina Collet may fail. Then where are we?"

Grandison shook his head and smiled. "Without going into details I may say that Miss Collet is not the only one cultivating the Felbeck Foundation field. But for the time being you have had an answer to your enquiry . . . or rather a reasonable thesis to pass on to your worthy underlings. Are you satisfied?"

"Partly, Sir Manfred."

Sir Manfred Grandison gave a great laugh and said, "How like you—so honest. Which I appreciate between us. Alas, for those below us . . . well it is too strong a virtue to be worn openly. But remember this—if the Felbeck Foundation can be plucked, then the fruit must fall into our basket."

*　　　*　　　*　　　*

At eleven o'clock when Seyton came back from having a final talk with the Rector about the memorial service for Punch, Mrs Shipley came to him and gave him a large manila envelope.

"Somebody pushed this through the door while you were out."

"Thank you, Mrs Shipley. And I shan't be in to lunch. I want to go to the bank in Hay. I'll get a bite there."

When she was gone he opened the envelope. Inside was a large sheet of cartridge paper and on it a pencil drawing which he at once recognized. It showed a small paddock beyond the Seyton chapel and in it Punch's chestnut mare with her small foal at foot. For some reason far removed from the brilliant naturalness of the study it raised a lump in his throat as he remembered the many times he had ridden alongside Punch hunting, Punch up on the mare, and going hell for leather; and vividly too other memories . . . Punch putting the old bull-nosed Morris at the ha-ha, Punch climbing the ivy on the chapel bell tower to take jackdaws' eggs . . . Recovering from his emotion, he turned the sheet over—knowing already who must have drawn it—and read the inscription on the back. *Acceptable, I hope, where the dippers weren't, and again my apologies. G. Collet.*

Shipley was just finishing washing down the Land Rover when he went outside.

"Just smartened her up a bit for you, Mister Richard. You off to Hay now?"

"Yes, Shippey. Thanks. You've made a good job there. By the way, have you seen that drawing woman around this morning?"

"Yes. She was up on the bank by the Quarry Pool some time ago."

He drove up the river track, but there was no sign of her near the Quarry Pool. He followed the track until he hit the road and drove on to Hay, where he did his few chores and then had a beer and some sandwiches in a pub. Coming back he turned down to the river and followed the bank and found her just below the Quarry Pool.

He said, "I came to look for you some time ago, but you weren't around."

"I went down to Bredwardine for lunch."

"Are you just starting something?"

"Thinking of it."

"I'd like it if you would come with me. There's something I want to show you."

For a moment or two Georgina was puzzled by his manner. There had been no polite greeting, no mention of her gift . . . and then, as he got out of the Land Rover and opened the door for her and she had a full view of his face, to her surprise she read him clearly. His was the emotional mood she had known well in her father when he was moved by some unexpected act or gift which touched him so much that he could find only gruffness or almost a lapse into gaucherie to signal his feelings. But what feeling here? She had devised a little ploy on her part to recover lost ground by the gift of a quick impression of a mare and foal—in fact, almost an act of desperation on her part, because she had this bloody job to do and, if it meant pushing, then she would push up to a point.

She said, "Of course." She picked up her sketching block and got into the Land Rover. And then as they drove off, recovered, and looking for any advantage, any lead to take her closer to her quarry, she said, "Have I done something wrong again?"

Seyton laughed. "Just the opposite. Your drawing moved me very much. You couldn't know it, but the mare was my brother's hunter. The whole thing just hit me . . . I don't know . . . it's not something I can explain. It just brought him back. Not in a bad way. You know . . . the loss and the waste. But in a good way. While he lived he had a full life and enjoyed it." He half turned and gave her a warm smile. "So I came looking for you, to say *thank you*, and to show you something which I know will give you pleasure."

"I see."

And she really did see now more than she had expected. That he was her quarry made no difference, that he was giving her a lead-in which she must now, and knew she could, exploit for bloody Quint and company was almost incidental for she was beginning to see—and respect—the true and inner man. It was like one of those moments which she had known when she had started to draw the mare, when hand, eye and brain fused, became something all compact and with their own fused qualities merely used her as a conductor. So now she saw and sensed the real Richard Seyton; not wealthy landowner, nor a business tycoon lately come who had out of innate instincts excelled those who had given all their working lives to making profits based on sharp or shrewd dealings, but the man himself wearing for a while his true heart and vulnerable emotions on his sleeve. Luck had given her the key to him, and luck, her father had often said—bad or good—was something that always operated independently of human control.

In the Dower House he helped her off with her coat and then led her into the dining room whose windows looked out over the park and to the sudden rise of the southerly slopes of the river valley.

He said flatly, "I knew that you would like to see these. Perhaps you knew that we had them?"

Her eyes already taken by the paintings and pencil drawings on the walls, she said, "No, I didn't." Then she moved away from him, forgetting him, into her own world.

The pictures were all the work of the ill-starred Herefordshire artist, Brian Hatton, who, in 1916, at the age of twenty-nine had been killed in action in Egypt, a man who had early been acclaimed the rarest of all things—true genius ... unique in the history of British art. There was a collection of pen-and-ink drawings, mostly with horses as subjects, a masterly quick impression in white paint on brown paper of two fighting stallions, some pencil drawings of hunting and country scenes, and over the great stone fireplace a large oil of a man in uniform sitting on a grey gelding with the Seyton private chapel and a glimpse of the Wye in the background. One glance at the man told her that he was a Seyton.

Behind her Seyton said, "That was my grandfather. He's wearing the uniform of the Hereford Regiment. I'm quite sure you know about Hatton."

"Yes, indeed. I've already been to the Hatton Gallery in Hereford. But like these, of course, most are in private hands and seldom come on the market." She turned to him. "They're marvellous and they make me feel . . . well, humble and inadequate."

Seyton shook his head. "I don't think you need be. Punch's mare could hold a place up there. Anyway I wanted you to see them. Any time you want to come back and study them just give me a call. Now, let's go and bully Mrs Shipley into giving us some tea."

With an unconscious naturalness he put out a hand and took her arm to lead her from the room, and in the few moments of being held she knew what was going to happen. Some unbidden but sure instinct told her that there was a compatibility, no matter how recently nascent, waiting to develop between them.

She had known it before in unconstrained and quite innocent encounters. That it should be happening now, in a situation which was quite artificial so far as she was concerned, bewildered rather than surprised her. Later, as they took tea and chatted, she detected too what had always been evident in the past with others. Given no unseasonable frosting the ultimate blooming was inevitable.

*   *   *   *

That evening Kerslake, after taking a call from Georgina Collet, reported to Quint's office. Quint was hunched up over his desk reading a particularly tedious report from the financial section on undisclosed benefits in cash and kind which various secretaries of some minor Trades Unions were, without reluctance, encouraging the accrual of to themselves. He was less interested in the cash than in the kind which covered a wide field of human and not always virtuous appetites from free double-glazing of their homes to the delights of the flesh and the table. Bored, he gave Kerslake a friendly nod and told him to sit down, saying, "The man I was about to summon. But with true generosity I shall let you get the weights off your own chest first. You look pleased."

"Yes, sir. Miss Collet has just telephoned. She's in."

"Is she indeed? How?"

Quint listened as Kerslake gave him the details and, when he had finished, commented, "Who says there is not a guiding hand behind our destinies? Benevolent or malign is, of course, a matter for argument. But we need not bother ourselves with that. So, she must be a happy girl."

"If happiness is the word, sir."

"Contrary to common thought it covers a multitude of states. It can be a dry crust to the starving, the meagre drip from a mossy rock in the jungle to a thirsty man, the elimination of an enemy struck from behind, or in her condition four legs in a bed and close pillow talk."

"You sound as though you don't care a damn for her, sir."

97

Quint smiled at this taking of rare privilege, a liberty Kerslake had over the years earned as an occasional concession.

"On the contrary, I am very fond of her. Shall we say though—only out of office hours; which, as you know, leaves little of the full twenty-four left once sleeping time has been discounted. However, Kerslake, let us be generous and chalk up a good mark to her. Perhaps you will convey our feelings to her when you go down there."

"Me, sir? To Herefordshire?"

Quint laughed. "You react as though I had said 'To Hades'. Yes, Herefordshire, Kerslake. The Hall and part of the grounds are open on Thursday each week. Tuesday, Thursday and Saturday in what is called the season, though season for what I don't know. But you will notice—not Sundays. It is a religious Foundation and I can only suppose the Sabbath is reserved for devotions to be screened from the vulgar gaze. I know that I am being tedious, but bear with me. We are the creatures of our moods and nowhere more so than in the sanctuary of our own offices. That is why men go out to work. Of course you know why I want you to go down there now?"

"Yes, sir. So that I know the ground where I might have to operate."

"Quite. No more than a few days. Be discreet, a little field mouse gleaning the stubble for the random ears of corn. Boring, but some time in the future you may well have to play a different role—not unknown to you—the adder lurking at the pathside waiting to strike. Seyton is not going to get his Hall back for years and years it would seem. But it also seems that there might be ways—unknown as yet to him—by which he could. If he does discover them—then he becomes expendable. We live in exciting times, Kerslake, and this office makes its full contribution to them. Perhaps you would have been happier, say, in an insurance office?"

Kerslake laughed. He quite liked Quint in this mood—just so long as he did not go on too long. And, anyway, he was by no means fooled by it. In this place each man and woman had an individual mode of consolation. For himself, after much trial and error, he had recently discovered his own way much to his surprise.

And much to his surprise he heard himself say now without any irony, "No, sir. This is my place, my home, my life. Outside it there are no true delights."

"Charming. Expose the young to the right influences and environments and they adapt to them as the chameleon to the colour of the rock on which it flattens itself. You spoke as I might well have done. But now—to be again serious—before you go to Herefordshire tell the people in the Commercial Section that I want a run-down on Seyton Enterprises, or whatever they call themselves, with particular reference to their sources of private information, international and domestic. The authorization is there." He indicated a sealed envelope on the edge of his desk and, as Kerslake reached for it, added, "Since there may well be a way to break the lease apparently then we must cover the possibility that Seyton may come to know of it and take action to get some sort of arcane proof to use to win him back his ancestral home. The gardener Adam and his wife may indeed well smile at the claims of long descent, but I assure you that neither Seyton nor Satan does. That's all, Kerslake. Good night."

Kerslake picked up the envelope and went to the door. With his hand on the knob, he turned, looked Quint full in his grinning face, and said, "Tennyson?"

"A little cobbled. But, yes. The beloved of Queen Victoria, whose statesmen in council 'knew the seasons when to take Occasion by the hand, and make the bounds of freedom wider yet'. We live in a sad age, Kerslake."

*   *   *   *

The memorial service for Punch was held a few days later in the second week of April, a day of high winds and fast, scudding rain squalls that raced down the river valley, stripping young leaf and buds and setting the rooks wheeling high to gambol and fight in late courtship displays. The lesson was read by

Nancy's father, and one of the Canons Residentiary of Hereford Cathedral gave the address. The chapel was full and afterwards Seyton had a few of Punch's and his own friends to lunch with himself and Roger who had come down from school at Cheltenham.

That evening, as he sat in the study with his coffee and brandy and, for sole company, his son who was reading a book by the fire, but not—he guessed—with much enthusiasm since he would have preferred the television, yet sensed—correctly—that he was in no mood for it, Seyton was remembering something the Canon had said of Punch ... *He was an open and frank man and, not unnaturally, from the innocence of his own nature valued these two qualities when he found them in others and had an abiding charity of compassion and understanding when he failed to find them in some. To all men he offered kindness, knowing that the powers of light and darkness have for their battle ground the human soul. I am sure he would never have expressed this to himself in these words. Most of you here can probably supply his non-canonical version. He was ever ready to give a man ... anyone ... more than one chance ...*

But was it all true? Not quite, he thought. When Punch found true evil, and that not to be changed by any kind of charity—then he could become implacable. To maltreat man, woman, child or beast and to continue to do so against remonstrance brought out a severity in him which had far more to do with the Old than the New Testament.

From across the fireplace Roger broke into his thoughts by saying, "What are you smiling about, dad?"

"Was I?"

"Yes."

"I was thinking about Punch. Something he did once."

"What was that?"

Seyton hesitated for a moment or two and then said, "Well, you'll probably hear it from someone else some time so I'll tell you."

He told how when he and Punch were young men there had been a gamekeeper on the estate—a good gamekeeper—who would drink too much at the inn some nights, get drunk and come back to his lodge and beat up his wife and children. So one evening Punch picked the man up as he was leaving the pub and drove him home to his wife and children. The game-keeper, very drunk, thought he was just getting a lift. But no. Punch went into the lodge with him and there, in front of his family, whipped down his trousers and gave him the beating of his life.

"Gosh, what a thing to do. What did his wife say?" asked Roger.

"She didn't say anything. Before Punch had little more than started, she picked up a big vase from the table and hit Punch across the head with it."

Roger rocked with laughter. "And what then?"

"Punch had a bump the size of a melon on his head. But the man never beat his family again. He was with us for nearly ten years afterwards. Excellent chap. And I don't want you to try and guess his name."

"I can guess, but I won't say." Roger was silent for a moment or two and then went on in a speculative manner, "There've been some funny people in our family from time to time, haven't there, dad? Like Sarah Seyton. She was a goer, wasn't she?"

"That's no way to talk of your great, great, great aunt."

Getting up and crossing to the far wall near the window Roger said, "I think you've missed out a great, dad. Anyway, what was with her? For instance—why did she do the sampler this way?"

Seyton went and stood behind his son. On the wall, framed and fitting exactly into one of the small wainscoting panels, was an eighteenth-century sampler—known in the family as the Satan Sampler—which had been worked by Sarah Seyton at the age of thirteen. In lay-out it followed the conventional design of samplers. It was worked with coloured silks on linen. At the bottom was her name—Sarah Glendower Satan. Although the family by then called themselves Seyton, Sarah had here reverted to the original spelling. There followed her age—thirteen years, and the year 1740. Then, from the top down, came the alphabet and the usual row of numerals from one to ten. But the alphabet and the numbers had been laid out at random following her whim of discord and chaos which obtained everywhere else in the sampler. Adam under the Tree of Life was beating his Eve with a stick while the serpent with a bearded and fork-eared head of Satan looked on. Instead of the usual pastoral motifs of birds and flowers there were snakes, toads, wasps, a bloody-jawed wolf devouring a lamb, a stallion —plainly—rearing up to the hindquarters of a mare, and sprays of deadly nightshade, clumps of toadstools and poisonous fungi. In a spirit of rebellion or sheer wickedness Sarah had reversed convention and—presumably—by doing so had soothed something of her restless and rebellious spirit. At the bottom of the sampler were four lines:

> *Tis not Religion that can give*
> *Sweetest pleasures while we live*
> *Wiser far praise Earthly joys*
> *And eat the fruit no blight destroys*

Answering Roger, Seyton said, "She was a restless spirit and a born rebel."

"Even so, dad—I wonder the family kept it. I mean it's a bit off, isn't it?"

"So it is. But the story is that she was the apple of her father's eye and he humoured her. He wasn't exactly orthodox himself. There are good and bad in all families and in ours we seldom bothered to sweep the . . . well, less savoury things under the carpet. History—and we're proud of ours—is not a matter of selecting and censoring. The whole truth and nothing but the truth. Anyway, Punch and I found the sampler useful. We made a language out of it, a secret code."

"Oh . . . How did that work?"

"From the jumbled up alphabet and numbers. If you write them out as they are and then put over the top of them the way they should be you've got a code—a simple one, but it was good enough for us. So the word CAT for instance would read OJP and the number 7 would be 3. We used it a lot and had it off by heart." Seyton smiled. "You've no idea—it came in very handy at times."

"It wouldn't be very difficult to break, would it?"

"No, it wouldn't, but it served us all right. At school we used to write very rude things in code on walls about the masters and fall over ourselves with laughter every time we passed them."

"That's an idea."

"I don't advise you to try it. You might just pick the wrong master—some crossword fiend, or perhaps a chap who'd done cipher work during the war." Turning away from the sampler, Seyton went on, "Well, that's enough of that. We've got an early start tomorrow. Bed for you."

The next morning Seyton drove to London, dropping Roger at his school on the way. Figgins, who had come down for the memorial service and was staying on for a few days to see her family, had made an appointment for him to meet Helder in the early evening of the same day. She had said, "He'll call at your club—six o'clock."

"Hasn't he got an office?"

"No. He lives in a flat. Hampstead way. I always get him by phone and he likes to meet people in public. You've never met him, have you?"

"No."

"He's a useful man. But don't try to push him. He likes to do his own summing up. Then, if he thinks he should talk—he will. But if not—then you might as well be banging your head against a brick wall."

That evening at six o'clock precisely Helder arrived at the club and was brought to Seyton by a club servant. He was sitting in a window alcove of the large lounge bar on the first floor overlooking Brook Street. Helder was a big man in his forties, wearing dark, heavy tweeds, an immaculate white shirt, a knitted black tie, and highly polished black brogues. He had a soft, muted manner, a flat, toneless voice as though he had long learned to eradicate all feeling from it, aiming perhaps at an inscrutability which was marred now and then by the shadow of a smile which would take the corners of his mouth unexpectedly.

Their greetings made and a large gin and tonic ordered for Helder and a whisky and soda for Seyton, they sat together at their relatively isolated table in the window overlooking the slow crawl of evening rush hour traffic in the street below.

Clearly not one for irrelevant chatter, Helder said, solemnly, "Miss Figgins tells me that you are interested in the Governors of the Felbeck Foundation. A very worthy institution, very worthy."

It was then, as Seyton said that this was indeed the case, he realized what it was the man reminded him of—a prosperous undertaker, an expert at avoiding distress to anyone's feelings, but still quietly dedicated to getting on with the job in hand.

"I am indeed interested."

"May I say how sorry I was when I heard the sad news of your brother?"

"Thank you."

"Ebullient, straightforward, and with a spirit as clear as crystal. However . . ." He sipped at his drink, and waited for Seyton to speak. Clearly if there were to be a meaningful conversation he meant to initiate no more than his opening statement.

Amused, but deciding not to show it, Seyton said, "You've let Miss Figgins have some stuff—which, of course, I've seen. I was wondering . . . well, if perhaps that was only the tip of the iceberg, so to speak."

"Nicely put, Mr Seyton. Yes, I would say just the tip."

"Is it possible to dive deeper—either into the depths or into, say, your files?"

Helder considered this for a while, and then replied, "It would be, of course, Mr Seyton. But being an honest man I think I would have to say that the farther into the depths I went it would only be to surface eventually with more of the same. If you know a man has stolen money and got away with it—then it's a fair assumption that he's either done it before or certainly will do it again. Translate that to other areas of human fallibility and the answer is the same. Against this, may I say that a man may be a lecher or a swindler and still have a genuine concern for the starving hordes of the Third World. In other words, Mr Seyton, you would only be asking me to dig or dive deeper into an already familiar environment. You would get nothing that will help you or that you haven't already got. To break a lease no matter under which clause—you must have facts that will stand up in law, facts and proof of those facts. Not hearsay, not gossip. Am I being discouraging?"

"Somewhat." Seyton spoke with a touch of sharpness for he felt that the man was being unnecessarily didactic. "Anyway— I've said nothing about breaking a lease."

Helder smiled and said, "No—but your brother, Mister Harry, did—some months ago—sitting, which I find curiously appropriate—in this very same room."

"Punch said that to you?"

"Yes, Mr Seyton. His actual words were—as usual, refreshingly blunt, 'Helder, you've got to help me. I've got to find a way to break the bloody Felbeck Foundation's lease on the Hall.' I remember them clearly."

"Good Lord! Did he tell you why?"

"No, Mr Seyton. And I did not ask him. I don't ask clients direct questions like that. What I guess or assume is my own affair."

"But there must be more to it than that?"

"Oh, indeed, sir. Along what lines, would you think?"

"Damn it! That's what I want you to tell me. You wouldn't be breaking any confidence."

Helder finished his gin and tonic, looking very thoughtful, and put the glass down on the table a few inches more forward of himself than necessary, but making sure that the signal should not be overlooked by Seyton.

Seyton, holding himself in check now, knowing that he must go at the man's own gait, signalled to the waiter to bring them fresh drinks, and then said, "Punch would want me to know."

"I'm sure he would, Mr Seyton. But I can't give you a direct answer because I don't have it. Not a full answer, that is."

Seyton was silent for a while, a silence without embarrassment to Helder for that individual turned and looked out of the window as though the passage of traffic outside was of absorbing interest to him. Seyton was sure that there were things, or something, the man could tell him but would not unless he could hit the needed note to set the key for the tune he wished to have sung to him.

Finally, and almost at random, he said, "If Punch talked to you about breaking the lease—did he by any chance show you the lease or a copy of it?"

"Yes, he did, sir." The shadow of an approving smile touched Helder's lips.

"And then ask your advice as to which clause—given your knowledge of the Governors of the Foundation—would be the one to go for?"

"No, sir."

"I don't follow."

"Then let me put it this way, sir. Which clause would you think might offer the most rewarding prospect?"

"Damned if I know. No, that's not true. Number seven, I suppose. Punch was after that, was he? Oh, come on, Helder—stop playing games with me. I want help and I want it from you—and I don't care if there's only the flimsiest chance of turning up something. I want those bastards out of the Hall."

Helder smiled broadly. "Remarkable—I mean the family likeness. I refer to your last sentence. Only—there is a slight difference. Mister Harry went further, and added—*I've an idea what I can get under clause seven and I want you to get me the means to record it.*"

"You said *record*?"

"I did, sir."

"By what means?"

"Technical, of course. Sight and sound recording."

"To be used where?"

"There could only be one place, I imagine, Mr Seyton. Though to be sure Mister Harry didn't say as much. At the Hall."

Seyton drew a deep breath. He realized now that Helder, out of some long-established quirk of character, was enjoying himself. Maybe he always had to have that to compensate for the work he did which, on any level, could only be described as sordid. So, his own growing exasperation forcing him to it, he said bluntly and vigorously, "All right, Helder. You've had your fun. And, by God, I see why you need it at times. But now cut out all the bloody nonsense. I've got an account rendered at home against Punch from a firm in Hampshire . . . Andover, I think. They're photographic and high fidelity specialists. It's for a fair bit, too."

"Simmonds—Andover?"

"That's it."

"Well, the man who runs it won't be fussing about the money. He knows a good customer when he serves one. And, anyway——" Helder smiled avuncularly, "——I took the liberty of phoning him with the sad news about Mister Harry, but assured him that you would settle in the fullness of time. I hope that was not a liberty, sir?"

For a moment or two Seyton stared at Helder, not in amazement, but in the ambivalent hold of shock which was compounded of quick excitement and also a fierce rising confusion of thought.

Then, not wanting to over-betray himself at this point to Helder, he said very deliberately, "Punch bought photographic and recording gear to use at the Hall?"

"Yes, Mr Seyton. Bought or hired."

"So it may be there still?"

"One might presume that, sir. Or should presume it, perhaps."

"I bloody well do presume it." Then, acknowledging the slow lift which was taking his spirits to optimistic levels . . . like a man, perhaps, seeing or imagining the pin prick of light at the end of a tunnel, he said, "Perhaps you'd like another drink, Mr Helder?"

"That's kind of you, sir. Yes, I would. Also—since with every respect—I may say that I am more experienced in these matters than you are, and know the possibility of hidden pitfalls, I would suggest that when you get back you tear up the account from the worthy and highly expert Mr Simmonds of Andover. I will settle it for you and include it in my fee which your splendid Miss Figgins will settle in cash with me eventually."

"Of course." Then, smiling, Seyton added, "And, of course, you have no more to tell me?"

Helder lightly fingered the knot of his black tie and stayed silent until the club waiter whose eye Seyton had caught had brought their drinks and departed. Then he said, "No more facts, Mr Seyton. Some advice. Tread gently and do what you must, but take no one into your confidence."

"Not even you?"

"Least of all me. If anyone should ever ask me why I met you here—and it could happen in this devious world—I shall say that you wanted whatever private information I could supply about the Felbeck Governors. A perfectly legitimate curiosity on your part since it is or will soon be no secret that you would like, if possible, to break the lease, one way or another."

CHAPTER SIX

IT WAS, THOUGHT Kerslake, a neat little bungalow. He had driven past it the day before, merely to establish where it was. Now, he could take all the time he chose for no matter how far her association with Seyton might have gone there was no risk of any untoward play of coincidences . . . a play which operated far more often than people imagined . . . as Seyton was safely in London since yesterday.

Early wallflowers coloured the beds on either side of the door. That she was at home was clear for her car was parked outside the neat asbestos garage. In the centre of the small patch of mown lawn was a bird-table with bread crusts, bird seed and a hanging half-coconut from which a tit flew away as he went up to the door; a coal tit. He was born and raised a countryman. The bell push operated a set of chimes inside and he smiled to himself, knowing they would not be her style. The old gamekeeper's cottage was her scene.

She came to the door wearing close-fitting green slacks and a crumpled, stained studio half-coat open over a loose khaki shirt and her auburn hair was a little ruffled. Although the clothes did nothing for her—except to suit her style of work—she looked good, very good. In the moment or two before either spoke, he thought—I could have stayed in Barnstaple, solid cop, and had someone like this to take to the annual Rugby Club dance, and other things . . . a parked car on the sand dunes, maybe a small bungalow like this at Instow with the piping of oyster catchers for music in the early morning when we woke. No regrets. Just a few thoughts, shredding away like tobacco smoke in a breeze.

She said, "Good Lord! What are you doing here?"

"It's all right. Your Mr Seyton is in London. Or was two hours ago. Not even he could drive that fast. Even supposing he would be coming here. Do we talk here?"

She stood aside and he went past her.

She said, "Straight ahead. The kitchen."

It was small, neat, clinical almost and without comfort. An electric kettle began to whistle. On the table was a tray with a mug, milk, sugar and a jar of Nescafé. She waved him to a chair, bentwood but cushioned, and offered him coffee.

"No, thanks."

She made coffee for herself and went and perched herself on a high stool by the sink, and then said, "You didn't answer the question. What are you doing here?"

"Sight-seeing. The powers that be decided I should have a look at the ground. Pay a visit to the Hall. Which I did today."

"Did you enjoy it?"

"I went round and was duly impressed. I can tell a cope from a chasuble and my grandfather lived in a half-timbered house in a poor part of Barnstaple which was standing when Drake went out to take on the Armada. I'm staying at the Talbot Hotel in Leominster and I shan't get in your way. But you send your reports to London just the same. So—what has happened since Seyton invited you in to see his pictures?"

"Nothing."

"No meeting? No seeing—even at a distance?"

"Only once. He drove by in the Land Rover and gave me a wave of the hand and toot on the horn. Could that be significant?"

"Doesn't rank in the Mata Hari class." He meant it as a joke. She had her legs crossed, the mug of coffee cradled in her lap, and his imagination—taking him unawares—reconstituted the picture without the slacks.

Flatly she said, "Bugger your Mata Haris."

He gave a little laugh and a shrug of his shoulders. To his surprise he was enjoying himself—which was rare, but when it started there was no stopping it, only concealment. He said,

"If you wish. You use field glasses, don't you? For your work. Observation and all that? No comment to be seen carrying them?"

"I always have them and sometimes use them. No comment, as you say. And, for Christ's sake, why don't you come to the point? Old Quint is bad enough but at least he's amusing with it. And why don't you look at me and not my legs when I talk to you?"

He liked that, but made no show of it. Lifting his eyes to her breasts, he saw them naked and then, recognizing danger, with little effort switched off this extra-curricular pleasure and said, "For the supposed purposes of your work do you think you could go up to a high place—I noticed one or two such—and use your glasses unostentatiously?"

"Up to a point, yes. And what would I watch?"

"Seyton, of course. The Dower House. Comings and goings. Cars calling there. Type, registration numbers if the glasses will give them, and descriptions of callers. Don't make a big thing of it. Don't over-do it. And don't try to assess the importance of anything. Just let us have the facts and we'll do the rest. Have you got a good memory for faces?"

For a moment she was silent. Although Kerslake made her angry now and then—and this because of her own predicament more than any overt word or act on his part—there was something about him now, she realized, that stirred some first movings of pity . . . something she had known with her father and Quint . . . in fact, the whole bloody lot. The fact that he was sitting there, slowly undressing her in his imagination, meant nothing. With some men you could always tell when it was happening and you made or did not make whatever you chose of it. Underneath everything though she knew—or guessed?—or divined?—a process which her father had made familiar to her, though he had little guessed it. It existed in embryo in this man. Self-disgust working in slow motion. Sometimes the growth died. Sometimes it flowered. Smiling now, she slewed round on the stool, not caring what of legs or thighs or breasts emboldening her blouse she presented and took from the kitchen draining board a house-keeping pad with a pencil clipped to it.

She said, "You went over the Hall today? Yes? A guide took you round. Nice little man but a hustler. Well . . ." As she was speaking she was sketching rapidly. "Here he is for you."

She tore the top sheet from the pad and handed it to him, and the look that came on to his face amused her.

He looked up at her and said, "That's marvellous!" He could have been a small boy, delighted by some sleight of hand. "You just do as many of these as you can and make a note of how often or infrequently they call."

"I see—and when am I going to get my own work done?"

He grinned. "You know what your real work is. You'll have to fit the other in."

"As you say, sir."

He laughed, the sound surprising him. He was more surprised when she went to the front door with him and, as he was on the point of leaving, said, "Why do you do it?"

"Do what?"

"You know what. My father was a near scratch golfer. He suddenly gave it up. When I asked him why—he absolutely adored it—he said he hadn't given it up. It had given him up."

"I'm not with you."

"Oh, yes you bloody well are. Why don't you come back in and undress me properly?"

For a moment Kerslake, the whole of his body taut with anguish, could have hit her. Then he said, "All right, you know why. It just happened after the first time that I ever put someone out of circulation. Like your father. The real thing just gave me up. But it will come back one day—I trust. Hilarious, isn't it?"

He walked away down the garden path, and left her hating herself.

* * * *

Seyton stayed a further night in London after the evening on which he had met Helder since he had unavoidable business discussions and decisions to make with Max Beaton who was running the London office for him. He and Max were very close and once or twice Seyton—feeling the need for some reliable confidant—was tempted to talk to him about the information which Helder had given him, but in the end decided against it. Curiously enough, because he felt that Helder—had he been consulted—would have positively advised against it. Helder's world had no place for unsought or whimsical intimacies. You kept information to yourself until you could either sell it profitably or use it for your own purposes. There had never been anything like that between himself and Punch; they knew all about one another, and took comfort or strength in sharing confidences or problems. Which was curious, he thought, as he drove back to the Hall through a blustery April day, because if Punch had really got hold of something which would break the Felbeck lease then why the devil had he not written or got in touch with him about it? No matter his own wanderings, sooner or later a letter or an overseas call would have found him. Good Lord . . . old Punch going so far as to be playing around with all that technical equipment. Something must have stirred him up, and that something had to be positive. Punch would never have chased any hopeless hare. Not that technicalities would have given Punch any trouble. He loved gadgets and only had to be shown once how to work something and it stuck. Spent hours tinkering with old clocks, radio sets . . . his big hands suddenly possessed with the sureness of a surgeon's. Well, one thing was for sure—and the thought gave him a big lift—all that stuff from helpful Mr Simmonds of Andover had to be around somewhere, and he was going to find it.

He made a detour on the way back and called to see Nancy. He had tea with her and, in the course of it, she said, "Have you had an invitation to the Harecastle do at Clyro this month?"

"Yes, I have. You're going too, aren't you?"

"Yes."

"Then we'll go together. I'll take you over."

"Thank you, sir." And then, her blue eyes quizzically on him, she went on, "Where are you?"

"What do you mean?"

"I know you. Something's on your mind. Not business, because you're always poker-faced about that. But kind of small boy stuff. Ants in your pants from suppressed excitement. Oh, it's all right. Most other people wouldn't spot it. But you let it slip a bit with me. Do I get to know?"

"If there was anything to tell, I'd tell you. But there isn't."

"Liar. But we'll leave it at that."

Almost as an excuse, though there was truth in it, he said, "It's all this Hall business. I can't stand the thought of those sods being there for years . . ."

"You'll get used to it. What can't be cured . . ."

Driving away he wondered if he should have told her, and then knew that it would have been unwise. He was going to trust no one until he knew much more about things himself. Bloody old Punch, ferreting away and never letting on . . . Suddenly he had one of his now rarer and rarer spasms of longing for Ruth. He could have talked to her, discussed things, and asked for help or comfort and known that no confidence would ever be broken. In business you could easily keep things to yourself because fundamentally all that was involved was money—which in the long run didn't mean a damn. Though, by God—he grinned to himself—it was nice to have.

As he went up the drive to the Dower House, the evening shadows long now as the sun was setting behind the distant hills of Wales, a familiar car came towards him and, on an impulse, sudden, but backed by reason, he blew his horn and then stopped and waved it down. As she came alongside him and leaned through the window the red sunlight took her hair and turned it to flame.

"Packing up for the day?"

"Yes."

"I've just got back from town. I wonder . . . would you care to come in for a drink? I've got something to tell you. Just a quick one, yes?"

114

"I'd be very happy to."

Why not, she thought, the farther you're away from earth the nearer you are to heaven, and he was heaven of a kind, her reward if she could make it so, and life so much easier for dear Daddy. And—oh, Christ, anyway, she was really getting sick of this business. It was ridiculous and demeaning. Why should she have to be even mildly accommodating to people like Kerslake, pretend to be amused (sometimes) by Quint, and be stuck with a Mata Hari role with this lusty shoot of the landed gentry? Not that she'd achieved anything real here yet, but every chance offering had to be gratefully—if not fulsomely—acknowledged.

He left his car with hers and they walked to the front door together. As he unlocked it and let them in she said, "Your housekeeper?"

"Ma Shipley? This is her day off." He smiled, reaching to take her raincoat before she was adjusted to aid the courtesy. "She and Shipley go off to Hereford for the afternoon . . . shopping and what have you. Then they stay on for the night's bingo sessions. Bow down and worship Bingo. Who says we don't have our native gods?"

She caught what she thought might be the edge of excitement, or something in him because his manner, rising like an unexpected zephyr, was a little forced. Basic shyness? Or perhaps the unexpected prospect of being able to force the tiny tip of growth she had divined in him when he had shown her the Hattons. Well, what or whichever, she must serve her masters and get—why not—all the pleasure she could from it . . . him? Crudely, a damn sight more potential than, say, someone like Kerslake could offer. Poor sod—and she knew her pity was real—turning assassin and castrating himself. She briefly, as he showed her into the study, wondered, if successful, how the gods would mark her.

He said, just touching her arm to seat her in a chair, "Hang on a tick. I'll get some ice and—would you like crisps or a biscuit?"

"No, thanks."

When he was gone she stood up and walked to a small gilt mirror that hung between the two main windows. She briefly touched her hair and smoothed down the front of her none too fresh working pullover. There was a Napoleonic Imperial eagle over the top of the mirror and the glass was slightly foxed. Been in the family, she thought bitchily, since the day old Boney was shipped aboard the *Belerophon* and the imperial dream crumbled into rubble. Suddenly the possible, distant prospect of getting into bed with Seyton in the line of duty made her feel rebellious. To disperse it she allowed herself the balm of the first obscene swear word that came to her mind and then felt better to the extent that she told herself that it probably would not be too bad. Good even. Splendid perhaps. The triumph of the flesh over spirit. Good old Mother Nature. Oh, what the hell and blast you Daddy Collet!

She gave him a warm, but nicely calculated smile as he came back carrying a tray.

"I hope you don't mind. I was just poking around and admiring myself in this lovely mirror." The acting bit, but she knew it was going over quite naturally.

He said, "What will it be?"

Glancing at the tray she said, "Pink gin, please. With ice."

When he brought it to her, he said, looking over her shoulder at the mirror, "Yes, charming, isn't it? A Seyton brought it back from Waterloo. He was on Wellington's staff. Went through the whole day without a scratch. Charmed life, but not for long. A year later one of the farm dogs went rabid and bit him. He died of hydrophobia." He smiled—and she liked him when he did for it lighted up his face—and added, "At least that's the story."

"Poor man." She raised her glass to him and sipped, and went on, "You said you had something to tell me?" She walked to the window seat and sat down. Outside the sky was a glowing furnace from the sun already hidden below the hills.

"Oh, yes. Well, I've been in town for a few days. I went to see your publisher. You know the drawings you showed me?"

"So?"

"You know what I'm going to say?"

"Of course I do. I never doubted that you were the kind that just said things and then forgot them because they were only guff to fill awkward gaps in talk. But I didn't realize that you were so quick off the mark, Mr Seyton."

"Well, I was up there and had an hour to spare. I've bought them. Do you mind?"

"On the contrary. I'm delighted if they're going to be here. Maybe not in the same room—but close to far more exalted company." A nice speech, she told herself, but genuine. And, for God's sake, why should she not be pleased? She liked a man who knew what he wanted and went for it. Most of them today horsed around watching the effect and waiting for applause. Even in bed the moment it was over, saying, 'Was I good?', I . . . I . . . I—always bloody I.

"I'm so pleased you're pleased," he said. "It was a bit pushing really, but I must confess I'm rather like that. See something that's good and I must have it."

She stood up and, to cover her sudden surge of emotion, moved so that she stood with her back to him looking at a framed sampler which was fitted into one of the wainscoting panels. She said, "I see nothing wrong with that if you can afford it. But what happens when you see something you want and can't afford it?"

He laughed. "I save up my pennies until I can."

She heard him move and he came up behind her as she studied the sampler which—despite her emotion—had now attracted her attention. He was far from close to her physically, but that made no matter because she knew what was happening to her; the opposite to the mental and physical stir that Kerslake and others could rouse. To give herself breathing space she said, "You've told me about the Wellington one. What about this one?" She nodded at the sampler and then turned to face him.

"Oh, that. She was a distant great-aunt. A rebel. Chip on her shoulder. Great beauty. She lived just simply for what there was in life with no thought of the hereafter."

He gave her that big, masculine grin and he put a hand on her shoulder with the lightest of touch and reached past her with his free hand and said, "It covers a dodgy bit of business. It's really the front of a small cupboard. Years ago there was a little concealed peg you had to press, but that's gone. Now you've got to use your finger nail. Like this."

Smiling at her he inserted the tip of his first finger nail into the wainscoting join and pulled the sampler away from the wall on its hidden hinges.

"Very neat." Not only the sound but the words she knew were banal, but she could not help that. The man was having a familiar—but long distant—effect on her.

"I think—or so they say—it used to be a wig cupboard. Not used for anything now." Looking at her, ignoring the little cupboard, he went on, "She's buried—Sarah Seyton that is— in the chapel. She couldn't avoid that. You must go and have a look at her memorial stone. There was no deathbed repentance. No last-minute reaching for grace or hope. She went out crying woefully against the great darkness into which she was going."

"At least she was consistent. No fickle, mind-changing woman. A familiar slur against our sex."

Seyton smiled. With a touch of his hand on her elbow he moved to the fireplace and they sat down. Looking at her in silence for a moment or two, liking her and knowing his admiration for her talent, he hesitated to speak what was in his mind and then decided that he must. He said lightly, "A chatty sort of fellow, your publisher . . . not everyone's cup of tea, I should say. Do you agree?" He smiled to cover a sudden embarrassment.

Georgina guessed at once what might have happened because it had happened before with others. Her publisher was an inveterate gossip. She decided to gamble that her instinct was right. So, to ease any diffidence in Seyton, she gave him an opening which he could or could not develop according to the dictates of his own nicety.

She said, "My publisher is a great old gossiper. Not the

kind to be trusted with a secret—however great or small."

"Why do you say that?"

"I think you know why, don't you? My father. But it doesn't upset me." She shrugged her shoulders. "It has happened to me before. Sometimes just because people remember. There's a kind which takes a vicarious pleasure, or even concern, over other people's misfortunes and just the name will trigger their memory bank. In your case—I would say not. But my gossipy old publisher, with your fat cheque in his hand, would not have been able to resist filling in a little the background of a protégée so profitable. Are you with me or have I misread that thoughtful pause after you had sat me down here?"

Seyton laughed suddenly, and said, "My God, you're as good as a witch."

"No witch. Just recognizing a now familiar situation. My father, isn't it?"

"Yes."

"Well, don't worry. Or rather you shouldn't worry. Your family has been liberally sprinkled with men and women who from conscience or desire have cried out, not only against the great darkness waiting for them, but also the great darkness which in life gathered round them. That's what my father did. He worked for the Ministry of Defence. A nice, kind, gentle man whose conscience suddenly grew too big for his comfort. That's one way of putting it. Another is that he suddenly went loopy. God knows. But he got himself into a mess—and now he's paying for it." She laughed, genuinely knowing she was safe with him, but wondering when *they* knew whether they would give her the relief of pulling her out of all this, though knowing they would not if she could turn it to advantage, which was what she now guessed was going to happen despite herself. She added before he could speak, "I shan't poach your game or steal treasures from the Hall. I just——" her voice rose "——bloody well wish it hadn't happened for his sake."

He put out a hand at this and rested it on hers.

"For God's sake! What do you think I am? I just wish the silly old fool hadn't told me. But I just couldn't stop him.

Here——" he took her empty glass and went to the tray of drinks. Over his shoulder, he said, "You went too fast for me. Yes, I was going to mention it. Simply because I believe in honesty. I could tell the silly old fool probably regaled everyone with the story. Some kinds are like that. Colourful background stuff to the author's or artist's life. How the devil you could read my mind so quickly . . . Yes, I see. Because it's happened so often. Well . . ." He came back and gave her the drink, smiling down at her. "Just forget it. And if you want to poach my game, please do so."

Taking the drink, she knew an overwhelming desire to kiss the hand which offered it. Nothing to do with bloody Birdcage. Just to do with her and his transparent decency; and knowing too that in all probability at the last moment he would never have made any mention of her publisher's gossip, might have decided to but would have stopped at the point of speech. To calm her own mood and ease his, she said, "And the treasures at the Hall?"

He smiled. "When I get the Hall back—which I'm damned well going to do—I'll find something for you."

"That's going to be some time, isn't it? What can you do but sit it out?" She spoke quite naturally, but hating herself because that innocent muddler her father was where he was, and because of him she was here with her part to play still. Loathe it or not, she knew that every part of their conversation would have to go to *them* . . . Kerslake who undressed her in his mind, Quint with his tiny kitchen, and the stained paperback of Escoffier sauces, who, too, undressed her imaginatively but in a nicer way, and then all the others—and sod the lot. But not this man. She knew that he could have what he wanted from her . . . that not only she, but he, had all that to offer which was so banally wrapped up in the overworked, shabby, tired word *love*.

She drove back to her bungalow, taking a long route, giving herself time to calm down and to find again that larger part of her posing self so that she could telephone London and pass on to them her version of what had happened between them . . .

all the obvious truth but none of the essence of her feelings or—less certain—his. And one thing she knew for certain was that they would not take her off this assignment because he knew about her father. Sometime, somehow, it might work to their advantage they would hope.

As she eventually turned into the little drive entrance of the bungalow, Seyton came back into the room where they had been having their drinks carrying the tray of cold supper which Mrs Shipley had left for him. Setting it down on a small table before the fire, he went to the dining room and brought back a decanter of red wine from the sideboard. He was about to sit down to his meal when he noticed that the Satan Sampler wig cupboard was partly open still. He went to close it but as his hand rested on the sampler, the light from the room fell full on the inside.

Nobody had ever used the cupboard except Punch. For him it was a sort of magpie nest of odds and ends. He had had for years the habit of cutting articles and items from newspapers and often in an argument would get up and rummage for something he had read and kept to make his point. In addition there were the usual old pipes, watches that he intended to repair but never did, a whole hoard of things that 'might one day come in useful'. Mrs Shipley knew the cupboard was there but had never touched it after a first early attempt to tidy it when Punch came to the Dower House to live. There was nothing secret about it. It was just Punch's cupboard.

And now, as Seyton was about to push the sampler door shut, his eye was caught by a long white foolscap envelope lying on top of the junk with his name written on it and addressed to him care of Beaton's office in New York.

He took it back to the fireplace and sat down. The envelope was unsealed and inside were two sheets of lined foolscap paper. The first sheet was dated the day before Punch had been killed in the car accident, the day on which Nancy and her father had come over to have dinner with Punch, though this last fact—unlike the date—did not immediately recall itself to Seyton.

The letter read:

Dear Richard,

Figgins has been trying to get your address or bloody whereabouts for me without any luck, so I'm sending this to Beaton who, she says, will get it to you. For God's sake why can't you be properly organized like other folk? Anyway, what I've got to say I don't want to take any risks with—and I don't think I'll get to finish it tonight because Nancy and the old man are coming to dinner. Anyway from here on in I'm going to have to put it all in dear old Sarah's fancy work—which I'm sure you won't have forgotten, having that kind of mind.

From this point on the rest of the letter was written in block letters in the Satan Sampler code which they had used for years when they were boys and young men. Ignoring his cold supper Seyton poured himself a glass of wine, drank half and then got up and rummaged for fresh paper on which to decode Punch's letter. For a little while it was difficult and he was tempted to refer to the sampler on the wall, but refused this aid since it was a challenge to him. It was not long before it all came back.

It took him some time to decode the rest of the front and back of the first sheet of paper which read:

The thing is, I know I wouldn't take your help originally to finance me when father died and the Hall became mine. Thought I could make it on my own. Bloody stubborn fool I was. And again a BF when I accepted the Felbeck thing against your wishes. But it seemed a good idea at the time. Anyway, the point is now that I really need your help—on the cash side eventually. No time for any stupid kind of pride now. But more urgent is that I need you here and your advice because you see, Richard, there is a way now that they can be turfed out. I've got enough proof of their real goings on to get their lease broken legally if they want it taken that far—which they won't. Though, God knows, there's more involved than simply breaking the lease because it could be a bloody dangerous business considering what part of their real set-up is. That's why I need you and the thing must stay just between us until we've worked out the proper line.

Frankly it's all too big for me alone. I need you at my side. Even writing like this I won't go into details—for safety's sake—but I can tell you that they really have been sods and worse. I've got some of it on tape and film and frankly I'm boiling over.

The first sheet ended at this point and, taking up the second to decode, Seyton saw that only part of the first side had been used. It read:

You see it isn't just the Hall and us. It goes far beyond that, and if it hadn't been for a pure accident I'd be sitting here like an innocent still.

It all happened when I was doing the quarterly check-up at the Hall with Shanklin and he got an urgent phone call to go and fetch some visiting big-wig who had arrived at Shobdon airfield. So I was left alone to finish the rounds. Well when I was down in the wine cellars just for old times sake—and nobody around to know—I thought I'd pop up the way we used to as lads to take a peek at the maids in their bedroom. Well, I spotted at once that someone had been using that way. More I won't say—except that, after what I found up there, I had to take some bloody risks. So you see you've got to come back hell for leather and hold my hand. But just in case anything goes wrong this end before you can get here all you have to do is to look in that place where we used to each . . .

Here the letter finished, and it was not difficult for Seyton to guess what had happened. Nancy and her father had arrived and, before going to greet them, Punch had put the unfinished letter in its envelope and shut it away in the Sampler cupboard to finish the next evening. But by the next evening Punch was dead, his car skidding off the road at six o'clock on the way home from Hereford with Shipley at his side.

Seyton put the letter back in the envelope, folded it in half and put it in the inside pocket of his jacket. Ignoring his glass of red wine and the cold supper, he fixed himself a large whisky, and then sat in front of the fire, staring at the red glow of the slow burning oak logs. Now, slowly, as he went over things in his mind—not letting himself get in the slightest degree emotional—he realized why Nancy and Roger and a few others had marked a change in Punch. Even Shanklin at the Hall. Punch was not good at containing his feelings. Then, slowly, a grim vein of excitement began to throb in him. If Punch said he had found proof, and recorded it—then that proof still existed, or at least there was a heavily weighted set of odds that it would; and what Punch had hidden he was damned sure that he could find. He sat there blankly staring at the fire and started—curiously without excitement—to think back over the old days as boys and young men when he and Punch had been so close without secrets from one another.

*　　*　　*　　*

The following evening at half-past six Sir Manfred Grandison, dressed in an old-style dinner jacket, came into Warboys' room and said without preamble, "I'll have a glass of your indifferent Marsala to put me in the mood for the company I shall be having at dinner . . . pretentious and insincere, the new élite riding that old shire horse which dear old Lowe years ago branded with the cartoon initials T.U.C. That is to say . . ."

Warboys smiled. "The Prime Minister, and the Secretary of State for Employment—or should it be Unemployment?"

"His specific brief is responsibility for Government policies affecting the working life of the country's population and the needs of potential workers, plus, of course, the promotion of good industrial relations blah, blah, blah . . . They both aspire to the reputation of gourmets and both feel that they could, did he now live, give André Simon a run for his money. Fish and chips and a glass of stout would become them better and certainly please me more."

"Our Lords and Masters." Warboys moved to provide the Marsala for his superior and served himself with a brandy.

Grandison took his glass, raised it and said, "God bless them. Democracy gives us strange bedfellows. Which brings me to the point germane of this courtesy call. I've just read your report on Miss Collet with the query you raise about her."

"More a comment."

"Truth is a great ally—if kept in a subordinate position. He found out about her father through her gossipy publisher. All very natural. Men are sympathetic to women in distress and will, as a consequence, often be moved to unusual chivalry or concern. The Ministry of Defence is one thing. He knows about that. We remain—and so do Collet's connections here—beyond the veil. Let her run, I say. And you?"

"I'm inclined to agree."

"Incline more and be positive." Grandison drained his Marsala, made a face, took the silk handkerchief from his breast pocket and began to polish his monocle.

"Positive then. I think Seyton has a certain simplistic view of women. An emotional man underneath. Sentimental—particularly about the family. When she did the drawing of the mare with foal one might think he over-reacted. But not at all. He's like that—if the atmospheric conditions are right. My verdict is that she has already got him hooked but is playing him so delicately that he has yet—but we hope never—to feel the barb. Or do we?"

"Your metaphor is a bit sloppy. So I'll cap it in the same vein. That depends on which way he swims so we won't count our chickens until they're hatched, dear Warboys. Anyway, let her run."

"She is doing that already. Ten minutes ago Kerslake passed on a report from her that Seyton spent one hour and ten minutes in the Seyton family chapel today. So devout a man?"

"If you have a private chapel—why not use it? *Domine, dirige nos.*"

"To where? The report further adds that during the course of these seventy minutes and about twenty minutes after entry he left the chapel, went back to the Dower House, and then returned carrying a long pole."

Grandison frowned, and said crossly, "What kind of report is that? How long is a pole and what is a pole?"

"Kerslake—who made the same enquiry—says she thought the length would be over six feet and under twelve feet, and that the pole was . . . well, not whippy like bamboo, but rigid in the way a curtain pole would be. She was watching through glasses at a distance of nearly two hundred yards. Interestingly when he left the chapel he did not have the pole with him."

"What the hell could he have been doing with that?"

Containing his surprise, not at the bluntness but the tone of the question and the hint of an angry frown which went with it, Warboys said, "I have no idea—except that he might have been putting up curtains of some form in the chapel. And, except again——" he was enjoying himself, "——Seyton is not the type to do things like that by himself when he has workmen who could do it for him."

Grandison suddenly smiled. "Good. Now stop enjoying yourself at my expense and tell her to find out, if she can, about the pole. The chapel is never locked. I know that."

"I've already told Kerslake to pass that instruction to her. But you know——" Warboys was loath to deny himself a little further enjoyment, "——there's probably a simple answer. It's spring. Maybe some bird was nesting in there and he wanted to knock down the nest. Bird lime on the family memorial tablets of the Seytons? *Lèse majesté.* No?"

"There, yes. And also to some extent here now. And now, too, what about the report on Seyton's business affairs?"

"Interim only. Impeccable. No question of 'Collar 'im tight in the name of the Law!' "

Grandison gave a broad grin. "Don't tell me. Kipling, I should say."

"Sadly, no. Max Beerbohm. However—to return to our muttons—there is one little ray of sunshine. He—or perhaps more correctly his firm—use a man called Helder. You won't know him. We've never used him, and never should—except in some extreme situation—because he suffers from an old-fashioned disease known as loyalty to his clients. If I sent someone to have a chat with him about Seyton—then Seyton would know within a few hours. So—should it be necessary to have a chat with him—then we would have to keep Helder in durance vile until whatever had to be done had been done."

"You mean such men still exist?"

"A few—but they don't breed often. I think their honesty makes them sterile. So do we leave him in peace?"

"Reluctantly, yes, unless ultimately forced." Grandison sighed and then, shaking his head and chuckling good humouredly for a moment or two, went on, "My goodness, and I had thought that on our side of the fence all men like that had 'died in the young summer of the world's desire; Before our hearts were broken—Like sticks on a fire'." He finished, his eyes challenging Warboys.

"Not difficult, but a guess, not from knowledge. It must be W. B. Yeats."

With boyish pleasure clear on his piratical face, Grandison shook his head. "It should be, shouldn't it? But it isn't. It's Chesterton, a parody of W.B. And now I go to take dinner with Our Lord and Master and his sycophant. How sad it is that in this country political assassination is out of fashion and that the stupidity and vanity of one man can slowly destroy a nation." Then with something approaching a look of anger on his face and his voice rasping, he went on, "I'm tired of the whole sorry mess. I say a pox on *vox populi*."

When he was gone Warboys finished his brandy and helped himself to another and sat quietly at his desk, not deep in thought, nor speculation, but aware of the beginning of some slow powerful tide of intuition, rare and signalled by small signs as were the tides of the seas as they turned . . . a shift of wind, a new pattern in the flight of shore birds, the sea anemones slowly rebuttoning themselves against the coming touch of air and sun and the small green crabs seeking the shelter of bladder-wrack havens under the rocks. And then slowly into his consciousness came the figure of sorry, sad Collet. Nobody, he thought, was invulnerable; that would be contrary to God's creative pattern. Each man was left to find his own way. There was no escaping that—neither for Grandison, for himself or for anyone else in the whole wide world of the human ant heap.

*   *   *   *

127

That same evening Seyton lay in his bath wishing that Nancy and her father were not coming to dinner. His mind was still full of the discovery of Punch's letter and he would have preferred to stay alone with his thoughts and speculations. The coincidence that she and her father had once drastically—tragically—interrupted Punch's letter to him, gave rise to a faint superstition in him. Was it a good or a bad omen?

Lying, soaking, he remembered the solicitor Bellamy handing over the heavily waxed sealed envelope to him—the ritual gone through with every Seyton succeeding to the Hall. In the family more ritual than secret. *He who would leave the Hall unseen must go down the Master's way. He who would enter the Hall unseen must pass by long silent Sarah.* The Master's way was from the set of maids' bedrooms on the very top floor of the old Tudor part of the Hall. A narrow, secret stairway had been built into the enormous block of the central Tudor chimneys and this gave access to the cellars and from there along an underground tunnel to the chapel. According to family tradition a seventeenth-century Seyton forefather, after a tankard or two of malmsey or Canary wine, had used the chimney stairway to go up to the maids' quarters to exercise his *droit de seigneur*. The chimney way was no great secret, but the tunnel to the chapel—its opening concealed by a pivoting wine-rack—was. He smiled to himself as he remembered how he and Punch, not long into their teens, had used the Master's way at night to go up and watch the maids undressing through the ventilator grilles set high in the bedroom walls. Their own giggling and clumsiness had betrayed them and had earned them a determined leathering from their father and the door in the cellar had been padlocked against them. The leathering, he thought now, had been too severe to balance fairly the benefits of their Peeping Tom exploits for they had seen very little.

There was no way that he could go openly to the Hall and examine the Master's way. From now on his attitude and manner to all at the Hall had to be unexceptionable. But that day he had gone to the chapel to check the condition of the passageway to the cellar. Twenty yards from the foot of the narrow flight of steps that led down from the chapel floor level he had found that one side of the Tudor brick-lined tunnel had collapsed and blocked the passage. He had gone back to the Dower House and taken a long, stout ash pole which Mrs Shipley used to knock down the martins' nest from over the back door of the kitchen quarters. "You can have 'em anywhere on the rest of the house, Mister Richard—but not over my back door. Makin' a mess—and not only on the steps, but sometimes in my hair!"

Back in the tunnel he had pushed the pole through the heavy dark soil. The pole was nearly twelve feet long and it was into the pile well over half its length before he felt it move easily, free of obstruction. It would take a good few hours' work to shift the fall and spread it back along the tunnel towards the steps. That done, and hopefully there would be no other falls, he could get into the cellar at night—they still had racked and binned there a lot of their own wines and ports—and then go up the Master's way to find—with luck—what Punch had found there and which had, clearly, spurred him to action. After that he would have to find the film and tape which Punch must have hidden away somewhere. Already that day he had gone through all the likely places in the Dower House without success and had ransacked their old playroom over the stables, but that had not surprised him. Punch had a jackdaw mind and had been good at hiding things and himself when they had played their boyish games . . . But for the time being he wanted first to get into the Hall.

That evening after dinner Captain Hope, stimulated by good food and port, and now further indulging himself with a large glass of brandy—carefree, as Nancy knew, because, cautiously abstemious she, having lost the toss between them, was to have the duty of driving home—got on his favourite hobby horse: the state of the nation. Not that the state of the country did not merit most of his strictures, for this was the tailing end of a winter of discontent; crippling strikes in industry and the social services, hospitals struggling to survive, schools closed, the Trade Unions militant and unable to control their own members and getting no firmness from a Government whose Cabinet Ministers were chiefly their subsidized lackeys . . . troops called out to run ambulance and fire services while pickets at factory and hospital gates bullied, assaulted, and intimidated workers who would have worked and volunteers who still knew the difference between human decency and human greed and envy, while all the while a nation once great and a country where once it had been safe to walk the streets at night slid nearer—his words, "The edge of the abyss at whose bottom lies Chaos, Corruption and the stinking Cesspool of all human evils. Where have all the virtues gone? Love thy neighbour? An honest day's work for a fair day's pay? I tell you this nation is destroying itself and the disease is an imported one as much as ever the Black Death was. All right, you may think I exaggerate. But, I tell you, we don't just stand at the parting of the ways between a civilized state but are already well on the road to a Socialist shambles—and all deliberately engineered by crypto-Communists, pinko-Intellectuals and power-seeking politicians who take orders from their masters either in Moscow or the Trade Unions. But never fear, sooner or later—because this is the law of opposites, the law that keeps the stars and planets in their courses—One will arise, some new Churchill, aye, or some Cromwell to tear down the false ideologies and to drive out of this once green and pleasant land all those who would turn it into a garbage heap where they would have our people root like pigs for scraps while their swineherd Marxist masters enjoy the spoils of tyrants and the fruits of privilege . . ."

At a side table where she was helping herself to fresh coffee, Nancy smiled to herself. She loved the old boy when he talked like this. He enjoyed letting off steam so much and it did him a lot of good. Looking round she caught Richard's eyes for a moment and winked at him and saw the corners of his mouth move in sympathy with her. He had been a bit subdued all evening she had thought and now—though he was used to it— he was being put through the hoop by her father, for the old boy had a way of lecturing that always seemed to imply that the one to whom he talked was to some extent responsible for the conditions he was condemning.

"Where now do you find the only remaining concept of duty, honour, and unswerving loyalty to this grand old country? Not in the Church—weasel minded and mealy mouthed, more concerned with starving Asians and something they call the Third World when under God's grace there is only one world and this country, one to which all the rest of mankind owe so much. No—keep your bishops. True virtue lives still in the Armed Forces of the Crown. Crown, I say—and what a dirty word these bastards try to make of that. The Armed Forces—underpaid, God save us, but loyal. No striking——"

"Mutinies have been known," said Nancy over her shoulder.

"Damn it, yes—but because of bad officers. But on the whole—and you know damn well what I mean, my girl—they stand firm for Queen and Country. I tell you that one day—and not far off—it is going to come to a show-down between——"

Crossing to him Nancy dropped into his lap a drawing roughly mounted temporarily on a stout piece of cardboard backing and said, "Richard's heard it all before and I don't want to drive you home in a state of apoplexy. What do you think of that?"

Her father gave her an angry frown and then, as his eyes went to the drawing, all sign of his spleen slowly vanished to be replaced by a smile. "My God . . . That's bloody marvellous. It's old Suzie to a T. And the foal. Feller that did this knew his stuff."

"No fellow," said Nancy. She pointed to the signature. "Georgina Collet." She looked at Richard. "Who is she—and how come?"

Seyton shrugged his shoulders. "Oh, she's some artist type. Asked permission to wander round the place to do wild life drawings . . . for a book or exhibition or something. She turned up with that. Kind of *thank you*, I suppose."

"And a very nice one too," said the Captain. "Think she'd come over to my place and do something for me?"

"I wouldn't know. I rather gather she's got her hands pretty full at the moment with commissions."

"Well, if she's still around, could you ask her? Or if not—then let me have her address."

"Well, I suppose so, yes."

"What does the 'suppose so' mean?" asked Nancy, and as she spoke she knew from the faintest change in his manner and voice that some small ripple of emotion had disturbed him from the moment she had dropped the drawing into her father's lap. "Is she here still or has she gone?"

"Oh, no . . . I think she's around still from time to time."

"Well, the next time you see her, will you ask her?"

"Yes, of course I will. I'll ask her to give you a ring."

Amused, but hiding it, knowing her Richard and the irrelevancy of any jealousy on her part, Nancy could not deny herself the mild but loving malice of a further small probe. Bed they shared now and again, but unashamedly she longed to make it a marriage bed. No other man could stand alongside him so far as she was concerned. But she knew herself no fool to build high hopes. Just a few small ones which she hugged for comfort now and then. So, looking full at him, and letting her voice tease him with a note of well-known gentle raillery, she asked, "What's she like? Young? Old? Ravishing beauty or one of those hair-drawn-back types and never use anything but soap and water on the face? Come on, give."

Seyton laughed, knowing his Nancy and genuinely amused so that he sought no escape from truth. "She's bloody marvellous. Thirty-odd. Splendid auburn hair. Super figure. But more than all that she's got that gift." He nodded at the drawing which the Captain still held.

"I don't care a damn what she looks like," said the Captain. "Two heads as far as I'm concerned. But you ask her to give me a ring."

"Yes, do that, Richard," said Nancy. "I'd like to meet her. And now, my tub-thumping father—get on your feet. We're for home."

"You can joke, my girl. But you wait until the day of decision comes. That won't be any joking matter."

Looking at the drawing after they had gone Seyton smiled

for a moment or two, thinking of Nancy and her gentle but unnecessary probe, and then the drawing of the grazing mare with foal brought Punch back to him, excluding all other thoughts. On a night like this, with the Captain and Nancy here, he must have stood when they had gone and could have gone back to finish the letter to him but had probably been too tired and a bit full of good drink to feel like it. And why not? There had been all the time in the world ahead of him . . . tomorrow and tomorrow . . . but there always had to come a tomorrow which no man could outlive.

CHAPTER SEVEN

THE NEXT MORNING it was raining hard with a cold wind from the north-east. Kerslake telephoned Georgina from his hotel room before going down to breakfast, and came quickly to the point.

"Don't go down to the Hall today."

"I had no intention of doing so—for obvious reasons. I couldn't do any drawing or observing."

"Exactly. But I'll go. I can watch the chapel from the bluff across the river—not on his land. I wonder what the hell he's doing in there?" It was no serious question, merely he knew a device to keep her on the line a little longer, wondering whether she stood now, a dressing gown loose over her nightdress, her bold, firm body sun-browned, warm from sleep . . . he let the pictures of her slide through his mind and at the same time was bored and calmly disgusted with himself, as though he had picked up some well-thumbed girlie magazine, flipping through the nudes and wondering why the hell he did it.

"Maybe he's taken up brass rubbing."

"I think the whole damned thing's a nonsense."

"My dear father used to say that seventy-five per cent of the time that's all it ever was with . . . well, the firm he worked for."

"Maybe . . ."

"Wrap up well and fill your whisky flask."

He knew she had no true concern for him, but found a little comfort just in the words. "I'll do that. And I was wondering . . ."

She laughed but without unkindness, he felt, and said, "There's no need to. Call in on your way back and have a drink."

"That's good of you."

"Not really. I get flat too. And any company is better than none."

"That's a bastard thing to say to a man." He spoke without edge to his voice; oddly, too, relishing her words as a true step towards compassion—of which he had no need.

"I know. But that's how we have to be at times, isn't it? I'll try and remember to think of you while I'm working here all nice and bloody cosy. Don't forget—you made your own choice. I didn't. That gives me the right to say bastard things to you."

He was on the far side of the river by half-past nine. The water was beginning to colour up with the run-off from the rain. He sat just inside a young spruce plantation with a clump of broom bushes for cover and had a clear view of the front of the chapel. He sat there until half-past eleven when he was rewarded with the sight of Richard Seyton, wearing a mackintosh and cap, leaving the chapel. The man walked without hurry, head down a little against the rain, back to the Dower House.

Going back, Kerslake thought, to a couple of stiff pink gins and then a hot lunch. He sat under the dripping spruces, had his first pull at his whisky flask (drink meant nothing to him; he could take it or leave it) and then ate some of the sandwiches the hotel had made up for him. They were pork luncheon meat and disgusting, but he ate them mechanically, hardly knowing he did so. Long ago he had learnt the art of just sitting and watching. There was a mental trick to it, like going into a trance. Not once had he given himself the passing relief of thinking about Georgina Collet or wondering what Seyton was up to, if anything, and, if something, why Birdcage should be showing an interest. His lunch eaten, he relieved himself, and then went back to his watching point. The river was running in rising spate, the brown waters curded with yellow froth. Two cormorants flew overhead with slow, piratical sweeps of their wings. At the head of a run of fast water a salmon showed momentarily and he wondered if the small rise in water had set it running or whether, like himself, it was reacting to boredom in the only way it knew.

At half-past two Seyton came back, head down against the driving rain, and went into the chapel and from the way he handled the door it was clear that it was not locked which confirmed what Georgina had once said that it never was. But it would be interesting to know now, he thought, whether once inside Seyton had locked it. God's house never barred to mankind. Come unto me all ye that are weary . . . An hour later a fallow deer came along the edge of the line of spruces, her coat lacquered with rain, and disappeared down a small track over the edge of the river bluff. He thought of the red deer of his own Exmoor and remembered the first time he had ever met Quint. In a bedroom of the Imperial Hotel in Barnstaple. That had been the beginning. He had realized then what he had wanted, had worked for it and got it, and was here now with no true regrets and would, one day, pass into Quint's place and, if the dark gods were kind, beyond . . . Warboys' place. But never Grandison's. His background, breeding, education . . . practically every bloody thing you could think of was wrong. He had seen Grandison many times, but only ever talked to him alone once. That had been after he had killed his first man.

Grandison had said, 'You did well, Kerslake.'

'Thank you, sir.'

And then he had gone on as though the subject of his commendation had no importance . . . no more than a weed pulled up, a fly swatted, an idle pot-shot at a roof sparrow . . . gone on to talk about Devon, asked him if he missed being there and, when he had said he did not and was glad to be away from it, had quoted something to him which he had never heard and which Quint—who had demanded a blow by blow account of their interview afterwards—had told him was from Herrick of whom he had also never heard. The words ran in his memory now. *Such discontent I ne'er have known since I was born than here where I have been and still am sad in this dull Devonshire.* And that night when he had taken his secretary to the theatre on tickets given to him by Quint and later had got into bed with her it had happened and went on happening until in the end he had given up trying. Sometimes he had had the odd intuition that Quint had guessed. Maybe that was why from then Quint had lifted their relationship to one in which he had been given greater licence in his speech with him . . . nothing great, but enough to be marked and appreciated.

At four-thirty Seyton came out of the chapel and walked back through the rain to the Dower House. At five he saw him drive away from the Dower House in the Land Rover. Without relief or hurry Kerslake walked back through the woods to the lay-by where he had parked his car. He got into the back seat and, uncaring of any casual traffic which might come along the small back road, he stripped his wet clothes from him and put on a change he had brought in a suitcase and then drove off.

As he came along the road towards her bungalow he saw the Land Rover parked outside. He drove by and a hundred or so yards down the road parked in a lay-by. He lit a cigarette and switched on the radio. He sat listening to it and, without really needing it, finished the last of his whisky. Twenty minutes later the Land Rover came down the road and passed him, disappearing into the fast-fading light and the still-steady rain. Kerslake drove back to the bungalow. Before he had reached the front door she had opened it to him.

He said, "Is he likely to come back?"

"No."

She stood aside and he went in, and from her manner he knew that some sort of concordat had been created between them. Nothing that would ever come to any flowering. It was all he wanted.

In the small, rather prim drawing room of the bungalow she offered him the choice of whisky or brandy and he chose brandy. As she got his drink she asked, "You took a change of clothes with you?"

"Part of the drill. Did your father never tell you?"

"Until it was too late he never told me anything. I thought he was a pukka civil servant. What happened today?"

"He spent time, morning and afternoon, in the chapel. At his prayers, would you say?" The new easiness in him was pleasant but never to mislead him. They were both what they were, and he knew, too, that they would both recognize the boundaries not to be crossed when they came to them . . . or, perhaps, and he was momentarily pleased at the aptness of his conceit, that there was no question of boundary crossing because they were both trapped and the pet shop owner had just happened to put their cages side by side. Birdcages.

Bringing the brandy she said, "He's the kind who reads the lessons. But I doubt whether he would ever wear out his knees with prayer."

"You like him, don't you?"

"Yes."

"Well, that's a bonus. I'm glad for you."

She sat down in a chair opposite him, crossing her legs under the working smock she wore and he was happy just to look at her and think of her breasts being nakedly exposed to him, as though it might be something she would do with a happy generosity to please him.

Casually, as though confidences had long ago ceased to be any novelty between them, she said, "What's happened to you?"

"I'm not quite sure. But I like it."

"Well, when you get round to finding words for it you can tell me."

"Maybe I will. Anyway, if I told it to anyone I'd like it to be you. What did Seyton want?"

"Some friend of his saw a drawing I did of a mare and foal at the Hall. He asked Seyton to ask me if I could do something similar for him. His name is Captain Hope and he lives around here somewhere. It's all on the telephone pad over there if you want it."

"We've got it already. The Captain's daughter, Nancy Hope, is his girl friend. A relaxed, unserious arrangement."

"Those are the best sometimes." She grinned then and went on, "Sitting out in the rain all day has done wonders for you. You're almost human."

"Almost. Will you do anything for the Captain?"

"No. I've got enough on my plate."

"Would you say there's any change in Seyton?"

"Not really. Well, yes, perhaps some. Or it could be imagination. He seemed . . . Oh, I don't know."

"Why didn't he phone you about this Captain Hope?"

"He could have done. He knows my number. But he didn't. Perhaps that's what I mean. A slight shift out of character. I wonder how long he'd been in the chapel before you got there this morning?"

"God knows."

She was silent for a time, watching him sip at his brandy, his eyes on her all the while. There was something about his manner she realized now that oddly reminded her of her father, a gentle strain of what? Melancholy? Perhaps. Because somewhere in the past the smallest of coincidence's tricks or a little time-shift of being somewhere he had not expected to be sent had set up an unexpected mood and no choice of ways because Fate was fingering him. That's what her father had said once. He had come down with a science degree, ready to go into medicine and then, with a few months to spare, to relax and recharge himself before going to Guy's he had gone touring in France with Quint, an older friend in a Government ministry who had talked him round to taking a job in what was then the Admiralty and his subsequent seduction had followed.

She said, "Yes, undoubtedly God does know. But do you think Birdcage do?"

"Could be. Could be not. That's not the point as far as I'm concerned."

"Don't they tell you anything?"

He laughed. "You know you shouldn't ask that question. But, yes—they tell me something. But in my experience it's not often the truth. But right now I know nothing."

"And you don't mind that?"

"Not at all." He rose and said, "I'd better be going. He might come back this way and see my car. I don't want that to happen. He could be the kind who remembers and if he sees it parked anywhere around the Hall area——"

"I suppose so."

At the door before she opened it for him he turned, standing close to her, and said, "I shall be phoning Quint. Is there anything I can say about your progress?"

"With him?"

"Yes."

"Well, women are always supposed to have an instinct about it, aren't they? Yes, I suppose I could say, given the right conjunctions of time, place and mood—and the mood the most important element—he'd take me to bed. But there's one thing I don't think he will ever do and that's talk to me confidentially about his affairs. He walks by himself—a little bit of human and even loving slap and tickle on the side could arise. But real talk—the kind you're after—No. He's a Seyton. The men of that family have always kept women out of their affairs."

"You never know. Anyway, thanks for the drink and so on."

She stood at the door and watched him drive away, sorry for him, liking him now, and knowing perfectly well what he had meant by thanking her for, not the drink, but the 'and so on'.

*   *   *   *

Warboys lay back in a leather armchair, his head just high enough for him to mark the lights of cars passing up and down the distant Mall, their movements distorted by the rain which smeared the window while Quint sat at his desk talking on the telephone to someone about a routine matter, its substance of no interest to him. He had had lunch that day at the Savoy and was remembering now the distant days of his young manhood when he had danced there many an evening to the music of Carroll Gibbons and his Savoy Orpheans, and of one girl in particular whose death had changed the whole of his life. Her father had been the owner of a world-wide engineering firm . . . a self-made man, charming, and with a finely honed intellect which he had much admired. They had taken to one another and no objection had been made to him and the girl becoming engaged and, tied to that, an opening to be made for him in the firm. The whole thing had been a dream—and a sharp lesson in the workings of adult human nature, almost his first, but this one never to be forgotten and to lay the foundations of the twists of time and chance which had him sitting now in this armchair. Peggy . . . common sort of name, really. But a delight and modishly generous with her favours. A large town house and an estate in Hampshire with part of the Test running through it and the days those when there really was a splendid mayfly rise and excessive water abstractions and pollution had still to come. Hunt balls . . . *Tiptoe through the Tulips*, and marble table tops after midnight sticky with spilled White Ladies. A summer night, both of them a little tipsy, and she sitting on the stone balustrade of the steps that led down from the terrace to the precisely laid out herb gardens, each bed neatly bordered with close and low-cropped box shrubs. Then one joke, slightly risqué, told by him, which had made her laugh and lean backwards. He had been too late to reach her as she went over and fell, the distance to the ground no more than eight feet. Fate had decreed that she should drop precisely between two rhododendron bushes, either of which would have cushioned her fall and saved her from hitting her head on the paved stone walk. Dead instantly. Lying there like someone disposed unmoving in an act of charade, the fingers of one hand entwined in a loop of her pearl necklace, her dress—black velvet—undisturbed, even modishly and a little seductively arranged as though she were posing for some fashion magazine. And that was that. The father had wiped him out of his existence. Twelve days later (why did the memory of such trivial detail persist?) he had met Grandison—then an M.P.— on the terrace of the Houses of Parliament where he was having tea with his father, Sir Eustace Warboys, also an M.P. Had liked him and so one thing had led to another and then to Birdcage. Which had fascinated him largely because he had so early learnt that life was of no importance. Merely a game which everyone had to lose sooner or later.

Quint put down his telephone, slewed round, and said, "Sorry about that. You were saying that——"

"I had lunch today at the Savoy with Grandison and Felbeck. Arranged, of course. I'd only met Felbeck once before. It was felt that I should come a little closer. Boiled turbot with a Scharzhofberger and then saddle of mutton with a Château Léoville, this last 'A shapely filly out of Scharzberg Flint by Phoebus Apollo; the sire passionate; the dame highly bred but so cold.'"

Quint grinned. "Only one man could ever have said that. Dear André Simon?"

"Quite so."

"And did you come closer?"

"To Felbeck—no. We remain in our own orbits. All was polite and interesting. He talks well. Mostly about himself or his Foundation for which he bears a commendable, I suppose, passion. Meanwhile our Lord and Master sat jocund and benign and . . ." he eyed Quint with a sly look, ". . . I would have given a lot to have been able to read his mind. Or even to know it at second-hand. Somewhere in all this there is a very ancient and fish-like smell, or I deceive myself. I say no more. As for the solid foundations, the brick by brick facts, well . . . Time will or will not tell. You are with me?"

"Lagging a little. But I understand the possibility. And I thank you for the confidence—behind which I hope there are no true facts for concern."

"*Folie de grandeur?* It comes with age. But here there is not even ground for guesswork—always a delightful exercise. Only let me ask this. In the past there were practised many quite barbaric cures for madness. Will you won't you join the dance? If we have to—and this is a passing whiff of fancy, no easily defined true Havana—you would, of course, join me in the treading of a medieval measure?"

"Of course." Quint smiled. "Purely for self-protection. But quite honestly I think either the Scharzhofberger or the Léoville has played too large a part."

"In no way. Fancy I admit, and without definition. But in

this service one acquires a nose for every lurking pride which can find a lodging in the human soul."

"A little mixed, but I take your meaning."

"I accept the 'mixed' but am glad you take the meaning. Grandison, as you may or may not know, brought me into all this at a time when I had a low opinion of human nature. That has been modified a little in detail but not in the main content. A few notable exceptions, of course."

"Myself one?"

"Of course, or I should not be talking so to you, my dear Quint. But, anyway, enough of that. What news have you from the banks of the Wye? A beautiful river, but give me the Test. The salmon may be king, but the humble trout is God's darling and His eyes' delight."

Quint told him of Seyton's two visits to the chapel and of his call on Georgina Collet and of her assessment—passed on like the rest—by Kerslake that evening, and finished, "Do you want this taken further? If he goes in again tomorrow then Kerslake could play an inquisitive tourist and try the door to see if he has locked it. I understand from Miss Collet that the door is normally never locked. The local people are free to use it when they wish."

"No. Leave him undisturbed. And only use Kerslake in bad weather. Otherwise he keeps away. But tell Miss Collet to have a look inside when the weather allows her to be at the Hall about her business. There's no fear that she will run into any trouble. If Seyton is up to anything he will have taken precautions to protect his activities. She has just got to be what she pretends to be. Kerslake is bad weather only and not now to go into the park or anywhere near the Hall."

"But why should he spend so much time in there?"

Warboys shrugged his shoulders. "I said just now that nothing positive occurs to me. But I could provide you with a Gothic hypothesis. You don't read romantic historical novels, do you?"

"Not often."

"Well, I do. Always when travelling by air. They take my

143

mind off a constant fear that the wings will fall off. I'd rather travel like the mole."

Quint was silent for a while, not from want of speech but from admiration and the pleasure that Warboys could sometimes give him by the pure brilliance of his deceptions and the lightning reach of his intuitions. With deliberate vulgarity, he said, "You've been sitting there all this bloody time and all the while you've bloody well known. You are a sod."

Warboys put his head back and chuckled with pleasure. Then shaking his head, he said, "You give me too much credit. I don't know. But there's no harm in a wild guess. Or even a preposterous conjecture. After lunch I went along to the British Museum Reading Room. A delightful place to sit and recuperate from a good lunch. I did a little reading too—in a delightful book written in the eighteenth century called *Marsham's English Eccentrics and Notabilities*. There is a very interesting account in it of the Seyton family, and particularly of one Sarah Seyton—who even then retained the old spelling of the name. But more interesting was a description of the Hall, outlining the various stages of construction over the centuries, and with this a lot of tittle-tattle of legends and family secrets and scandals. Priest holes and secret chambers. They were—still are—Royalists. In Good King Charles' Golden days and before—and, who knows, now?—it was always handy to have a way of coming and going without being seen. I say no more than that. But it set up a romantic train of thought. So I began to speculate about Seyton going into his chapel yesterday with a stout long pole."

"And where did you get?"

"Nowhere specifically. Except that the book mentioned a rumour that there was a secret, underground way from the Hall to the chapel. Fascinating?"

"Not particularly. If Seyton wants to go to the Hall he can go in through the main entrance."

"Ah, now you're being deliberately obtuse—or perhaps more accurately, you won't play at wild guesses. You must have one small fact before you let fancy take flight."

"Well . . . assuming you are right. Why go mole-like from A to B?"

Warboys smiled blandly. "I have no idea."

Quint shrugged his shoulders. "Well, what do you want me to do? Suggest this possibility to Kerslake and Georgina Collet?"

"No. Not to anyone—above or below our station in this organization. We will just sit and cherish the possibility of the mole theory between ourselves. It may well turn out to be one of those 'barren optimistic sophistries of comfortable moles'. No?"

Quint sighed openly, and said, "Ah . . . now I have lost you."

"It has little aptness. Just a fancy to top off our conversation. But I think you cheat. 'Thou smilest and art still, Out-topping knowledge'?"

Warboys heaved himself slowly from his chair and went to the door and looked back smiling at Quint as he half opened the door.

Quint suddenly chuckled and shook his head. "All right— since you must be fed. Matthew Arnold. But call me a light half-believer of your casual creed. Also I doubt the existence of the British Museum book you mentioned. You just had a quiet doze to settle your lunch."

"That too."

Warboys went. Quint sat, and found himself thinking of Grandison and Felbeck, and feeling suddenly very tired and very old.

*   *   *   *

Since dinner time he had been sitting broodingly in front of the fire, relaxed and thinking of Punch's unfinished letter, and particularly of its last unfinished sentence. *But just in case anything goes wrong this end before you can get here all you have to do is to look in that place where we used to each* . . . To do what? Hide things, clearly. But there were dozens of places where over

145

their years they had hidden things; in the Hall, in the country around, in the Dower House and in the farm and estate buildings and as some became known or unsuitable finding new ones. Bulk, too, was a factor—in the present circumstances a helpful one because if Punch had acquired film and tape and for these would want a projector and tape player then the hiding place had to be reasonably commodious. Already he had been through the house without success, except for a collapsible film screen which had been on top of Punch's wardrobe. Tomorrow if he finished his work in the chapel tunnel he would begin on the farm and estate buildings. Though he had a feeling that Punch would not have wanted to cache his stuff too far afield where by chance someone might come across it. Old Shipley, for instance, would be quick to notice anything unusual in places like stables or barns.

Hearing the rain beating against the windows he hoped that it would continue through the next day. While he was safe enough once in the chapel and down into the passageway, there was always the chance in good weather of some local or someone from the Hall coming into the place. As it was he had decided against locking the door once he was in the chapel. Before first light on his initial working visit he had taken up shovel, pick and working dungarees to the passage and had left them there. And today, too, he had made good progress, spreading the fallen soil back along the tunnel. Three or four hours tomorrow should see him through.

Feet sprawled to the blaze of the fire, a half-drunk glass of whisky forgotten on the table at his side, he found himself thinking of Georgina Collet. Late that afternoon he had decided to go into Leominster to buy himself a more powerful torch for use in the tunnel, and on the way had called on her to tell her about Hope's request. It had meant a small detour and he was mildly curious with himself for making it when he could so easily have telephoned her. Company? A little relief from all this chapel lark. God knew. All he knew was that he had done it. Odd, too, that he probably would never have bothered if he had not remembered Nancy's look when he had told the

Captain about Georgina. Things must have been pretty bloody for her when her father was taken up. Not the kind of thing you'd choose to want to live with—though he could not feel that she let it worry her much. Or perhaps she did and just kept it on a tight rein.

After a while he went to his desk and began to write his weekly letter to Roger. Remembering his own father's irregular and not very informative or interesting letters to himself, he had always made a point of putting himself in Roger's place and making his letters the way he would have liked to have had them from his own father. Writing now he could wish that he might be able to tell Roger about the chapel tunnel business. He would have loved it. Well, perhaps one day he would be able to tell him. Just as he finished the letter Figgins, who always rang late, knowing that she was more likely to catch him, telephoned to clear up some business points and some queries which Beaton had raised. He answered them mechanically, efficiently, aware that although they were important his real interest in them was now remote. The time would come again to take up the reins . . . Hall back or no Hall back. It could never be self-supporting on its own unless he turned it into a bloody circus. Better to stick with diamonds than that . . . what in God's name had turned up that money-making flair in him? Ruth's death? Punch's pig-headed decision to go his own way?

With her business queries finished Figgins said, "What are you doing with yourself . . . generally, that is?"

"Oh, mucking around. Tidying a few things up."

"That tells me nothing. You know what I mean. The Hall. Is there still a bright little gleam in your eyes?"

"Could be. I must look."

"There probably is—and that would tally."

"With what?"

"Well, let's say, with someone not just going to accept that there's an end to things about the Hall. Felbeck, for instance. Who knows you're not the kind to give up."

"Spell it out."

"Oh, you know the way they do it. Suddenly Tax people and Customs and Excise chaps become a little more efficient. Not probing. All very gentlemanly—as far as they know how to be. But taking another look at currency transfers and foreign dealings."

"We've nothing to hide. And anyway Felbeck wouldn't have that kind of pull."

"I don't know. You could have made him uncomfortable." She chuckled. "Perhaps he asked the Archbishop of Canterbury to have a word with the Chancellor of the Exchequer."

"He can get on the hot line to the Archangel Gabriel as far as I'm concerned. We've never played funny tricks. I can't think——"

"What gave me the feeling? About you?"

"If you like."

"Well . . . towards the end Punch was up to something. First Helder and then badgering the life out of me to try and find out just exactly where you were. And now—oh, I'm as good as a Welsh witch—they're the best kind. You're brooding and I don't think it's on any china egg. And I'm very fond of you, Master Richard, sir."

"Ditto, in reverse. But you've got nothing to worry about."

"And Felbeck?"

"Well, he's got all those starving millions and the preservation of such Church treasures as he can get his hands on."

"He's a gamecock. Mind how you ruffle his feathers."

"Why don't you get on your broomstick and fly off to a jolly midnight coven?"

"Too rainy for flying. So it's bed."

"Good night."

Ten minutes later, when he had finished his whisky and was thinking of going to bed, Nancy telephoned.

"Richard, would you mind very much if I stood you up?"

"About what?"

"You know . . . the supper dance thing of the Harecastles over at Clyro."

"No . . . But why?"

148

"That bloody boring tax exile brother of father's in Monaco has asked us down for that week. He always sets out the dates very precisely. Father wants to go but not without me. You know I always have to play umpire for them when they get going. I've never understood why they bother to visit each other. But I know the old man could do with the change. Would you mind very much?"

"Of course not. Do the old boy good. And you."

"You're a darling. What will you do?"

"Dunno. Probably send a nice regret letter and stay here and sulk—thinking of you lying in the sun."

"Stick-in-the-mud. Ask somebody else."

"Any ideas?"

"Well, what about your glamorous artist girl? Georgina Something?"

"No, thanks."

"Oh, come on. Give the girl a break."

"Don't be an ass. I hardly know her."

"No? Well, she phoned this evening to tell the old boy that she just couldn't take on any new commissions at the moment. I must say he took it very well and very soon put on his gallant, chucking-under-the-chin act—metaphorically that is. But if you don't fancy it, you don't. But it was good of you to phone her about it. The old boy sends his thanks."

Seyton said nothing for a while, deliberately letting the silence between them hang, a theatre curtain imminently to rise. There was no malice in her. Just Nancy enjoying what he now recognized had been a carefully well-worked-out ploy. Then he said, "My dear Nancy, did she really say that I had phoned her?"

"No, she told father that you'd called on your way to Leominster."

"So I did."

"You're honest. And I'm a bitch. But it was fun—and I've won a quid from the old boy. He said you would say you had. But I knew better. Do you fancy her?"

"Are we going to start one of those inquisitions?"

149

"No. But I just like to keep abreast of things. Why don't we get married? Then I wouldn't have to bother."

"I'll give it thought. Perhaps you ought to know that I called on another woman, too, on my way to Leominster."

"Who?"

"Mrs Shipley's old sister at Weobley to drop in a pair of mittens Mrs S. had knitted for her. And don't think she hasn't still got a twinkle in her aged eye. She had two illegitimate children before she was twenty. Good night."

He rang off to the sound of her laughter.

The next morning he had an early breakfast and was in the chapel by half-past eight. By half-past ten he was through the blockage and walked the tunnel as far as the cellar entrance, but—as it was daytime—made no attempt to go into the cellar. He left the chapel at eleven o'clock, leaving all his gear behind him in the passageway. As he came out he saw that the rain which had persisted all night was now fining with a shift of the wind to the east and would soon stop.

Kerslake, who had stationed himself in the trees on the edge of the high bluff across the river at first light and had seen his entrance and exit, went back to his car and changed most of his clothes and then drove to a country pub for a bar lunch. Afterwards he telephoned Quint from a roadside call-box. Their conversation was short and surprised him.

Driving back to Leominster, the rain now gone and patches of blue sky beginning to show, he called at Georgina's bungalow. She was working in the sun room which overlooked the garden and small stretch of orchard which ran down to the river. She greeted him pleasantly and then returned to a large drawing board where she was working up from her rough field sketches a final composition of a bankside with a pair of nesting dippers.

"I'm not disturbing you?"

"No. In fact I don't mind being talked to while I work. Is this an official visit?"

Sitting on the arm of a small settee, he said, "Yes. Quint has called me back to London."

"Today?"

"Yes. I'm going back to collect my things from the hotel."

"Does that mean I might have to sit out in the rain watching Seyton?"

"No. Just carry on your good weather work. He was in the chapel for quite a while this morning."

"Perhaps he really has got religion."

He smiled, watching her as she stood back a little from her board and eyed her work critically. He had the feeling that she was only half with him.

"Maybe. But I got the impression from Quint that he didn't care a damn what he was doing or might have got. Not that it's any of my business anyway. Sometimes I've spent weeks marking a man and then suddenly I'm called off and never hear another word about him."

"Frustrating."

"Used to be. Now . . . well, it's part of the play. Still . . ." He went silent, watching her, and realizing curiously without surprise that he was just watching her. No more than that. No undressing; just a very good-looking woman, auburn hair untidy, taking high points from the light of the angle-poise lamp, the loose stained overall masking her body, only her legs bare, sun-browned, her feet in canvas tennis shoes, one of them unlaced. Almost sluttish—yet conveying a feeling of warmth and ordinariness.

She said, "I like that. '. . . part of the play'. That's what my father used to say it all was. Towards the end, that is; when he was beginning not to bother to hide things from me. Oh, it was done obliquely I see now. A kind of letting his hair down but still keeping his face hidden."

"I never met him."

"You wouldn't have had much in common. You don't suffer from his kind of doubts." She turned then and moved away from her work, smiling at him. "You just suffer. Only a little. And only now and then. Like now—hating being called off. Hating not knowing what it's all about?"

"I suppose so."

She came up close to him, smiling, a faint wetness on her red lips, the edge of white teeth showing momentarily and then hidden by her lips closing with a little nervous tremble. Then she gave a small shrug of her shoulders, laughed briefly, and said, "Well, take a little comfort—or maybe kindness. I don't know . . ."

She put her arms around him and kissed him gently on his lips. For a moment or two he submitted and then slipping his arms around her shoulder and waist, held her fiercely, but briefly, and then let her go.

She walked away from him back to her work and asked, "Better now?"

He laughed, not at her, but to mark the lift in his spirits, and said, "You're an odd so-and-so."

"It's a nice compliment. But don't think the comfort was all one-sided. I'm the one who is being bitched up—not you. At least, as far as you are concerned, I have a free choice. To give or not to give. But not with bloody Seyton if the cards fall that way. Whoring is respectable commerce by comparison. And now——" she took up a red chalk and leaned over her board, her hand moving surely as she began to thicken the shade and detail of a stream boulder, "——back you go to your masters."

"Yes, of course. And thank you." He turned and began to walk to the door which led into the tiny hall. She kept her back to him, working at her drawing. He paused momentarily and wished he could find something more to say, but there was nothing in him to give except a surprising compassion for which he had no words.

*   *   *   *

Shanklin called on Seyton just after six o'clock that evening and had drinks with him. Big, bluff, assured and almost perceptibly wearing a halo that came from good works and self-satisfaction, he explained that he had been away for a holiday . . . a much-needed break to recharge the batteries before the new season began when the Hall would be open most of the week except Sundays.

"Also Felbeck is coming down towards the end of next week. We wondered if you would care to come up and have dinner?"

"Yes, of course." No matter his feelings towards these people now, Seyton realized the unwisdom of any overt change in his manner.

"That's splendid. Also this summer we're having an International conference at the Hall and as we are anxious to provide accommodation for quite a few of the visitors we were considering one or two minor structural improvements . . . wash basins, and two bathrooms, all that kind of thing on some of the top attic floors. There would be nothing radical, but naturally under the lease we must have your approval. Perhaps you could spare some time fairly soon to come up and see what we would like to do?"

"I don't see why not. Punch used to make a quarterly inspection, didn't he?"

"Oh, yes. You just say when you want to do it." Shanklin paused, eyed his glass of sherry as though, like some crystal gazer, he might be expecting to get some glimpse of the future from it, and then went on, "Pardon the question, Mr Seyton—but I understand that you have considerable business interests abroad—chiefly in the South Americas?"

"Yes, that's true. Why do you ask?"

"Well, it's an area in which the Foundation has not been significantly active. Mostly because of the large Roman Catholic presence there. We—that is the Foundation—were wondering if when we have this International conference you would perhaps care to come and say a few words about . . . well, your experiences there. Your feelings about the cultural and social aspects. We're going to put quite a large body of field workers over there. But I'm not suggesting you talk about religion. Oh, no." He smiled broadly, a big, open-hearted man of the world Christian. "Just a few general *dos* and *don'ts* about everyday life and . . . well, pitfalls to be avoided and any helpful notes about the handling of social and official approaches. It all

153

might seem superficial to you, but to someone going out there for the first time a small mistake in etiquette or bureaucratic niceties means a lot, or could do."

Seyton shrugged his shoulders. "Well, it's hardly my cup of tea."

"We'd all be happy if you gave it thought. Please do."

"I'll think about it."

"Good." Shanklin stood up. "Well, I must be on my way. But before I go I would like to say—and this quite privately— that I'm sorry the Governors' votes went against you. Oh, yes, indeed. I understand your deep feelings about the Hall and sympathize with them . . . but I may say that were I a Governor of the Foundation and not just its servant, I would have given you my vote."

"That's very generous of you."

"More than that. You see, my family had a small manor house in Dorset for two hundred years. When I was at school my father had to sell it as a result of stupid speculations. A nice man, but very gullible. It broke his heart——" he grinned, "——and considerably bruised mine."

"Well, that's the way it goes. But I suppose I'm luckier than you. I only have to sit out the term of the lease and then I shall have the Hall back. Tedious, but inevitable."

With Shanklin gone, he sat with a drink, and wondered whether Shanklin's visit had been genuine, and his words equally sincere, or if the visit had been designed to explore in the obliquest of ways his own feelings. Probably the latter, he thought. But if so, why bother? Unless—as he knew now through Punch's letter—they knew, too, that there was something which did exist to give him cause for breaking the lease and, remote though the possibility might seem to them, they were taking no chances. Shanklin could well have come looking to catch straws in the wind. From his own business experience he knew well how the most astute of men could betray themselves with a word or a smile and never know it. And he was prepared to bet now that Punch's turning against them, undisguised, had had them worried. What they wanted to know now could be whether he had come into the same category. Going to the Hall tonight would be nothing. Punch had done all that. The real problem was to find the proof and all he had to help him there were Punch's last written words . . . *all you have to do is to look in that place where we used to each* . . . What place? God knows he had searched around enough. A place where they used to—what? Hide things. And the little word—*each*. Where they used each to hide things? Well, there had been plenty but from all he had drawn a blank. For a moment or two—since he had not asked either of them about this—he wondered if Punch had confided in Mrs Shipley or old Shipley when he hid his stuff and they were now waiting for a word from him. But immediately he had to discount this. Punch would never have involved them in anything like this. *It could be a bloody dangerous business* . . . Punch had written. Then he certainly would never have put either of the Shipleys at risk.

Out loud, he said, "Sod it!" Thinking of Nancy and the old boy turning up just at the wrong moment. Well, in a few hours' time he might be a wiser man.

* * * *

When Quint had telephoned Kerslake that day to recall him to London, he had also invited him, no matter how late he got back, to come to dinner. An invitation in view of the 'no matter how late' Kerslake had interpreted as an order. But it was one which he was glad to accept and obey, one because he liked and respected Quint and was over-indebted to him, and two because it would save him from the bleak foraging with eggs and bacon and baked beans in his own flat or the bleaker interval of a service station meal on the motor-way.

Sitting now with brandy before them, and behind them a fresh salmon mousse and then fillets of sole *à la panetière* followed by dry biscuits and Camembert cheese, the whole accompanied by a bottle of Chablis, Quint said, "Well, all that was very enjoyable, though I say it myself. But, of course, as you realize, the invitation was not without a purpose."

"Of course, sir."

"We can forget the *sir* for a while."

"As you wish." Kerslake spoke lightly, sensing that he was to be allowed some limited licences—rare concessions but always welcome to him.

"It is five years, almost to the day, since we first met at the Imperial Hotel in Barnstaple, and you became—you will understand my correct meaning—my man. Not the first by any means. Long years ago Georgina's father was one. Others too. Some now dead, alas. The pleasant thing is that—since recruitment is mostly brought about by personal contact at some propitious moment—there usually is formed a highly loyal, not to say esoteric, bond."

"Father and son?"

"Or brother and brother. Some family tie within a larger bond. Warboys, for instance, and Grandison—younger and elder brother."

"And you—to whom were you son or brother?" He spoke knowing quite well that this preliminary—typical of Quint— was merely a sentimental, good-natured gambit. Something— for which he was well content to wait—had to follow.

"Long dead, my dear Kerslake, and much regretted. Dying I may say peacefully and in retirement. One day, I hope, you will stand in relationship to someone in the same way as I do now to you. A minor—but often invaluable—loyalty within a loyalty. You follow me, of course?"

"Exactly."

"So I speak frankly without need to say for your ears only. One's absolute loyalty, of course, is to Birdcage, not to any individual in it. To the service, no matter how much justly or unjustly maligned or praised, condemned or commended. The state of nations is such that none can safely exist without their Birdcages. Deplorable—but without them open barbarism would flower grotesquely. One could draw a parallel between a king and his country. If he takes his people's loyalty for granted and abuses his own to them then hell is only a few steps away. *L'état, c'est moi*—said Louis the Fourteenth. He could not have been more mistaken. The State is an intellectual and meta-physical conception. Abstract. Unable to exist if a body of people inhabiting physical or political boundaries reject their true obligations to such a necessary idea. Are you following me?"

"Rather more than less. But far from feeling that you are just entertaining me. I'm happy to wait until you put it in plainer words. Or perhaps as a simple instruction."

Quint put his head back and laughed delightedly, and then said, "And to think that—with all respect to you, my dear Kerslake—I once thought that you would perhaps only turn out to be a solid, plodding leg-man, exchanging a monotonous beat in Barnstaple for an equally boring one—since you could aspire to no more—in Birdcage. So you would have it in simple words? Why not try to formulate them for yourself—and aloud to me. The night is reasonably young, the brandy decanter three-quarters full and you can leave your car outside and take a taxi back to your place."

Kerslake was silent while Quint replenished their brandy glasses, relishing the move to a closer relationship with this man—for whom he already bore deep affection and gratitude, despite the fact that on him he could have blamed his own present impotence—a disability not, he now suspected, likely to be permanent. As he raised his glass slightly to Quint's to mark with an almost symbolical flourish the onset of a possibly dangerous and deeper loyalty, he had a picture in his mind of a sloppy, untied tennis shoe, a long smock making a body shapeless, and bright April sunshine streaking auburn hair with moving fire. He made a passing attempt to imagine her naked and failed.

He said slowly—reaching for the words and ideas as deliberately as he would have reached with care to pluck a raspberry cane to avoid clumsy fingers crushing the soft fruit—and with his eyes never leaving Quint's to mark any signal of trespass or over-boldness, "The C.I.A. did it—almost. *L'état, c'est moi*—or should be. That was the thought with them. One has seen other organizations in other countries appear to have achieved it.

Iran? Power doesn't only corrupt. It just gives an insatiable appetite for more power. I think you have in mind that, whereas in past days all the best things were exported from this country to keep the globe coloured red practically all over, now . . . well, we import a lot of the bad things. My mother was always talking to me about being a good example. All dogs have fleas. What happens when all fleas think they should have dogs? No, Christ, that's not what I mean, but——"

"Don't worry. I'm receiving you loud and clear despite the occasional static. And I'm very pleased with you. Go on."

"All right. True stability is sanity. Law and order, no matter how debased, must be kept. You can't have the night-watchman robbing the bank." He paused for a moment or two, genuinely confused by the flux of his own thoughts and his effort to reach Quint with a far from adequate stock of presentable, yet subtle, verbal felicities. Then—throwing caution from him, he said bluntly, "I think you are trying to tell me that something is wrong with us. With Birdcage—and you bloody well—and maybe others with you—aren't going to bloody well stand for it."

Quint beamed and said softly, "Out of the mouths of babes and sucklings. Oh, dear Kerslake . . . much tried and tortured in your training . . . you and I have sinned against God—but that doesn't put us in outer darkness without hope. God by now will have learnt that the sermon on the Mount needs some rewriting. Or perhaps He has turned mathematician and gives due weight to the proposition that a smaller evil is justified to prevent the larger."

"And where does that leave me, sir?"

"It leaves you saying 'sir' again occasionally and with this preliminary comment. It is not a question of the night-watchman robbing the bank. It is the danger of the bank manager wanting to manipulate the bank for his own . . . well, for his own *self-aggrandizement*. Are you with me?"

Kerslake said, "I get the pun. But—surely that's an impossibility?"

"Annus mirabilis? And wonders will never cease. Men have

walked on the moon. Nothing is impossible. Just give man the time and the will. From these he will breed miracles. Let me add that there is a large element of speculation in all this. No hard proof. Just unseasonably a rare and unexpected touch of spring in the air that makes the winter-thin robin charm the frosty day with a rusty scrap of love call. If we wait for hard facts we sometimes wait too long." Quint shrugged his shoulders. "I'm sorry. You asked for simple guidance. You have in the past received direct instructions from others superior to myself in this organization. Carried out their orders without reference to me—which was right and proper. But now—which has been the main burden of our talk—I want it differently. Any instruction you receive from anyone else, higher or lower in our establishment, I wish to be made privy to before you act. And I promise you full protection, unfailing protection. An honest promise because I should never ask of you, or maybe never need to ask of you, anything which in any way outrages or contravenes the dark ethics of our profession. Do I need to say more?"

"No, sir. Not as far as your plain instruction is concerned. But am I allowed to ask a few questions?"

"Ask. But I may not answer."

"Is all that has been said in this room private to us alone?"

"At the moment, yes. But given certain remote shifts of circumstance, it may not remain so. But that would not jeopardize your standing in Birdcage."

"I see. And now, strictly between ourselves, am I allowed to ask whether all this accounts for my being recalled from Herefordshire?"

"Partly."

"And has something to do with this Seyton business?"

"It could have. But only as humbly as the flare of a match lighting the touch-paper of a rocket is compared with the high burst and fiery splendour of the rocket's apotheosis, a lowly, but vital servitor, a peasant without whom the Fire King can never rise to royal exaltation. *Gloria in excelsis.*" He leaned forward and served Kerslake with more brandy, and then beaming with good humour, went on, "It is sad when Time's chafing proves that what one thought was gold is no more than gilt. Now, while you finish your brandy, my dear Kerslake, I shall play you a little Handel."

CHAPTER EIGHT

THE FIRST CUCKOO he had heard that year was calling, the echoes of its notes coming back from the high river bluff making it hard to decide exactly where the bird might be. Not that he cared. He had gone through the day withdrawn into an almost surliness of manner so that Mrs Shipley had said after lunch to her husband, "You watch your Ps and Qs. He's in one of those states. Like when he was a young man and something hadn't gone right for him."

He sat now on a large drift log close to the edge of the river, his salmon rod propped against its end and lying on the grass a fresh run springer around the twenty-pound mark. Not that he had deserved the fish, he thought. Today he deserved nothing because he knew that he was letting his mood master him as long ago it had used to do until with manhood he had learnt to meet and check it soon after birth. He had fished without finesse or wisdom, not caring whether he was covering a known lie or not . . . just slinging the yellow-bellied Devon out and then working it back without regard to current or river depth. Punch, he told himself, would have kicked his arse. And at the moment, metaphorically, he could have kicked Punch's arse. Other people, too, deserved, though still alive could never receive, some sort of castigation. Nancy and her old man for cutting Punch's letter short. The fish had run like a young colt and, instead of playing it, he had just held on to it. He should have had a line break and lost it in the first few seconds. Instead he had manhandled it to the bank, tailed it by hand, since he had brought neither gaff nor tailer, and killed it with two smart raps of a stone.

He sat with disappointment sharp in him like heartburn. He

161

had gone in through the chapel at one o'clock that night and had made his way by torch easily to the cellar. Hooding his torch he had found that the stairway door—once a sliding panel, but replaced before his time on account of dry rot—was bolted shut on the cellar side and easily opened. He had made his way up the whole system of uneven stairs and narrow passages until he had reached the end in the small roof space which abutted on to the run of maids' rooms. Nowhere had he found any signs of disturbance or recent use—except by rats, mice and bats. Going back to the cellar he had tried the door which led into the Hall and, as he had expected, had found it locked from the far side and had found no flicker of nostalgia or amusement as he remembered his and Punch's delight when they had discovered where his father had kept the key which they had imagined would open the vicarious delights of venery to them, their youth precluding any thoughts of Bacchic pleasures which lay readier to hand.

Not that he had expected to find anything more than he could guess Punch must have found . . . some place where his brother could have, unobserved, filmed and taped the movements and talk of people in one of the Hall's above floor-level rooms. But so far as he could tell by torchlight none of the brickwork or rough boarding on the walls of the stairway had been disturbed. And if he had found evidence, he told himself now morosely, there would have been no advancement to his advantage because what he really had to find were Punch's tapes and films. Still . . .

The cuckoo stopped calling. A shoal of minnows in shallow water broke surface in panic as a young pike chased them. A high flying jet drew a great vapour trail across the far hills. Suddenly his own surliness—which he knew Mrs Shipley must already have noticed—riled him. Men gave themselves away too easily by not being able to suppress or mask their moods. Business life had long ago put the final polish to that by no means easy performance. He reached for a cigarette and told himself not to be a fool. Whatever there might have been to find in the Hall was of no importance. Punch had been there long before him. What he just had to find was where Punch——

A voice from behind broke into his thoughts.

"Is it Patience on a monument, or Rodin's thinker?"

He knew the voice and, turning, let a smile mask his face. He said easily, "I'm not sure. Perhaps a combination of the two."

Because of the fineness of the day she was not bundled up in anorak and waterproof trousers as she so often was, but wore a high-necked green sweater, a silly scrap of a green cap on her head, and a tartan skirt with two or three of last year's burdock heads clinging to it.

"You've been fishing?"

"You could call it that."

"No luck?"

He pointed to the far end of the log and she moved so that the fish came into her view.

For a moment or two she said nothing, but he caught her sharp intake of breath and then she said, "My God . . . what an absolutely beautiful thing. Would you mind if I . . ." She hauled the haversack slung round her back to the front and began to open it to take out her large sketch pad and then paused. "I may, mightn't I?"

He laughed. "Of course. Perhaps you'd like to have it? For eating, I mean. Sketch first—eat later."

"I could never eat all that."

"Put it in the deep freeze."

"All I've got is a refrigerator the size of a matchbox."

"Well, I'll tell you what we'll do. When you've finished your sketch, you can come back to the house with me and I'll cut you off a piece."

"You're very kind. Thank you." She moved past him and sitting on the end of the tree trunk began to sketch, and asked, "Is it a cock or hen?"

"Hen."

He sat watching her as she worked and was amused as well as impressed by the way she had now switched to a total absorption in her task. It was quite clear to him that for the time being he had been forgotten. When she had finished they walked

163

together back to the Dower House. She came with him into the kitchen where Mrs Shipley was busy preparing his meal, and stood by him while he gutted the salmon and then cut her off a generous portion behind the shoulder which Mrs Shipley wrapped for her to take away, a not very talkative Mrs Shipley but quite content to abide with her private thoughts. He had gone out one man and come back another. And it was no surprise to her when she heard him ask her to have a drink before she left. Both he and Mister Punch had ever been ones with eyes for pretty girls. One day, she thought, might well bring a sad day for Miss Nancy Hope—he would fall for some young woman like this—and the sooner the better if he were to start having the kind of moods which she had known in him early after his wife had died.

Over their drinks, he said, "What do you do with yourself every evening in that bungalow?"

She shrugged her shoulders. "I don't know. Cook my dinner. Work a little perhaps. Read. Listen to music. And sometimes I just sit."

Following a thought which had begun to stir in his mind, not simply at random but born out of his own present frustration and nurtured by the sight of her relaxed in her chair, legs crossed, all woman and—he supposed—as unattached and subject to the same moods and emotions as himself, he said, "Would you like to go somewhere with me where I can show you a couple more Hatton paintings?"

She smiled almost provocatively, and said, "Of course I would. But I get a feeling that the Hattons are just bait."

"Well, yes. There is a little more involved."

He told her quite frankly of the dinner dance at Clyro and how Nancy had been going with him, but now could not.

She said, "I'd have come—without the Hattons. I love dancing and you've been very kind to me, Mr Seyton."

He grinned, not attempting to deny himself her attractions, the thought of dancing with her, holding her, a pleasure which he would want to have in other than an imaginative role.

"Well, that's splendid."

Driving back with her cut of salmon she thought about him and found herself comparing him with Kerslake. The one twisted up and going to take a long time to untwist himself. And this one—born with a silver spoon in his mouth and able to drive straight ahead for what he wanted without having to blinker himself to anything happening to either side of him. She knew the power and attraction of her own body, appearance and intellect. And so did Quint for there must be others he could have chosen to put in this role of hers, but for one reason or other they had been rejected. Dear Quint was no fool. And Miss Hope—was the name one of good or ill omen for her? No hopeful and pretty woman would ever lead this man by the nose. Virtues he undoubtedly had but his strongest clearly was knowing what he wanted and going for it. It would be interesting to know what lay behind all the concern that Birdcage was showing over him . . . Just for a while she let herself play with the fancy that Birdcage had no existence, that she really were here in truth from her own volition and professional needs. Dear Quint. Bloody Quint. But anyway she would have gone to a dinner dance with a man with two heads for the chance of seeing some more Hattons.

Back at her bungalow she telephoned Birdcage and found herself talking to Quint, and telling him about the invitation.

"That's splendid. Moonlight, we hope. Dancing, for sure, and if music be the food of love, and so on."

"Bugger you, Uncle Quint. The only thing I'm really looking forward to is to see the Hattons."

"Why not? In the same category as come-up-and-see-my etchings, no?"

"It's easy to be flippant from where you sit."

"Don't be fooled, Georgy. Anyway, you could have said *No* to me right from the start."

"You know I couldn't. It might help a bit if I knew just a little of what all this is about."

"Ah . . . well, it might help me too. Though I do know minimally a little more than you. What will you wear for the dance?"

He was teasing with an element of cruelty in it which was unnatural to him so that she knew he was uneasy but that did not hold back her own sudden resentment. She said brutally, "Topless and a bloody grass skirt!"

"Ideal." He laughed gently and rang off abruptly, which she knew was an act of charity to stop her from saying more.

*　　*　　*　　*

Some days later Seyton went up to the Hall to have dinner with Felbeck and Shanklin. With them also was the Hall housekeeper. This last was a widow in her late thirties, a Clarissa Hampton, whom Seyton had not seen around at all during his previous residence at the Dower House. Over drinks before dinner this absence was accounted for by his being told that she had been making an overseas tour of the Foundation's various hostels and centres. The term housekeeper, too, he learned was only a loose description of her duties. She was a catering and dietary expert and, before joining the Foundation, had held important positions in the hotel management world. High-powered she might be in her work, but in appearance and manner she was far from outstanding. She was a quiet-spoken *jolie laide* with a good figure and a retiring habit which lay somewhere between shyness and reserve which—Seyton thought—might disappear altogether when she got down to her professional work. She had dinner and then coffee with them in the library and then quietly withdrew. Not long afterwards Shanklin went too and Seyton sat, monopolized by Felbeck.

He had a feeling that the whole arrangement had been designed to give Felbeck his sole company. In no time at all the man was happily immersed in a monologue which chiefly concerned itself with the state of the world—bad but not without hope—and then the state of their country—a bloody mess—but not such as to lead to despair if the right remedies were applied soon and with rigour. Curiously enough these remedies only included the briefest reference to the exercise of the Christian spirit and ethic which might have been expected from him. Largely he called for the return of true discipline, less tolerance and wishy-washy attempts at 'understanding' and 're-education'. The time had come, or was soon to, for a more Spartan approach from authority to stamp out the evils which had attached themselves and flourished like lice on the body of the Welfare State. He was like—Seyton thought—a terrier at a rat hole, quivering with anticipation, and the odd thought occurred to him that the man was speaking either from some hidden stress or a slightly unbalanced mentality—something, anyway, which he had not noticed in him ever before. True impatience and something like near rage seemed to be working in him. This country was being cut to ribbons industrially and commercially by strikes and the amorphous power of the Trade Unions. Its peoples were being turned into zombies and work-shy degenerates who flourished like rats in a sewer on the easy pickings offered by Social Security. The laxity of sexual morals got his whipping, the degenerative effects of television, disco-theques and bingo halls he scourged with a fierce passion, and the growth of crime, he declared, was nurtured and flourished by the gross misconception that 'understanding' and 'constructive regeneration' was what the evil-doers needed to rehabilitate them rather than draconian punishment . . . the restoration of the death penalty . . . bring back the lash . . . flog the rapists. And then—with a sudden sigh and a heave of his shoulders—he smiled, spread his hands and said, "Oh, my dear Seyton—forgive me. But just now and then it all boils up in me so that I feel quite primitive and need the outburst. Of course, you must discount a lot of what I've said. But in the main I'm sure you will agree that this country is in one hell of a state. Blowing off steam—a man must have a chance to do that sometimes. I'm sure you will agree."

"Yes, of course." Seyton said it without knowing whether he did or did not agree. Politics, unless he had to handle and manipulate them in the way of business, were of no interest to him. But he did know that he sympathized with the man. "Still, it hardly fits the Christian principles of the Foundation, surely?"

"No, of course not. But don't forget that Christ took a scourge to the money changers in the Temple. The real trouble is that the state of the world *is* intolerable and religion *doesn't* seem to be able to do anything really effective about it. I inherited this Foundation—just as I inherited my wealth mostly—and I love it, but I begin to doubt its effectiveness in any significant degree whatsoever. We are in the middle of the Christian dilemma. Kindness, understanding, charity, love one another, I'm beginning to think just don't work. Not because they can't, but because—for the time being anyway—Anti-Christ is back and reigns and that is an enemy which must be fought with the only weapons it understands—power backed by punishments which match the committed sins." He sighed. "Sometimes I really do wish that I had never inherited this responsibility. I'd like to hand back the Hall to you tomorrow and walk out. But that is impossible for many reasons, but principally to me for a sole one which you will understand. Family tradition. What a Felbeck started all those years ago must be carried on. It was a noble conception. I have it in trust and can't abandon it or hand it over to anyone else."

"That's why I want this place back."

"I know. Two solid traditions finding themselves in opposition. Is that not the work of Anti-Christ?"

Smiling, knowing sympathy for the man, Seyton said, "I don't give a damn for Anti-Christ or for the Felbeck Foundation."

Felbeck shrugged his shoulders. "We both have our problems —and there is no immediate solution to them."

Looking straight at Felbeck, Seyton said firmly, "Are you giving up the Foundation?"

"No."

"And I'm not giving up the Hall."

"Well, there it is. But at least we are being civilized about it."

As Seyton walked back to the Dower House under the bright April night stars, an owl calling from the direction of the chapel, a slow mist risen knee-high over the pastures, a figure came up the driveway towards him. It was Clarissa Hampton wearing a light coat and with a head scarf wrapped over her dark hair. She stopped in front of him and, as though they had already met and were in conversation, she said, "He talked a lot, I imagine? And probably quite out of character?"

"Yes, he did."

"I know the signs. You must discount most of it. Oh, we all know how it goes. But it is just a safety valve."

"That's clear to me, Mrs Hampton."

"Yes, of course."

"You've been waiting for me to come out?"

"Oh, yes. I know when the strain is going to hit him. I just wanted to hear for myself that you understood. He could retire from it all. But he won't."

"Can't is the truth. He's tied."

"Yes. It happens to a lot of us."

She was silent for a moment or two, and then said, "I wasn't here at the time—but I'd like you to know how sorry I was about your brother."

"Thank you." He had the impression that she did not want to let him go, but could think of no way to keep him talking.

"What will you do? Settle down here?"

"I don't know. I've got a business to run. Without it I couldn't keep this place going when I get the Hall back."

" 'When'—so much in life hangs on that word, doesn't it?"

Suddenly irritated by her, he said, "It doesn't bother me. *When* can be in an hour's time or ten years' time." And then quite bluntly, he went on, "Are you trying to say something to me—because if so I'm not with you?"

She laughed—a surprisingly gay sound in the night—and shook her head. "Oh, dear, no. This is only about Mr Felbeck. Circumstances have trapped him as they do all of us in some degree. I knew he was going to be a bit overwrought tonight. I just didn't want you to misunderstand . . . well, that it's his way of shedding tension."

"I knew that right from the start. I know something else too. You're in love with him, aren't you?"

"Oh, yes, of course." Her voice lifted with a frankness that held an almost joyful note. "I'd do anything for him. Anything he asked me. I frankly worship him. Anyway, he's married and very happily. So, there we are." Her tone was free of any self-pity. "All wanting something which we may or may not get." She looked up at him and smiled and he sensed for the first time the force of her dedication to Felbeck and also the effort it must have taken to overcome her natural pride and self-esteem to have waited to waylay him to make excuses for Felbeck; an exercise which, so far as he was concerned, was quite unnecessary. He did not care a damn for Felbeck—except as an obstacle between himself and the Hall.

He gave her a nod and a smile and said quite genuinely, "The gap between wanting and getting isn't fixed for ever. Life has a way of upsetting what we think are cast-iron certainties. That's why betting is a mug's game."

She put out a hand and touched him briefly on the arm, and said, "You're a very nice, but hard man. Good night, Mr Seyton."

By the time he had got back into the Dower House he had forgotten her.

* * * *

There were times—more frequently of late than before—when Felbeck found himself wishing that he had never met Sir Manfred Grandison—though that first meeting, some years ago now, had saved him and the Foundation from very considerable embarrassment and scandal. Any large organization, no matter what safeguards it adopts, is open to manipulation from the clever and dishonest. One of their most trusted overseas administrators had for two years misdirected the use of the Foundation's funds to his own profit and—like so many peculators—had grown overbold and confident so that his guilt had inevitably come to light. The loss of money from the Foundation's funds, though large, had presented no difficulty since he had made that good from his own private fortune. Suppressing the inevitable bad publicity—which would have come from the facts being widely known following a prosecution

—had presented a problem which Felbeck was determined to overcome. Good works spoke for themselves—and so drew charitable donations and bequests which were vital to keep the Foundation viable. At stake had been its good name. And imminent had been the prospect of a public prosecution . . . and Grandison had saved the Foundation.

Listening to him now in the flat overlooking Regent's Park, Felbeck remembered with irritation the casual way Grandison had made light of the difficulty, remembered too—though by now he was well used to the mannerism—his quotation tricked-out comments. *But he that filches from me my good name, Robs me of that which not enriches him, And makes me poor indeed.* At the time Grandison had been known to him only as a then Member of Parliament and a public figure with considerable influence in Government circles. He knew better now. At the time—when through Grandison's influence the question of a public prosecution had been dispelled and the whole business settled without ruffling the calm of the charitable waters— Felbeck had been deeply grateful and indebted to Grandison. Over the succeeding years, though at first not recognizing it, the debt had been slowly paid back. That process had been painless because everything asked of him was within his gift and within his will. Only recently had he realized that Grandison had skilfully suborned him to *his* will, and left him not only uncertain of his compliance, but fearful of the position in which he now found himself. And 'only recently' meant since the return of Richard Seyton to the Dower House and his inheritance.

From the window where he was watching the strollers in the Park, Grandison, without turning, said, "You have nothing to fear but fear itself. What we have done had to be done. In this day and age if you wish to do good you have—sadly, I acknowledge—sometimes to first do ill. And anyway it has been done under the aegis of authority."

"Whose?"

"Mine. As the Head of a Government organization. I am answerable for all that. Not you. But culpability is not the point. Since there is nothing for Seyton to find—then there is nothing to fear."

"How can one be sure that there is nothing to find?"

"Can you suggest anything?"

"No, but . . ."

"A small, unfinished phrase. Like a broken ritual chant . . . meaningless. So he pokes about in the chapel for hours at a time? Meaningless to you—but worrying? Forget it. I had an uncle who would sit in a cold barn all night because he was interested in the feeding habits of barn owls with their young."

"You don't find barn owls in a church."

Grandison turned and laughed. "It's too positive a statement. Life is full of surprises. My uncle found that. He confessed that while he learnt a lot about the feeding habits of owls he also learnt a great deal about the copulatory patterns of the local lads and lassies. A small bonus—mentioned only to cheer you up. Seyton may be secretly and deeply religious and spends hours on his knees seeking expiation for real or imaginary sins. There's none so odd as folk. Or he could be considering where to put a memorial plaque or stone to his brother. The place is overcrowded with such already or——"

"I wish you would be serious, Grandison."

"But I am. However, if you wish me to be particular, then I will. What we have done—from the most worthy of motives—and what we intend to happen at some time in the future—from the most practical and patriotic of motives—is vital nationally. The end we seek justifies any means. If the future is to be bright then we must accept that the continuing present must sometimes be shadowed by stratagems which taken in isolation would appear to be—and indeed be to the victim—drastic and final."

"What in God's name are you talking about?"

"You know what I'm talking about. Removing obstacles from our path. Should the unlikely need arise, then Seyton would be removed. And we should remain, as Ovid said, 'blameless in life and clear of——' I interpose the words *all detectable*—'offence'."

"You must be out of your mind!"

"Not in the sense you mean, my dear Felbeck. Only in bothering to calm your momentary and quite phantom fears. Given the real need it would be done, I promise you. But I am sure that the necessity will never arise."

"You really mean this?"

"Felbeck, the phrase demeans you. Sport I may with words and phrases but never with their meaning. You know at the head of which Service I stand. Do you think all trouble-makers and traitors come to a just trial? Our courts are burdened with too long a backlog of cases as it is. In our service there is no need always for twelve good honest men to decide. There are things honest men should not be plagued with. Their honesty is too often only misguided sympathy, or tainted with the dialectical hues of their own political convictions. I assure you that if Seyton should ever—which is as remote as the snows of Everest top to most of us—find proof to plague us with . . . well, then he would go without pause for absolution."

Felbeck nodded. "I know all you say is true. It's just that there are times . . ."

"When the spirit flags and courage falters? Well, then, since the hour is six, there is a timely remedy. What would you like to drink? Brandy, whisky, gin—or a timely cup of hemlock?"

Felbeck laughed, a little shakily, and then said, "Whisky, I think." Then with a sigh, he went on, "My God, Grandison, you are a most extraordinary man. It's a human life you've been talking about."

"And in this case one which, I swear, has nothing to fear from me. Seyton is a good work horse. He wants to break your lease. He wants his Hall back. Blinkered, he looks neither to right nor left. Dead ahead. All right. Let him work his heart out. There is nothing he can do but work out his term of years until the lease falls in. Our one-time ancillary use for the Hall is done with. It remains now the headquarters of one of the world's noblest and most Christian organizations—without blemish or aught to fear from any calumniator."

*   *   *   *

173

When he called at a quarter past seven Georgina, with a dressing gown over her underclothes, was making up her face. She went to the door and let him in, saying, "I won't be more than a few minutes. Go into the sitting room and fix yourself a drink. It's all there." Then looking over his shoulder and seeing the car outside, she said, "My goodness! A Rolls . . ."

He grinned. "Well, I am a diamond dealer and you a beautiful woman. Are you afraid of what the neighbours may think?"

"The nearest one is half a mile down the road. You go and make yourself comfortable while I get on with my make-up. Poke around and look at the drawings if you want to."

Back in her bedroom, she sat for a moment or two looking at herself in the mirror. She liked fun as much as any woman did. A good-looking man, a Rolls Royce and a pleasant evening to look forward to and even the possibility, if he were like that, not caring to drink and drive, that she could take the wheel on the way back, and then as soon discounted the idea. He was not the type who did the dirty shuffle on a girl who liked her drink as much as he did. Richard Seyton would, she bet, have some old-fashioned virtues. How many, she wondered? And not for her own sake. Stupid Daddy, and self-sacrificing daughter. Still, there was no Birdcage law to say that it had to be all work and no pleasure. Tonight, as far as she was concerned, she would wish it to be all pleasure. If work cropped up . . . well, too bad.

Not taking a drink since the evening was still young and driving after too much drink now a thing of his past, Seyton sat on the settee and picked up from a near table a portfolio of her drawings. Again he was impressed by her talent . . . perhaps genius . . . but certainly a kind of magic which appealed to him largely because she had the almost breath-taking felicity of catching and marking animals and birds in a precise instant of time, arresting it so that some fractional moment of truth lay exposed. Two lapwings caught falling through the air in courtship display above a field of young corn; and then a dabchick—quite a few of them around but not often seen—

moving up a stream, oddly more reptilian looking than water bird . . . between the eyes and the hand no faltering on her part. And then suddenly old Shipley's face filling the paper, cap pushed back, sweat shining on his cheeks, grinning, his old pipe sticking out of the corner of his mouth, made him chuckle. (Later, when he asked her, he was to learn that she had watched Shipley working through her glasses and then done it from memory, a memory sharp with retained truth.) After Shipley there was a drawing of the fourteenth-century pigeon-house in the Dower House garden, a great cloud of the doves hanging in disturbed flight above its roof . . .

She came in to him, a fur cape held in one hand, a small black silk evening bag in the other, her dress black, too, and simple, leaving her arms bare but coming close about her neck, the demureness challenged by the soft, full burgeon of her breasts, and to one side a small gold brooch, a multi-rayed star. Her auburn hair, a smouldering fire making him fancy—to his surprise for he was not so given—that the first touch of wind would tease it to flames. And, anyway, whatever his fancies, he felt within him the undeniable response of his body to the living presence of beauty . . . the nerve kick of his senses over-mastering him, a thing that lived its own life and—though quiescent for so long—now moved independently and seeming to challenge him to deny it living room.

He said, "You look absolutely marvellous." The words banal but undeniably sincere.

"Thank you, sir." She made a little curtsey, and then went on, "You've not had a drink."

"There'll be enough of that later. But what about you?"

"No, I can wait, too."

He said, "Miss Collet——"

She shook her head. "You get a choice. Georgy or Georgina. Then tomorrow, if you like, we can go back to the Miss Collet. Which is it to be?"

"Georgina."

"That pleases me . . . Richard."

He laughed and said, "And no return to formalities

tomorrow." Then, to ease the unexpected, almost immature emotional impediment to naturalness between them, something so far distant in his past that he would have thought it beyond rejuvenation, that adolescent pause which came between first attraction and first kissing, he held up the drawing of the pigeon-house in his hand still and said, "When did you do this? It's so good."

"One morning some time ago."

"There are a lot of these old pigeon-houses in this part of the country. In the old days the birds were a good source of food. Now . . . well, they are ornamental. And a bit of a nuisance. They breed so much we have to cull them."

"How?"

"Oh, Shipley shoots a few now and then. The old ones. But I remember that when Punch and I were young we used to go into the pigeon-house each spring with knitting needles and prick the eggs they'd laid. That kept them down fairly well——'
He stopped abruptly, his mood suddenly changing, maturing with a certainty beyond doubt because he had been here before with other women, always knowing the moment when the words you were using bore no relation to the emotions you were feeling or the honest desire that began to demand expression. He grinned suddenly and went on, "I'm gabbling away about doves and they're really the farthest thing from my mind."

"What is on your mind?"

"I think you know—and I hope you approve."

He stepped forward, put his hands gently on her shoulders, kissed her on the cheek lightly, and then moved back from her.

She laughed and said, "That was nice—and deserves a return. Since it reminds you of things you did with your brother I'd like you to have the drawing. No, no argument. And now I think we should be going."

*   *   *   *

Shipley was sitting in the Dower House kitchen waiting for his wife to finish work and walk the few yards home with her.

Usually when Mister Richard was out for the evening she would stay on for a couple of hours, ironing or cleaning the silver . . . God knows what she did, he thought. Women always found something. She was gone now to answer the telephone which had just rung. He lit his pipe. Mister Richard out gallivanting. Well, that was something, anyway. Like old times. Over Clyro way—that would be the Harecastles. Well, it was about time Mister Richard got out of his rut. About time, if it came to that, that he got married again. Young Roger could do with a woman around. Something was eating into the gaffer. No doubt about that. What was all this then, too—taking that drawing young lady to Clyro? Maybe he fancied her. Worth fancying too. But . . . no more than that, he hoped. But you never knew. Things so often went by opposites. Look at Mister Punch. He'd have sworn that he'd have married soon. Randy enough as a young chap. Both of them. Hellions at times.

Mrs Shipley came back from the telephone, and said, "I told you not to light that pipe in here."

"I knows you did. But I lit it, didn't I?"

"Like that are we?"

Shipley grinned, pinched her bottom and said, "I ain't so old that I have to stand back from anything I fancy. And neither be you. Fancy a glass of port?"

"You'll get the back of my hand."

"Don't tell me you don't now and then. What I smell on your lips sometimes you may call elderberry wine but it ain't. Who was that then on the phone?"

"Miss Nancy."

"All the way from France?"

"All the way from France, and not for a minute foolin' me. Wanted to know if Mister Richard was gone over to Clyro."

"Did she now, and quite right of her. What did you tell her?"

"What she wanted to know, of course. That he'd gone— taking that drawin' young woman."

"And what did she say to that? That you wouldn't have the bother of making his bed tomorrow morning? Wouldn't be the first time, would it? Aye, and Miss Nancy herself to blame in the past for it."

"You've got a dirty mouth, Shipley."

"Who, me? What's dirty about the naturalest thing in the world—a man takin' a woman, or tuther way about?"

"Well, maybe. But he should marry. He owes it not only to hisself but to young Roger. If I was Miss Nancy I'd go after him harder than what she does."

"Then you'd be wrong there. T'ain't natural for a ewe to chase the ram. Miss Nancy knows that."

"You and your ewes and rams."

"Well, what's the great difference? 'Cept they got four legs instead of two and don't send one another Valentines. I'll bet you he marries Miss Nancy in the end. But at the moment he's got something more than weddin' bells ringing in his mind. He's been going around all over the place—not thinkin' I notice, of course—mopin' and pokin' and peerin' and pryin' as though he'd lost something somewhere and not sure hisself what it is or where he lost it. Aye, he's so taken up with something, I can tell you, that he won't miss a drop of port or two from the decanter. So get us a glass, girl."

"Well, just one."

Shipley chuckled. "Aye, that'll do to begin with."

* * * *

She lay awake, relaxed, warm and far from sleep or wanting it. The part-drawn curtains showed a few stars over the branches of an apple tree in the garden. If she had been a cat she would, she thought, have been purring. The two Hattons had been marvellous. A ploughman leading shire horses down a muddy lane, and—she guessed from his days in France—a charcoal and wash of two French peasant women washing clothes at a stream side. The drink and food delicious at the buffet supper, tempting her to a mild gluttony. What was it old Quint had once said to her? *No one as lovely as you should show such obvious delight in eating. It's like a sudden false metre in poetry.* Sod Quint. She didn't want to think about him.

Music and dancing and forgetfulness, taking the night right out of the calendar of discontent and the secret self-humiliations she had suffered for dear Daddy. Not sod *him*. But just for a few hours forget his existence. Right from the beginning the night had begun to delight her, detached from any before or after. Oh, the after would come. But to hell with that right now because the night had a few more hours to run before dawn and morning when she would pick up the telephone and report to Birdcage. She hoped it would be to the answering service for she wanted not even the most tenuous contact with anyone there personally.

Nothing had been planned, or pushed for, or even hoped for on either side. The night term had been set, she felt, by forces outside, benign to the point of sweet indulgence; everything going the way a drawing so often did, a limited miracle, controlling and bestowing a shared felicity . . . so much so a miracle that she had even known what he would say and do next, felt too that behind words and actions some other silent dialogue was moving between them, that the Gods had said, 'Take this without question and enjoy it. The golden fruit of the Hesperides which must be plucked and eaten while it is still sun-warm.' She giggled softly to herself, a hand to her mouth to muffle it, not wanting to wake him, knowing that wine and the night's magic still lay potently in her. Perfection, in the only way human perfection could be, demanding nothing but giving everything with an open naturalness that was as swift and sure and gut-shaking as the high set and then breath-taking beauty of the falcon's stoop. Nothing could go wrong, she had known; and nothing had gone wrong. Driving back, her head against his shoulder, the smoothness of the Rolls paced by the smoothness in herself. And knowing nothing would go wrong with the night. Nothing could go wrong because the Gods had ordained this night free for her so that each step, each move, each word, each caress she had known and welcomed from fore-knowledge as benison following benison. Time out from stinking bloody Birdcage.

He had loved her as few others had done, richly and tenderly, and then again with fresh passion and both of them fierce in their demands and breaking the night's silence with their words and cries, and she lay now not caring a damn that it might only be for that night. He rested now with his back to her, sleeping, taking more than his fair share of the not too large bed, snoring now and then gently, his skin warm against her breasts and belly, and while he slept she kissed the back of his neck and her nostrils delighted in the smell of his skin. Dear Daddy, she thought, I'm going to save up for years and buy myself one like this to keep for ever. Dear Daddy . . . they sent me out a-whoring, but look what I've got. Isn't it a pity it has got to go back in the morning . . .? And, dear Daddy, don't think that in the midst of it all I didn't try to do a little work. Oh, with the lightest of touches and while we had a last drink in the bungalow before going to bed. Just a tease so that the evening would not be all play and no work, saying: *I was working in the spinney down river from the chapel one day and saw you go in. You were ages before you came out again. Have I got a praying man on my hands?* And dear Quint—when you come to listen to this, send me a note telling how to mark truth or falsehood in the words of a man who is looking at you with the sure knowledge that bed and its delights are close, since you've already embraced and his hands have been given willingly a licence to rove and his dress tie is cocked up at an angle and in a moment he's going to give it a tug and flip his collar stud free as he rises to come to you, and does rise, saying, already dedicated to other more important matters so close and fast coming to hand: *I suppose you could call it praying . . . anyway, looking for the answer to a personal problem. Did you know that the colour of your eyes just now is like wet emeralds . . . or at least that's what they make me think of?* Wasn't that nice? Though far from accurate. Yes, nice because he's no poet or fancy speaker, but a plain honest John. The good news from Ghent to Aix about his limit. But he's got some Hattons and loves them because they're alive and so is he. Good with his hands be it horse or woman . . . gentle, firm or masterly to meet exactly the challenge and mood of his steed. Bawdy, yes. But nice bawdy, dear Daddy and you dear Quint.

So that was that, and all that followed, my bloody business and nobody else's, except to say that I was (to raise a little smile from you Quint) *in nubibus*—and still am.

He stirred then, came awake and turned to her and said sleepily, "I thought I heard a cock crow."

"So you did—but once only."

"Would you like some coffee?"

"Later."

He put his arms around her and held her to him and, smiling at her, said, "Go or stay?"

"Stay."

An hour afterwards his hand on her shoulder woke her. He was standing at the bedside, dressed.

"You're going?"

"I'll call you."

He bent down and kissed her.

She said, "You're a monster."

"Beauty and the beast?"

"Could be. Don't forget to take your drawing."

"I'll find a place of honour for it."

She heard him go down the garden path whistling gently to himself, and then was reclaimed by sleep.

CHAPTER NINE

THINKING BACK ON it he realized that it had come to him with a slow inevitability as though it were being willed to him by some outside force. Maybe Punch clamouring from whatever realm he inhabited, calling to him not to be a bloody, blind fool. Or maybe just the workings of memory as the night's pleasures and joys, settling into place, left him with a clearer mind as he returned from Parnassus to the well-known surroundings of the Dower House. However it had come, though, he knew that fundamentally he owed it to her; that quite literally it had been her gift and his words which had followed his acceptance of it . . . words which had worked like slow yeast while he took his bath, memory haunting him while he dressed and there propped on the dressing table to one side of the mirror was the drawing of the dove house, and somewhere in his mind he could hear the echo of his own words . . . the whole thing so tenuous to begin with that he could not pin-point exactly what it was that his memory was trying to recapture, only knowing that it was important that he should—and willing to believe now that Punch in exasperation had shouted to him from some distant aerie not to be such a bloody, blind fool. And then the phrase swimming clear into his consciousness . . . *each Spring with a knitting needle*. And then that to be topped at once with Punch's written words . . . *look in that place where we used to each* . . . And at once he was there; and within ten minutes had proof for he went down to the back hall with its long key board, each set neatly labelled, and the hook under *Dovehouse* barren of any key.

As it would be if Punch had hidden anything there for he would have taken it into safer keeping. Not that it was all that much safer. It had been put on the key ring in the cut glass bowl in Punch's bedroom. Knowing Mrs Shipley to be busy with breakfast he had gone to the dove house and unlocked the door and had had to stand and let the dust and feathers settle as the birds had thrashed their way around and out of the house, only a few staunch early nesting hens holding their place, and on the small stage half-way up the house had found a large cardboard carton tightly taped and a medium-sized old suit-case, locked, but he guessed the key to be found where he had already found the dove house key.

He had left the cardboard carton and the case where they were, locked the house, and gone into breakfast, knowing that there was nothing to be done until he had the place to himself after dinner. But the gift, he knew, had been hers . . . first the drawing and then her asking how the birds were culled. His gratitude was not to be denied. He drove to Leominster, bought flowers, and took them to her.

*   *   *   *

At four o'clock that afternoon Kerslake, summoned to Quint's room, stood at the window. Although the sun shone clear from the western sky a fierce spring shower was pock-marking the surface of the lake and with the sun's help putting a fierce burnish on the blooms of the stately tulips in their beds. Listening to Quint he found himself wondering if the man had long sensed some of his feelings for Georgina Collet and was now—as sometimes in the past he had—taking a sadistic but polite pleasure in making him uneasy. Not that anything in his, Kerslake's, manner showed it, but then Quint had little need for outward marks of emotion; a man's silence or stillness often spoke plainly to him. In his own thoughts and emotions Kerslake acknowledged a variety of reactions and made no attempt to curtain off his imageries or his sharp jealousies. It was a new situation to him, surprising him, and testing him— though he had no doubt of the final resolution of this passing weakness.

"So," Quint said, "we move a little further along the line. The train may stop at all stations but the country in between has its divertissements. He takes her out to a dinner dance . . . country-house stuff . . . and they have a good time. Seyton proves himself human. Three times I gather before daybreak. He departs at what Warboys vulgarly calls 'sparrow fart'— bearing with him a small gift from her, a drawing of the dove or pigeon house at the Hall. But, lo and behold, by half-past ten the next morning he is back, bearing his own gift, a great bouquet of flowers. To be exact, which our dear Georgina is never less than, it consisted of carnations and yellow and blue irises. The carnations scarlet. All a little vulgar, I think you will agree—or maybe they are his racing colours. Anyway, I gather, though Georgy put it more politely, he mounted her again. At eleven in the morning . . . dear, dear, love should keep more romantic hours."

Bluntly Kerslake said, "Where is all this leading, sir?"

Quint smiled at him blandly. "To an opinion. Yours, I hope. But that can wait for there is a little more to be said—or rather read. I will give it to you in her own words—as transcribed from the answering phone. Here they are. I quote. 'In view of what had happened between us—which is what you have bloody well been angling for—I would have expected a shift in our relationship, but not such a big one. He was up in the air about something more than just our loving, and I got the feeling that it was something to do with my gift of the dove house drawing. He thanked me for it again and said that one day he might be in a position to explain to me exactly why it meant so much to him. In the circumstances I would have bloody well thought that the other gifts would have meant more. I don't know, but like a good little whoring girl I must give my pimps what they want, and I'm ready to bet that something has popped somewhere. I've been asked to dinner in two days' time, and have said *yes*. And then without either of us needing to ask for it we made love again but—since you love these details and they may be important—not entirely in the nude as before. Throwing aside all the titillating detail you

184

pretend to enjoy—or do you perhaps?—quite clearly something has happened to him. Whether it is significant or not isn't my business unless you make it so. Undoubtedly I shall receive some directive from you.' " Quint leaned back and gave Kerslake a mild smile. "Well, what do you make of all that?"

Himself now, all feeling purely professional, Kerslake shrugged his shoulders. "We've got the personal relationship which was wanted. Given a willing woman and an unattached man it doesn't rank as a miracle."

"A felicity. Go on."

"The dove house part is interesting. But for the life of me I couldn't begin to guess at the cause without more facts."

"Go wild then. Cut the pack and see what card is turned up. Let your imagination have its freedom. To paraphrase and somewhat distort a sixteenth-century poet who turned from the love of women to the love of Christ—licence your roving mind, and let it go, before, behind, between, above, below. There may be some new-found land, some wild truth waiting to be discovered. A guess, a fantasy which when put into words may have the sudden ring of truth. Truth may be stranger than fiction. But lacking truth tell me a fairy story, some preposterous proposition. We are in the dark so let us amuse ourselves with fancies." Quint smiled suddenly. "My dear Kerslake—I don't idly tease you, nor do I underestimate you. Just give me any fiction which comes right off the top of your head, or perhaps more precisely the tip of your tongue."

"Well . . . To begin with, what do we know? Seyton wants the Foundation out of the Hall. To do this there must be some legal way of breaking their lease—or, and why not, maybe they have already broken the terms of the lease in some way. More interesting is the fact that Seyton's brother in the period not long before his death turned against the Foundation. The turning was a personal one. He wanted to have no more to do with any man or woman there in the Hall. He was an honest, straightforward man—why should he take against them personally? Because they were or are up to no good."

"Why do you say that?"

"Because I have it from you. Why else would you give me an instruction regarding anything Sir Manfred Grandison might order me, in confidence, to do? For me that is as incomprehensible as Seyton getting excited about a drawing of his dove house."

"Or spending long hours in the chapel?"

"Yes. Unless——"

"You pause—does some wild flight of fancy put you down?"

"It's wild all right but that is what you are asking from me. So here it is. He could have been looking for something in the chapel. Let's say something which—through his brother or from some other source—he knew was waiting to be found. Perhaps something which would help him to get the Foundation out. Let's assume he didn't find it. He probably could have gone looking elsewhere for it—without any luck. And then . . ."

"And then—what? I wait for you to have the honour, though I could take it from you."

Kerslake grinned. "That's generous of you. And then, I say, the lovely Georgina presents him with a drawing of the dove house and, by God, he says to himself, maybe that's the place. Why didn't I think of it before? So the gift of flowers—which seems to me a little too soon in the day—is more than saying a nice thank-you for their evening. But what could possibly be hidden in the dove house of importance is beyond me."

"And for the time being I think it should remain beyond us. So what instruction do you think I should send to Georgina now?"

"You ask me that, sir?"

"I do, sir."

"Well . . . I'm damned if I know."

Quint laughed. "Honest, Kerslake. But you are right. No specific instruction. Just to let things run between them and to keep her eyes and ears open. And don't be deceived by the way she talks or frames her reports. There is much of her father in her—but she possesses the one quality he could never acquire. His work made him miserable to the point of disaster. Georgina —despite her outbreaks—knows the wisdom of making the best

186

and the most of a bad job. Nothing we can ask of her will ever really touch her. Do you agree?"

Kerslake shook his head. "No, sir. If you play with dirt you get defiled. You can wash your body clean but not your spirit. But it's no great thing to shout about. It happens to the vast majority of the human race. It's just one of life's common hazards."

Quint beamed. "And to think that but for me you would have stayed patrolling a small town's beats . . . chucking out pub rowdies, spotting illegally parked cars, collaring petty thieves and, for high spot once a year, the murder of erring wife or husband by jealous ditto ditto. Well now, all that remains to be done for the present is for you to telephone her with her instructions; to push nothing, to probe for nothing, to foster the sweet romance, and to give us a daily report, so far as she is able, of Seyton's activities, of their verbal and otherwise conjunctions, and of any acts or emotional displays which seem to make him pass out of character."

"Yes, sir."

When Kerslake did this a little later from his own room, he spoke precisely and unemotionally, yet picturing her clearly at the other end of the line, wearing a stained working smock, her auburn hair tousled from her habit of working her pencil end through it as she considered the effect of a line or some detail of shading and suddenly knowing quite clearly—and for the first time in his life—that he had fallen in love with her without hope, and wanting none. The emotion itself was enough.

She listened patiently to him until the end and then said with a lightness which sounded genuine, "What a marvellous time you both have. I suppose one day, if you run out of my kind—or maybe when you retire—the two of you will be reduced to visiting peep shows on piers . . . What the Butler Saw . . . The New Parlourmaid . . . The Midnight Bathing Party . . . Dear, dear, dear—and to think that Quint when he left Oxford was determined to turn Roman Catholic and become a priest. Well, he's become a Father Confessor of a kind, hasn't he? And what was your bucolic ambition, dear Kerslake?"

"I had none until I met Quint. And now—through him—I've achieved it. But . . ."

She caught his pause and indecision, and asked, "And *but what* now?"

He laughed gently. "Perhaps to have met you at a Rugby Club dance, and married you, and to have been a good policeman and a better husband. We all have pipe dreams. That's mine for the time being. Thinking about it puts me nicely to sleep at nights."

"And when it wears thin you'll find some other dream."

"Of course. Dreams come cheap. Anyone can have one."

"There speaks the true, good Birdcage man . . ."

She put down the receiver at her end and for a moment or two he was left with the thin static and hum of a bad line.

* * * *

That evening after dark and when Mrs Shipley had left after dinner he went to the dove house and brought down the suitcase and the cardboard carton from the half landing. One or two of the birds flapped around bedazed by the light of his torch, but most of them sat tight. He carried the case and box to the yard at the back of the house and cleaned them free of dust, feathers and droppings. He took them up to Punch's bedroom, slit the carton open with his knife and unlocked the case with the key which—as he had suspected—was on Punch's ring. He made no detailed examination of the contents, but saw enough to satisfy him that they were what Punch had wanted him to find; knew, too, that there was no point in needlessly risking curiosity on the part of Mrs Shipley or the daily maid who came in from the village. He had to have time to himself. The next day was the Shipleys' Hereford day—cold supper left for him. He would have the house to himself from lunchtime onwards.

Excitement now had abated. In some ways he had already regretted that morning's lift of feelings which had taken him to Leominster for flowers and his time with Georgina afterwards. He wanted to share nothing until he knew what he had to

188

share. Anyway, as far as she was concerned there could be no possible cause for worry. He could only be grateful to her, and that emotion for a while he had not handled too brightly. From now on he would not risk showing any difference in his demeanour to anyone. Not that the sudden shift in their relationship meant nothing to him. Something had happened more than a gay evening and getting into bed with one another. Oh, he had known that before with other women since Ruth . . . with Nancy—but not ever sensing a spring of emotion that took him out of control, or sent him flighting into a reconsideration of his own state and way of living. But something in the responses they had set up in one another was, he felt, uncommon . . . and perhaps at this moment likely to prove unwelcome. Well, whatever . . . But without doubt the stuff he had found hidden in the dove house took precedence over everything. One step at a time.

He locked the case and the carton away in Punch's wardrobe, and went down and poured himself a whisky. Before he had finished it the telephone rang. It was Nancy from France to say that she was coming home at the weekend.

"Did Mrs Shipley tell you I called last night?"

"Yes, she did."

"Oh, dear, I know that tone of voice. She told me that you took that little artist piece to Clyro."

"That's a bald, but not entirely exact description."

"You mean 'piece' isn't exactly exact?"

"By no means."

"Did you stay for breakfast?"

"For God's sake, Nancy!"

"What's wrong with the question? I just wanted to know if you had a good time. Which clearly from your stuffiness you did. So what? I'm happy about it. Mind you, a little jealous too. But that soon goes. Anyway, what I really wanted to ask was if you would come over for supper on Sunday night. The old boy would like it as well as me. He hasn't enjoyed himself here much. The weather and the company have browned him off."

"Yes, I'd like to do that."

"Good. If you'd like to—bring your artist girl friend. I'd like to meet her and so would the old boy—he might get her to change her mind about doing something for him. Now come on—don't be stuffy. You ask her."

"All right, I will."

"Jesus. The line is just vibrating with your enthusiasm. Do I fancy that my dear Richard is, in fact, not the least bit interested in me, my dear bored papa, or even the lovely drawing lady? What's eating you?"

"Nothing."

"That's all right then. A nice polite lie, and I'll bet you've got the stiff tycoon look—straight ahead, your line across country quite clear to you."

He laughed then, though in himself there was a touch of irritation that he could—to her, at least—so easily betray his mood. With an effort, he said lightly, "My dear Nancy . . . I'll bring her over and we'll have a jolly evening. And that's all I had with her."

"I can believe that--and it makes me sorry for you. You need more than that. Being a big noise in the diamond world just isn't enough. Neither is wanting the Hall back. With only those two interests you're in danger of becoming a bore, and I couldn't bear that. Darling Richard, rather than that I'd gladly see you married to someone else than me. Good night."

The next afternoon, as soon as the Shipleys had gone off to Hereford, Seyton went up to Punch's bedroom. He set up the small collapsible film screen and—with the help of the maker's instructions still in the box—fixed up the projector. The projector with three spools of film were in the cardboard carton. In the suitcase were a tape player and three tapes. The tapes were marked *One* and *Two* and *Play this first*—all in Punch's hand.

Knowing his own excitement, he schooled himself to deliberate, unhurried action and put on the tape marked—*Play this first*, keeping the volume down. Punch's voice came alive in the room and the sound, for a moment or two, shocked him with swift emotion, setting the blood tingling in his cheeks.

'. . . Richard, I've got so bloody worked up about all this that I can hardly trust myself to speak about it. But I must take precautions. In case, by the remotest chance, anything goes wrong somewhere. You never know, do you? After you've heard this and played the other tapes and seen the film—pretty poor stuff technically, but the best I could manage, you'll know what a boil I'm in—especially as I can't get in touch with you yet. None of this would have been necessary if you'd only set up a forwarding address or left a phone number where you could be reached. Sod you. The film's poor, not only from the conditions I had to work under but because I wasn't so hot in processing it. By the way I've chucked all that equipment into the river, and the camera I sent back to the Andover bloke because I only had it on hire . . .

I don't know, but I've got the nasty feeling that something will go wrong, so that's why I'm chuntering away like this. It's a sort of comfort really—as though I was really talking to you before going into all the details and showing you the stuff. Which, I suppose, is the best way to imagine it. As though I was really talking to you. You see, I managed to slip up the old back so-called secret way at the Hall on my own. Just poking about and I found that they'd taken a small panel out of one of the walls so that they could look into the grand bedroom. The one Sarah Seyton always used. And been bloody clever about it, too. They'd done it right behind that big gilt mirror with the cupid and satyr frame and I got the shock of my life because they'd taken out the mirror glass and fitted some see-through stuff . . . you know, the one-way stuff.

Well, you know me. At first I went up like a rocket, but I pretty soon came down again. So instead of going charging off to take old Shanklin by the scruff, I sat and thought. And then I went back down and checked all the inside wall with a torch and then I found something else. In the side wall of the library they'd cut a small square right through to the top row of the book shelves—but obviously hidden from the room side by the books and there neatly tucked away was a microphone and a coil of flex which they could run down the few steps to the cellar where probably they connected up the recorder and so on when they wanted to. All this from a religious organization! I can tell you I was hopping mad. All right—I know I can be a bull in a china shop, but not this time. I just went back to the Dower, sat down with a large whisky and did some thinking.

At first I didn't see my way ahead at all. But on my second whisky it suddenly came to me. I didn't have a bloody thing to worry about. I mean about being caught or found out if I had a shot myself at doing what they had done or were even still doing. And my God, when you come to that part you'll go over backwards. If I was to be caught I could just say—that's not the point. What have you damned well been up to, you religious Joes and bible-thumping bastards? I can tell you too that's when I thought here's the way out. I could get them by the short and curlies, get you to make good your offer to finance the Hall etcetera, and break their lease under the disrepute and so-on clause. I mean can you imagine if someone on their side gabbed in his drink and the word got round and one day in Hereford some chum of mine came up and said with all the good will and chumminess in the world, "I hear your tenants have turned the Hall into a high-class knocking shop"?

So I did have a go. Not for long but long enough. And all the damned time I'm trying to get in touch with you! I really did need you to hold my hand. Anyway it's all on film or tape and the moment I get in touch with you plain sailing. But I was nearly damn well caught. I never left any stuff in place. Always took it back into the chapel tunnel. But one night when I went over—and I didn't go over every night you understand, only when they had big-wig guests at the Hall and then not always—well, they'd put everything back in place, and a damned good job somebody had made of it too. You wouldn't have known. And I knew it was a damned good bet the mirror had got its original glass back in.

Well, that gives you some idea of what's in store—though I hope that all this is just me being over-cautious and that I can tell you face to face, you wandering bastard, and we can take action together. But even so I'm going to write you a letter to give you the full story just in case anything goes wrong. And who knows in this world what next is going to happen? And for all I know—though I was damned careful—the buggers may have twigged me, and I wouldn't put it past them to try something. Odd thing is, though—putting aside their methods—I'm a bit in favour of what they're after. But that's *something else. Well, with God's good grace, here's hoping you never have to listen to all this, but that we'll be sitting together and me telling you all about it. Funny thing, though—using Sarah's old room and her mirror. She'd have loved it all. Probably volunteered to play a part.'*

After the tape finished Seyton sat for a while, emotion high in him from hearing Punch's voice, and running with it a bitter sense of irony; irony that small details could play hell with people's lives. If only Punch had been able to get him early on the telephone then the odds were that Punch would have still been alive, would never have made his usual trip to Hereford . . .

He played the remaining tapes, but now there was no real surprise in him. In most of them just Sir Manfred Grandison and another person figured. But on some Felbeck was present. Most of the second or third people present were unknown to him entirely, some though were known by name because they were public figures, and two were people whom he had met at the Hall The theme was always the same. The victim—not always a man—had been prompted to indiscretions in Sarah's bedroom and these had been recorded on film. It was blackmail affably and sophisticatedly handled. The price to be paid was not to be made in money, but in future services when the need arose. Surprisingly very few of the victims made any resistance. One or two even treated the matter lightly, giving the clear impression that had they been approached directly they would have co-operated willingly. As an object lesson on human nature it left Seyton feeling sick. In all Punch had recorded only five conversations. Of the film sequences there were even fewer—just three. Their quality, as Punch had said, was poor, but without any doubt of the identity of the two people involved or of their sex and activities. It was clear, too, that Punch's film sequences were not concerned with any initial indiscretion. They were clearly from the manner of the individuals involved a continuation of an already established liaison and he recognized clearly the two women involved.

Sitting there he could hear Punch's voice saying . . . 'I'm a bit in favour of what they're after. But that's something else.' So it was, but he could understand Punch's momentary feelings. But more than that he recognized that Punch, going bull-headed after what he wanted, had run an enormous risk. Only good luck had saved him from being discovered at his work. And it was no good his saying he did not have a thing to worry about. They would not have quietly packed their bags and stolen away. There was plenty to worry about and now he had it all in his lap. The thing had to be handled properly and all along the line he had to look after his own safety.

As a start he locked the tapes and film away in Punch's safe. Then he got out the Land Rover, put the projector and tape recorder aboard, drove to the river and dropped them into a deep pool. One thing he knew for certain was that he was not now going to take a step without considering the risks which might arise for himself. And that needed thought. And—quite positively—he knew that he needed help and certainly advice.

He sat for an hour back at the Dower House thinking things over and sorting out a course of action in his mind. Excitement of any kind at the prospect of getting the Hall back was far distant from him at that moment. He could wait for the flags to be put out. In the meantime he had to find the right approach and to look after himself.

At six o'clock he telephoned Figgins in London and after a few moments business and social chat with her said, "Figgy— I've got a little job on hand. And I rather fancy I'd like a chat with Helder about it. But I don't want to come all the way to London. Do you think you could get in touch with him now and ask him if he could meet me in Cheltenham at three o'clock tomorrow? I'll be in the Rolls in the main car park across the road from the big store . . . you know . . . Cavendish House."

In her most non-committal voice Figgins said, "I'll try. But he's difficult to find at times. I'll ring you back. Will the day after tomorrow do if he can't make tomorrow?"

"Yes."

"Okay, then."

An hour later Figgins rang back to say that Helder would be in Cheltenham on the next day.

*　　　*　　　*　　　*

He rang at eight o'clock just as she had finished her supper of baked beans on toast and was about to listen to a symphony concert on the radio. She sensed at once that his mood had changed, but felt that it was to be expected. One could not live on the top of a mountain all the time, or coast blissfully along on the crest of a wave. From any blissful high there had to come some following low . . . and who knew, maybe in his case, a reappraisal of what had happened and, perhaps quite understandably, a wish that it never had; but at least he kept to a comforting verbal standard.

"Georgina, love . . ."

"Richard."

"What are you doing?"

Realizing that there was fresh ice to be broken, she told him, talking without change to her semi-intimate manner. He might sleep around occasionally but never with an indifferent promiscuity. Anything he did had to mean something to him, if only while it happened. Gossiping away about her day since she had seen him she had the wry but poignant wish that it could all have been and would go on being on a very different plane from the one from which she had been forced . . . bribed . . . to operate. Few women could really put from them the abiding, primitive hope that promiscuity, rare or frequent, might hold some promise, however remote, of love's permanence. Talking to him, surprised at the ease with which she could do it as though she had long rehearsed the dialogue, she knew in herself that given an innocent, uncomplicated freedom of will and emotions she would have wanted him for herself always. Just the clean, clear, simple and developing relation common to all lovers who were free to give themselves with honest, mutual desire and turn a passionate, physical relationship into an abiding force to which they both made a true

obeisance . . . love and marriage, children and mortgage repay-
ments; all the supposedly hum-drum trappings and bonds of
true sharing. To hell with Quint. The oddity turned like a
sharp pain in her breast . . . what if she suddenly came clean
with him? She had no idea what Birdcage wanted with or from
him. But she knew what she wanted. She could tell him the
truth and risk his reactions. Love, she speculated with a
moment's cynical sourness, might conquer all difficulties.
Might. But there was dear Daddy, and God knows what other
complications, equally dear to Quint, which could turn her
and his world upside down and lose for them both even this
small . . . a ghastly word, an occasional favourite of her father's,
surfaced . . . this small serendipity.

He was saying, ". . . Nancy—that's his daughter—you know
he wanted you to do some horse studies for him—wants us to
go over on Sunday to supper. Would you like to?"

"Would you like me to?"

"Of course. I know it was the wine and the music and all
that, love. But things have to start somewhere, or somehow. So,
yes, I would like you to. Well, you know I'm not really one for
delving too deeply into things right off. Things happen, but
then I think you have to stand back and see how they shape
up. Are you with me?"

"Oh, yes. There's really no need to rush into the future. I'm
happy that what has happened has happened. Let's both be
sensible and see what old Father Time comes up with."

He laughed. "You'd be bloody surprised sometimes."

"Nicely, I hope." But as she spoke she knew that there was
no hope. Just gather ye rosebuds while ye may. Old Time, sod
him, was already flexing his wings.

"Good. I'll pick you up. I shan't see you tomorrow because
I've got to go to Cheltenham on business."

"In that gorgeous great Rolls?"

"Yes. I'm taking Roger out to lunch and then I've got some
business to clear up afterwards."

"I'd like to meet him some time." She was now really hating
herself for what she knew she had to do. All was grist to the

Birdcage mill, and dear Daddy while not exactly picking oakum was having a bad time.

"I'm sure you will some time."

After he had rung off, she called London and Kerslake on late duty answered the telephone. She was brief and Kerslake let it stay that way. When she had finished, he rang Quint at his flat, and Quint who was mellow from a meal of omelet laced with a Grand Marnier sauce, listened while he was given the model, colour and registration of the Rolls and the location of Roger Seyton's school, and then said, "Have a driver around here for me at half-past nine. It's a long time since I've been to Cheltenham. How was dear Georgy?"

"Brief—not to say curt."

"How understandable. Share a bed and the molecular structures of the human psyche undergo some rearrangement. I think the time might well be coming when we will have to call her off. Women have an emotional logic and fidelity unknown to men, and a surprising capacity—given the right circumstances—of suddenly turning round and without heed for the consequences saying, 'Well, fuck you, Jack!' Or, more analytically explicit, she could be tempted to ditch Daddy and protect Seyton. Yes, we must watch dear Georgy less she should show signs of becoming 'A dancing shape, an image gay—To haunt, to startle, and waylay.' You agree?"

"Of course. I would never quarrel with Wordsworth."

Quint chuckled and rang off.

Kerslake, late-night duty ahead of him, put his receiver back and began to leaf through his latest copy of *Playboy*. Reaching the centre spread he stared at its naked subject with less interest than he would have given to a colour gravure of a red Devon heifer.

*　　*　　*　　*

He had a pleasant lunch with Roger, and was finally softly bullied into promising that the boy should have his motor

197

scooter to ride around the estate for the next vacation. For a moment or two during the lunch, too, he was unexpectedly touched with a sharp emotion, the rare now recurrence of a feeling of the loss they had both suffered when Ruth had died; knowing, too, that it probably bore harder now on Roger than himself. A man could find other comfort, to ease the deprivation. But Roger had none, and he was at the age when he needed a home with a woman in it. One nail drove out another, as some Italian had once said to him. Although he felt that could not ever be entirely true for him, he knew it could be for Roger. Just as he fast grew new body tissues, so he could—given the chance—grow new emotional ones. They had all the world before them, all their life—not just half a life to reshape and re-order. Thinking this, unbidden came the images of Nancy and Georgina into his mind. God knew it was not a matter of making a choice in any immediate future . . . Time would work it out. Or would it? In the end the choice would—and there was no arrogance in his conception of a freedom of choice—come and come with an insistence not to be denied; and might, too, concern neither of them.

He drove Roger back to school, masking all signs of his own mood, and then went to the main car park. Helder arrived five minutes late. As before he was wearing heavy tweeds, black brogues and an immaculate white shirt, but—maybe as a note of respect to Cheltenham—had abandoned his black tie for what looked like a regimental one, though exactly which regiment Seyton failed to recognize. He apologized for being late—he had been held for a while at the main check point by the queue of shoppers' cars coming in after lunch.

Their brief greetings done, Seyton said, "Helder, I want your help."

"Yes, sir."

"I can't go into details. You'll understand that?"

"Yes, sir."

"You have, I imagine, had or still have some connections with the police?"

"Yes, sir." Helder stared straight ahead, watching a woman

back her car out to leave, scratching the bodywork of the adjacent vehicle and then driving straight off.

"And, I fancy I've heard, with organizations which . . . well, let's say, operate for obvious reasons above and independently of the police."

"Would you mean in matters of State security at home and abroad?"

"Yes, I think I would."

"Well, sir, it depends what you mean by connections. There was a time when I have taken pay from such, but never been on a permanent payroll. I like to work on my own account—and in less exalted spheres. But sometimes one favour deserves another. Yes, I think we could fairly say that. But then again, sir—the field is very wide. If I give you a few options perhaps you might feel free to indicate which one would seem appropriate to the matter which is concerning you. But I should point out for ordinary mortals the standard procedure is to go to the police."

"Bugger the police."

"A view widely—but far from fairly—held, sir."

"All right then. Now give me your options."

For a moment or two Helder was silent, his face turned slightly away from Seyton, his regard on a large black labrador sitting in the seat of a sports car and assiduously licking at the tax disc on the windscreen. Then, clearing his throat politely, he said, "Well, sir . . . there are the Armed Forces, and then those concerned with foreign affairs, a few others of a far too esoteric nature, I imagine, to meet your requirements, and then the most important possibly, that which is concerned with the internal security of this country itself at home but which ranks—or can when it needs—higher than any of the others. Which would you fancy to meet your needs?"

"The last."

"You are sure?"

"Yes. The police are no good to me, nor any of the others. What I want is to have a quiet talk to someone who will see at once that I am not fooling around—and then will do something about it with discretion. And I don't want to talk to some underling the equivalent of a police station sergeant. I want to go right to the top or as damned near it as can."

To Seyton's surprise Helder sighed and said, "You've thought about this carefully, sir?"

"Of course I damned well have or I wouldn't be here. You get me what I want if you can—and you can name your fee. This is urgent and important."

"I've no doubt about that, sir. May I ask on what sort of common ground—if I can arrange it—that you would like to meet?"

"Anywhere, so long as it is well away from Seyton Hall and my part of the world."

"I will do my best for you, sir."

"You'll do better than that." Seyton grinned. "I know you, Helder. And as soon as you've got it fixed up, phone me and give me the details . . . where I can meet whoever it is. But I don't want any understrapper. Just give me a ring."

"Oh, no, sir. That would never do if matters are the way you've given me to understand. I'll do it through Miss Figgins. As soon as I've fixed it she'll phone you and give you a time and day to meet me in London outside Burlington House and then I will take you to your man. Will that be all, sir?"

"Yes, Helder, and thank you very much."

"No, thank you, sir. It's a long time since I've had a nice drive out into the country."

Helder got out of the car and began to walk to his own. As he came to the car whose paintwork had been scored by the incompetent woman driver the owner was standing frowning at the damage.

Helder said, "The good lady who did it was driving a white Rover 3500. Registration number—BOU 351K. BOU 351K."

He walked on to his own car, and sat in it until he had seen the Rolls Royce depart when he switched on his radio and drove off himself. Five minutes later Quint in his chauffeur-driven car followed.

Some hours later Quint was with Warboys in his room

enjoying a glass of Tio Pépé with his superior. Sitting sideways in his desk chair Warboys was gently flexing an ivory paper-knife in his hands and studying an arrangement of cherry blossom that stood in a large alabaster vase on the desk. The blossom was good this year. A cherry year, a merry year. But there was no merriness on Quint's mandarin face. Quint's face, he thought, in repose showed signs of strain. He must repose his own some time and take a good look in his mirror.

He said, "Do you think we ought to bring Helder in?"

"On what count?"

"Do we have to have one?"

"With Helder you do. Unless you held him in chains it would get back to Seyton. After all Seyton runs a big business show. He's used Helder a lot for that. This could be the same thing. What more natural if he goes over to take his boy to lunch than that he should meet Helder half-way for some business reason?"

"You think that?"

"No. But for comfort I would like to make myself able to."

"Something worries you?"

"And you, I think."

"Possibly. But then there is always something to worry one here. If you wish to be frank I am discretion itself."

"There's nothing. Only a feeling. No knowledge."

" 'Knowledge is the wing wherewith we fly to heaven.' "

"It might be hell."

"We approach a little closer. But close enough I think, dear Quint."

"I agree. But there are times I think when this sort of work turns one psychic. And it's not a feeling I like."

"Nor me. Still, we must let nature take its course. When the wind blows the blossom will fall from the tree. Shall I just say— let us wait to see if there comes a wind in good time?"

Quint smiled. "In God's good time?"

"Ah, now there's a point. And being a point gives us a full stop. So I suggest you go home and soothe yourself with the making of some simple dish."

"And you?"

"I shall sit and admire my cherry blossom for a while, and then go round to the Flyfishers' Club for dinner and talk with men who find happiness by their rivers, find tongues in trees, books in the running brooks, sermons in stones and good in everything. And remember—when there seems need to talk—it is often wise to remain silent."

CHAPTER TEN

AFTER SUPPER ON the Sunday night the two women left Captain Hope and Seyton to their port in the dining room with the strict admonition from Nancy that they had half an hour and no more to themselves.

Alone with Georgina in the sitting room, a late April gale buffeting at the windows, knowing that her abruptness would not be taken amiss, knowing—through some mysterious alchemy of understanding which sometimes two people can recognize instantly and welcome—that true jealousy was not in their natures because they were alike in many ways, and certainly in each other's independence of spirit and philosophy, she said, "It's long past the time that somebody pinned him down, Georgina—for his own sake and Roger's. I'd like it to be me, of course. But if not . . . well."

Georgina shrugged her shoulders. "I don't think you need worry about me. I like him, of course. And, no doubt, you can guess how far it's gone. But I'm not his kind. All this landed gentry stuff."

"Poppycock. What a nice word. There's no being anybody's kind. The world's full of examples of happily married couples who were not considered each other's kind. That's why nice girls marry rotters and whores marry aristocrats—and the results surprise you."

"I'm not talking about temperaments or vices and virtues. I'm talking about me which is what you want, and what I don't mind doing. He and I are too alike. We have obsessions. He wants his Hall back. Until he gets it or finally realizes that he's got to sit out the lease, he's not going to make any new venture. Oh, yes, I guess a pleasant evening or two, maybe a lovely week together . . . but nothing more. That goes for me, too. I'm perfectly happy with my work. Just being what I am."

"He's got a one-track bloody mind. That's his trouble—and the reason for his business success. I don't love him at the moment, but I know I could if I had the chance. My God, I do find hopping into bed is a bit like always making a dinner just of the hors d'oeuvres." Nancy laughed. "Can you imagine what those two in there would think if they could hear us? Men think women are bird-brained."

"Sometimes I think we are. But I'm glad we can talk to one another like this. He's nice. I like him, yes. Could love him, yes. But I know I'm never going to have him. What was his wife like?"

"Perfect. Madly good-looking. Always did the right thing. Never got in his way. Kind, generous, and worshipped him. But so dull. She only came alive when she was on a horse. I sometimes think that was when she escaped—went mad, just let some bottled up frustration in her run wild . . . too wild. It killed her in the end. But, I suppose, really she was right for him. My God, the way I'm talking about him. As though he were some juvenile delinquent problem case. Also I know that I'm covering up . . . Oh, Lord, I do get in a muddle sometimes when I really want to be straightforward. You see, whatever I've said, and you've nicely agreed with—the fact is that I want him, have for years, at any price. Now my back hair is really coming down. I might even sniff a bit to keep the tears back, if I could force a few—which I'm not very good at. You see I get the feeling deep in my bones that he's really going to fall for you and, whatever you say, he won't take No for an answer."

"He'd have to take my No—if that's what I said."

"There you are, you see. If."

Georgina laughed, though at that moment there was no humour in her, only a slowly growing confusion caused by the emotion so clearly underlying Nancy's hard-boiled talk. She said, "When I've finished here I'm going to America."

"He'd follow you there. He can be as stubborn and persistent as hell when he chooses. Both he and Punch were that way from the cradle. You take this Hall thing. He isn't going to sit by and let them work the lease out. Not him. He'll get them out one way and another. You heard him when father asked him tonight if he meant to stay here now, and he said of course he was. I know when he means something. He's a bloody Seyton, this is his place and he's going to have it back. All that diamond business stuff means nothing. He'd sell out tomorrow if he could walk into the Hall."

"Well, he's no immediate hope, has he?"

"I don't know about that. I know my little Richard, that touch of smugness and a look which means 'All in good time, you'll see'. And then, bingo, when you least expect it he pulls the white rabbit out of the top hat. I tell you, he's a worker but he's also a lucky bastard—things fall into place for him very often without his lifting a hand."

"Well, that's nice for him. And now, to cheer you up— which I don't think you really need—you can tell your father after I've gone that I'll do a few drawings for him before I leave."

"You will? Well, bless you for that. It'll mean so much to the old boy."

Driving back to the bungalow with him, although they talked quite easily about the evening and the two Hopes, there was in her an undercurrent of speculation about her responses to Nancy's forcing talk. Herself, she had been reasonably frank, but no more than that because her truth was a vastly different one from Nancy's. She knew without doubt that, being free, Birdcage non-existent, she would now be in love with him. Or rather was in love with him but barred from giving it completely free expression. My God, bed yes, and a closer, easier manner of disposing herself with him. Bed broke a few barriers, but too many remained. Even now she could not forget and knew she would report Nancy's intuition that he had some near hope of getting the Hall back, some rabbit perhaps already up his sleeve. Quint and his kind might reverence facts, but they were also greedy for fancies. The whole bloody thing wearied her so that she longed to be a million miles away . . .

205

somewhere where there had never been any dear Daddy, no Quint cloaking his own self-disgust with carefully chosen words—so often other people's—and escaping each night into a world of civilized and mildly epicurean delights and avoiding as often as he could looking into the mirror of truth, and no Kerslake who—frankly accepting his state and enjoying it— would have liked her to share board and bed, the union blessed or not by priest or some indifferent Registrar of Marriages flanked by vases of artificial flowers. Anywhere but here now, in this Rolls with him, because close though they were in flesh they were a million miles apart and she was wishing she could in a little while find the resolution to make some excuse for his not staying with her that night. But she could not. Would not for she lacked the courage of self-denial . . . and, damn it, why not? The job was a dirty one, but at least he was a bonus on the side.

He came in with her, and they sat over a last drink and talked, easily, pleasantly, and she threw off all her thoughts of the outside world and built a make-believe romance for herself and him and, while he made her laugh at his tales of local people and odd characters and of his escapades with Punch, she embraced self-indulgence, pretended to herself that they were engaged with all their friends to read the announcement in the *Daily Telegraph*, that she was to be Mistress of Seyton Hall, and let pleasure and fantasy run in her like some drug in the blood at once potent and benign. And when they were in bed and he had made love to her and his hand, touching her face, discovered the tears that were under her eyes he said nothing, but kissed them away. Then, when he went and she had heard the sound of his car die away, she reached for the telephone at the bedside and spoke a message into the recording unit at Birdcage saying that he was going to London on the coming Tuesday and would be there probably through Wednesday and part of Thursday, staying at Brown's Hotel. The purpose of the visit—business. Then she took two Mogadons and went to sleep.

*   *   *   *

Helder was waiting for Seyton outside Burlington House. They walked to the Piccadilly Circus tube station and rode to South Kensington station. There was little conversation between them. From the South Kensington station they walked towards Sloane Square and a few minutes later stopped before a small hotel.

Helder said, "You know what you are doing, sir?"

"Yes."

"Right. First floor. Room number Three. Just knock and walk in. He knows your name and what you look like. I took the liberty of giving him a photograph . . . a press cutting, but a good likeness. He may or may not give you a name. If he does it won't be his real one. But he's the man you want. They don't come much higher. I briefed him a bit about the background, but by now he will have done his own homework."

"Thank you, Helder."

He went in through a neat, soberly furnished, highly polished hall. A girl sitting behind the reception desk gave him a smile briefly and went back to her ledger work as he climbed the first flight of stairs.

In answer to his knock on Number Three the door was opened by a tall, elegant man, spare of flesh, his long pale face deeply cleft below the cheek bones, his hazel eyes large-lidded, the pink of his scalp showing warmly through his thinning white hair. He wore a light grey suit, a finely linked gold chain looped across his double-breasted waistcoat. A motion of a hand brought Seyton into the room and, as the door was shut, the man said, "Good morning, Mr Seyton. I'm Peacebairn——" a flicker of a smile relieved the rather solemn face, "——and I don't have to apologize for the dramatics. I gather it's what you would have wanted."

"What I want, Mr Peacebairn, is some advice and, of course, discretion." As he spoke Seyton sat in a chair, indicated to him by a wave of the man's hand. The room was double-bedded and on a small table was a tray with two glasses and an opened bottle of pale dry sherry.

Smiling, Peacebairn filled two glasses with sherry and said,

"What I want is a glass of sherry and no doubt you'll join me. Yes, of course. Advice and discretion. A well-matched pair, go well together, but need sympathetic handling." He handed Seyton a glass of sherry and then sat down in a small armchair by the window, gave a little sigh, sipped at his drink, and went on, "So—the floor is yours. I have of course briefed myself about you and the basic situation which exists at Seyton Hall between you and the Felbeck Foundation—the sight of whose back, I gather, would be a glad sight for your very determined eyes. Have you known Helder long?"

"Quite a few years."

"A good man—but beyond our tempting, sadly. And now, I am all yours."

"It's a long story."

"The day is ours—and one, I hope, which may produce more than 'a beggarly account of empty boxes'?"

"I beg your pardon?"

"Forgive me. A bad habit of cloaking my thoughts in other—and far more illustrious—men's words."

Seyton smiled. "Well, this is no account of empty boxes. It's of tapes and films, and adds up to a well-planned, still growing conspiracy of interests against our national security."

"Ah, then you have at once my attention. I shall sit and without interruption hear you out while you demonstrate to me the truth of Helder's statement that you were no man with a bee in your bonnet or a habit of chasing rainbows. I wait."

From then on he was as good as his word while Seyton told his story, beginning with the part letter in code from Punch which he had discovered and then going on to tell how he had discovered the tapes and films and the obvious deductions he had drawn from them . . . and the further, and to him, personal point, that they gave him every right to take legal action which would successfully enable him to break the Foundation's lease on the Hall. He finished, "That's the full story—and you can see quite clearly why I needed the advice and help of someone like you. It's not a thing I could just trot off with to my solicitor."

"Indeed not."

"I presume you know something of this Sir Manfred Grandison?"

"Quite a bit. May I say, too, that you did the right thing in coming to us."

"Well, I don't pretend that I don't have some sympathy for what they're after—even though they don't see it as an immediate thing. But all I'm really concerned with is getting the Hall back."

"Which I think I can say you will."

"I'm bloody going to get it back!"

Peacebairn laughed. "I don't think there's any doubt of that. But from now on—and you'll appreciate this—it is not a matter for any further action on your part. You shall have your Hall, but we must have the handling of affairs, and, of course, we must have the tapes and the film. Where are they at the moment?"

"Locked up in my safe at the Dower House."

"A pretty old-fashioned one, I should imagine?"

"Well, yes, I suppose so."

"Then they must be held with absolute security. That means you will have to hand them over to us. Not just from the security point of view. We'll have to run them through to confirm your story."

"That's what I want. To be shot of the whole thing and just told when I can walk back into the Hall."

Peacebairn smiled. "I like your obsessive directness. Are you not concerned about the political and national issues involved?"

"Yes, I told you I was. I take their point—but I can't go all the way with them. But somebody's got to do something some time or this country will go up the spout."

"Patriotism is a violent emotion. One of the many manifestations of the emotion love, or that even more violent one—religious faith. Excessive love is like excessive wine . . . an enemy to steal away men's brains. However, if I send a man down you will hand over all this stuff to us?"

"Yes. But I must have a firm promise that I get the Hall back."

"I give it. And I have your word that nobody knows any-thing about this except yourself—and now me?"

"That's so."

"And so far as you are concerned it will remain that way?"

"Of course."

"All right, Mr Seyton. I'll let you know when someone is coming for the tapes and films. I shan't feel happy until they are with us."

"Neither shall I. Just fancy those buggers sitting there, singing hymns, collecting Church antiques, and slashing out charity to all the world like confetti, and all the time . . . God, it beats me. I think Felbeck must have gone quietly mad to let Sir Manfred Grandison talk him into all this."

Peacebairn shrugged his shoulders. "We're all potentially mad, Mr Seyton. Perhaps because we all came from Chaos we have an ineradicable nostalgia for it."

"The only nostalgia I have is for the Hall. And I want it back."

Peacebairn laughed. "I realize that." Then his face moving to a severe solemnity, he went on, "But I must ask you to keep that subject a completely closed one as from now. Say nothing . . . not even the hint of a hope to anyone, no matter how near and dear."

"If you say so."

"Good—then I shall be in touch with you."

A few minutes after Seyton had gone the door opened and Quint came in. Without a word he helped himself to a glass of sherry and then sat down on the bed with a heavy sigh, and said, "Peacebairn?"

Warboys smiled. "On the spur of the moment. It amused me. Not overmuch, but enough to lighten what followed. What have we got on our hands?"

"Something with quite a few historical precedents. Another casualty caused by the corrupting forces of power. Give a man an acre of ground and soon he will want more. Give a man like Grandison the means to make a dream come true and he'll use them. After all we have had a winter and spring of discontent

. . . vicious, inhumane strikes . . . garbage piled in the streets, hospitals and schools crippled by strikes . . . road haulage men refusing to move goods, docks closed, picketing and all the petty and not so petty tyranny of the trades unions who have yet to learn how to keep an orderly house. Power from below instead of firm government from above. Hospital cleaners telling surgeons when they may or may not operate—no matter the urgency of any particular case. Decent workers scared to break a picket line—with reason for bang goes their daily bread. And all this merely a preliminary flexing of the muscles by the trades unions. Not even a rehearsal for the real thing to come . . . the historical process they've set in motion and no longer know how to control. The state of the nation suddenly a marvellous, fecund spawning ground for extreme types of ambition. Which way do you go? A Soviet state? Or a dictatorship? Or something in between—if there is anything in between? Well, you can see the option that Grandison and those with him have decided to pick up. Not yet, but not all that far ahead. Next winter, maybe."

"And how will it run?" asked Warboys.

"Along classical lines. At some crisis point—a winter of want, shortages of food and fuel because of industrial action provoked by militant shop stewards, and possibly rioting, the country on the brink of chaos—the Prime Minister will have a State of Emergency declared. The rest follows. A National Government. Key men in all the Services already committed. Some influential trade union leaders, hating their troublemakers, will take their stand with the Government—glad of the chance to crush their left wing elements. Three-quarters of the people of this country will back a show of force against the militant unionists. Bloody hell, and bloody strife for a while— and then, with the prospect of paradise more or less to be regained, this country enters a new era of discipline and decency. I tell you—the mood of the majority of people in this country is ready for it. It is a political evolution most people think is long overdue. They only wait for someone to fire the starting gun."

Warboys sighed. "How right Grandison was when he told me that his interest in the Felbeck Foundation was to find a way to use it for Birdcage. And he'd already found it. You get some Chief of Staff down there who's shying at the veiled suggestion of a future role that could be open to him and then you wine and dine him and pop him into bed with a woman while a hidden camera . . . God, he must be mad."

"On the contrary, he's absolutely level-headed. Democracy as we know it isn't working and won't work. It never has worked. Man is not a democratic creature. Nothing with blood in the veins and passion in the spirit can ever be. This is the eternal paradox, the everlasting problem. The answer is not a positive solution but a working compromise. That's the challenge of humanity to its own imperfections . . . to find the right, the least dishonest, the most benevolent state of balance between the law of the jungle and that of the judiciary. Either he thinks he's found it, or the means to it which—from what Seyton told you he heard on the tapes—sounds like some form of benevolent dictatorship, a myth in itself, or a period of draconian, near fascist direction to be slowly relaxed when human nature has been through a proper course of schooling. The time could be coming right for either to work. If I had to make a bet on one or the other I should be obliged to toss a coin. Grandison is no fool, nor will the others with him be. He and they might succeed, but that is not our problem. We are not in our service to make judgments of that kind. We have a clear brief. The maintenance of the status quo."

"Then what is the answer?"

"Oh, come, Warboys—there's only one. And you know it. We've got to clear up the mess, and it must be done so that there is no chance of a word being said against Birdcage. The processes of history will produce what they will. But no matter what sort of government we eventually get in this country there will always be a need for us—so we must keep our haloes intact. We do not make or destroy governments. We work with loyalty to the Government of the day. Once there arises any doubt about that—then we become nothing. Grandison has planned to commit the ultimate crime in our calendar—to use us as an active political instrument. But politics don't work like that. Politics must always be a natural force spawned by human society. We lose the little virtues we have if we start to use our power and privilege independently—as did the C.I.A."

"So what do we do about Grandison?"

"You must go to him and tell him everything. That's your right and your duty, not mine. Only one course is open to him and he must take it. Resign, retire to private life." Quint gave a slow smile. "Perhaps then he will find time to write one of the biographies he's always talking about. But like the August cuckoo—go he must."

"And Seyton?"

"He's no problem. He hands over the tapes and films and forgets them—having our word that the whole plot has crumbled to dust. A word from us to Felbeck will give him back his Hall, and he will live happily ever after—and keep his mouth shut."

Warboys sighed wearily. "My God, I'm not looking forward to seeing Grandison. We've been so close."

"I think you will find he will take it philosophically. He's gambled before on our behalf and lost and accepted the way the dice fell. Now he's gambled on his own account. To corrupt Pope a little, I do not think he will sit blaspheming his gods, the dice, and damning his fate. And when you send someone down to Seyton to collect his stuff, I suggest you tell Kerslake to do it. He knows the ground and he can go on and give Georgina her marching orders. Which will make her happy and certainly her father. A curious contrast, isn't it, between poor old Collet and Grandison. The one trapped by a surfeit of conscience and the other by the seduction of power?"

Warboys shrugged his shoulders. "What man lives who isn't the casualty of misplaced virtue at some time in his life?"

*   *   *   *

Warboys saw Grandison that afternoon in his chief's office at the top of Birdcage building. Grandison, hunched down a little in his chair behind his desk, listened to him without any show of emotion, his lips a little pursed as though he were gently restraining some inner stir of amusement. The smoke from the cigar in his hand rose in a fine, unwavering line.

When Warboys had finished speaking, Grandison was silent for quite a while. Then suddenly he smiled openly.

"So," he said, "my affairs have gone agley. All has foundered on an unexpected rock—if one might call Seyton's brother that. Odd and ironical, isn't it, that a plan to move this country to a different system of government should have been destroyed by a relic of feudalism? However, don't think that I won't accept your judgment. It is exactly what I would have expected of you and Quint. Nor would I waste my time now in trying to convert you and him to an acceptance of the absolute necessity of the change envisaged. For the time being it has proved still-born. But one day there will be another birth to bring a sturdier youngster which will grow to fruitful manhood. Political evolution is as irresistible as natural evolution—and neither of them are cramped by time. Time is the mother and necessity the father of such an offspring. It will come. As Coke said, *'Minatur innocentibus qui parcit nocentibus'*. That was my guiding principle broadly. He threatens the innocent who spares the guilty. We would have put down the truly guilty men, even though so many of them are unaware of their guilt. Though you clearly will never accept it, your conception of the true role of Birdcage is old-fashioned. You cannot sit aloof, beyond contamination by human affairs. Birdcage is part of the human condition and must move—as man does—with the times. However . . . I say no more on that point. I shall retire. It befits my age if not my wishes. So what happens now?"

"I shall send someone down to collect the tapes and film from Seyton."

"Who?"

"Kerslake."

"Ah, yes. A Quint man?"

"Yes. As I was and am sadly no longer yours."

Grandison laughed. "Speak no requiems. And when you have these tapes and films?"

"If they are what he says they are, then I shall have to see Felbeck and tell him that he must hand back the Hall as the price for his absolution."

"I see. Well the tapes and films will be what he says they are. Seyton is no man to bluff while holding a bad hand. But I think I am the man to talk to Felbeck—if you agree?"

"I do."

"Then I shall go down to the Hall and see Felbeck. He is down there this week arranging for some coming conference."

"How on earth did you ever get Felbeck into this?"

"My dear Warboys—no matter how high a man's dreams are set there must always be some private pleasure which occasionally sends him a nightmare. He is a friend and I cannot betray him now though I was ready enough to blackmail him once."

"And what will you do?"

"Your concern for my welfare is touching, but I know sincere. Well, I shall not fall on my sword and end things like a noble Roman since as a Catholic that is forbidden to me. No, I shall make an old dream come true. I fell in love once with a woman. And she long dead before my time. Now, since I shall have no excuses to stop me from celebrating her, and also I shall enjoy the irony of the way chance has brought it about, I shall write the biography of Sarah Satan."

Warboys laughed. "Yes, I really think you will."

"Without doubt, and with love in my heart because—with a little taming—she would have made such a splendid Birdcage person. So there it is. You need do no more. When I have seen Felbeck I shall announce my retirement. Until then I trust you and Quint to give no hint of its imminence."

"Of course."

"And one other point before you go. Perhaps not necessary, but I would like to make it. I bear no hard feelings towards you or Quint. But it would be idle to deny the bitterness in me.

For that I must find some cure more immediate than time."

"The biography?"

"Perhaps. But, at the least, and more immediately, something sweeter far than flowing honey."

"You quote?"

"Possibly and only partly, but it has a shadowy substance in my mind. And now you can leave me to sit here alone for a while to look back over a life so far spent with a rich share of delights and disasters that give me no cause for bitterness nor repentance."

*   *   *   *

On his way back from London he had made a detour and called on her. He sat now on the settee by the window overlooking the garden and orchard running down to the river. The daffodils were still in bloom and the first of the cherry blossom. A blackbird gave a before-dusk virtuoso performance. He sat sipping his whisky and watching her as she worked to finish a small drawing of a goldcrest on a spruce branch in the last of the good light. Although he was keeping it under control the change in him was only too apparent to her. Its source and nature left her without curiosity, but wondering what he would say, what his manner would be if she were to tell him now that she was soon to pack up and go. No reason had been given. She had just accepted the dictat, and accepted too the instruction that she was to say nothing of her going to Seyton. What she had wanted for her father was to be given. That was all that mattered to her. She could take up her life again, knowing that Birdcage could make no further calls on her.

But now this man sat talking to her and she knew exactly what was in his mind without needing it spelled out in black and white. Before he left here she knew he would ask her to marry him. There was no need of clairvoyance. The thing ran between them almost visibly, like a spark between two poles.

He said, "Things went well in London. I had a bit of business luck and feel like celebrating. Would you care to come out to dinner with me, Georgina?"

Back to him, working, she smiled at the use of her full name. Never once had he called her Georgy . . . not even while caressing her. And she liked it that way. Some names were not meant to be mutilated.

"Oh, Richard, I can't."

"Why not?"

She turned then and looked full at him and knew that she had no way of avoiding honesty.

"Because I don't want to."

"Why don't you want to? Have I done something? Upset you?"

She moved to him then, unable to stop herself, bent briefly and kissed him on the forehead and then stepped back.

"No, of course not. It's what you might do—and that's something I don't want."

Seyton grinned and shook his head. "You've got to do better than that."

She looked at him and breathed deeply to hold back the threat of tears in her eyes. "All right. I don't want to because of what I think is going to happen. You're going to ask me to marry you, aren't you?"

He sat up, surprised. "My God, how could you know that?"

She laughed then because there was no holding it back, and to spare him any hurt she leaned forward and kissed his forehead and let him quickly take her hands so that she stood close to him as she said, "Because it's written all over you. No——" she freed her hands, "——let me go. I've got to speak plainly and I can't do it if you're touching me."

"Now you're getting me worried. Yes, of course I was going to ask you to marry me. But I didn't see it coming out just as bluntly as it has. I mean . . . well, over dinner or . . ."

"Or what? In bed?"

"Would that be wrong?"

"Of course not, you fool. It would be lovely. But it's the marriage thing that's wrong. Yes, I love you—but it can't be. And it's nothing to do with you. It's me. I'd give you anything

217

else. Just as I have already. But not marriage. I'm not the Seyton type. Big house and estate and all that . . ."

"Nonsense. In this day and age? My God—you should see some of the types some landowners pick—Oh, Christ! I could have put it better."

"No. You put it right. I'm just not your type. Oh, yes—for a while like it has been. Or if you were unhappy . . . well, as your mistress. Or just a chummy affair like with Nancy. Now there's the one you should marry. She's right. So right that you can't see it."

"I don't want Nancy."

"And you can't have me. Not with wedding bells. Not with my father. Not with me all wrapped up in my work. And not with a lot of other things about me that make me so sick I'd die if I had to tell you. And, for God's sake, don't ask me to."

"If you say not, then I won't. But I'm not the sort who gives up easily. I'm sorry it has come out this way. It's not like I'd seen it at all."

She smiled, reached for his glass and took a sip of his whisky. "Oh, Richard—you may be inscrutable and damned poker faced when it comes to business. But in something like this . . . well, it's all over your face."

"There's something else you should know about me. I don't give up easily."

"Oh, I know that. And neither do I."

"I really don't understand you. I love you and you love me, but you won't marry me. That doesn't make sense."

"It doesn't have to make sense. Or be explained. I love you but not all the way to marriage. Why can't we leave it like that, and just enjoy what we've got while it lasts?"

"All right for now. But I'm damned if I understand all this. I shan't give up, you know."

She turned away from him and stared at her drawing, knowing that her face might betray her in the surge of temptation which possessed her . . . a deep urge to tell him everything. That she had been sent down here to work on him, that whether she did a bad or a good job she had the promise of a parole for her father as reward, that she was what she was and that made her as guilty as her father had ever been. Then she turned back to him and said, "Look, Richard . . . why don't we let it ride for a while? I don't want to go out to dinner with you . . . I don't want other people around. But I will have dinner with you. I'll cook something here for us. Fair compromise?"

He smiled. "Of course. A fair and sensible one. I guess I was rushing my fences a little. We'll do just as you say. But I'm not giving up."

"I know you're not. But from this moment that subject is out. Right?"

"Right." He stood up and took her in his arms and kissed her and then holding her from him he said, "Speaking quite unemotionally, I think I shall have a painting of you done. In that dress you wore when we went to Clyro . . . I can see it hanging in the library as a companion to the painting of Sarah Satan. You won't mind being in such bad company, will you?"

She laughed. "Why should I? I'm no stranger to bad company. Have you forgotten my father's in prison?"

"What does that matter? Plenty of Seytons have been in prison. You name a crime and we've probably got it somewhere in the family annals."

Later, while he slept at her side, she lay with a calmness now of spirit and body, facing and accepting the unalterable nature of their relationship. She loved him, would always love him, but the dark gods had long decreed that there could be no true fruiting of their love. For her . . . well, it was just a question of gather ye rosebuds . . . Long ago the trap had been set for her, a trap that her father had planted and which Quint had sprung. Take what you can while you can was the answer . . . for that same flower which blooms today, tomorrow will be dying, as Quint would probably have said, garnishing his own self-disgust with other men's fine words.

CHAPTER ELEVEN

AT THREE O'CLOCK Kerslake had a call from the reception desk that his car had been brought round and was waiting for him. That morning he had been briefed by Warboys to go down to the Dower House at Seyton Hall and to pick up tapes and film which Richard Seyton would have waiting for him and to bring them back to London. A little while ago Quint had come into his room and, clearly knowing of the instruction from Warboys, had asked for his briefing.

"I go down to the Dower House and collect tapes and films from Seyton—who has been informed—and bring them back here to Warboys."

"Nothing else?"

"No."

"Good."

Daring, remembering a past conversation, Kerslake said, "Did you expect anything else?"

"There was always a possibility. Loyalty, like love, has many faces. However, off you go and ride down through the fine spring which has surely come because walking across the Park this morning I could not put my foot down without stepping on three daisies."

"Lambs' turds we say in Devon."

"Equally poetical."

In the hallway Kerslake was surprised to see Sir Manfred Grandison standing by the reception desk, light overcoated, and a large brief-case in his hand. He would have passed with a polite nod, but Grandison stopped him and said, "Warboys is sending you to Hereford?"

"Yes, sir."

"Seyton Hall?"

"Yes, sir."

Grandison smiled. "We must practise minor economies. Look after the pence and the pounds will look after themselves. I'm going down to Seyton Hall and you can take me. When you have collected what you have to collect you will hand it to me."

"Yes, sir."

"Good. Then let us be on our way."

They walked out together into the primrose sunshine and Grandison sat in the back and Kerslake drove. For this small comfort he was grateful. To have had his Chief alongside him would have meant conversation of some sort and, at this moment, Kerslake was far from being ready to welcome that. They did indeed have a little occasional chat, but very soon Grandison opened his brief-case and began to work, and after that was done he settled himself and went to sleep, now and again snoring gently, and Kerslake was left to his fast driving and his thoughts.

Some three hours later Warboys walked into Quint's room, gave no greeting and sat down on the window seat and looked out over the Park. The day had turned sour and so had his mood since lunch. A fine drizzle, backed by a wind from the east up the river, was rolling grey veils of rain across the lake. Down in Hampshire on the banks of the Test, he thought—though it was the least important of his thoughts, often smothered by others—the wind and rain would be coming off the left bank and making quite a few normally easy lies difficult to cover. He watched a tall girl in the Park struggle with a wind-blown umbrella, her red mackintosh, sleek with rain, rising like a small parachute dome above her legs as a gust hit her. Not the girl, but the coat brought back another girl to him, the one who had walked so often with him wearing a similarly coloured mackintosh and whose face he had last seen looking up at him from below a balustrade, fallen petals of rhododendrons like red blood stains jewelling the grass and the flagged path. The past momentarily troubled the present, and then was gone. He looked up to find Quint standing beside him, holding a glass of sherry. He took it and smiled greyly.

Quint said quietly, "What is it?"

"I don't know—and that is the trouble."

"Kerslake's gone. Everything will be regulated."

"An ugly word—fit only for clocks. Yes, I saw Kerslake go from my window. And I don't think I was standing there accidentally. One of Fate's little fingers could have given me a small prod. A niggle in the mind. Sir Manfred Grandison went with him. I saw him. And I checked at reception—he met Kerslake there."

Quint was surprised but hid it.

"So—is that surprising? He had to go sooner or later to see Felbeck, who is at Seyton Hall. Now and again he has bouts of strict economy over cars. Waste big, economize little—the logic of all government departments."

"I need no comforting."

"Then I give none." Quint went back to his desk, poured himself a sherry and raising it admired the colour, compared it in his mind to a crystal ball and then dismissed any thoughts of finding any enlightenment in it. Warboys was the crystal ball.

And Warboys as though he had read his thoughts, said, "I have the feeling that something has been said to me which I should have understood. Or, no—maybe it was a slip. But I think not. I think it was deliberate."

"And what was said?"

"And there you have me because it has gone and I've been trying for hours to recall it."

"Said by?"

"Grandison, when I told him that the game was up."

"You are afraid perhaps that he will take the tapes and film from Kerslake when he has collected them?"

"No. He could do that, of course. Kerslake would think it nothing odd. He's still the great Panjandrum—except to you and me. And the tapes and film mean little now. Except that they would be useful on file for some time in the future and in connection with quite unrelated matters to the one we have in hand. The material for blackmail is always useful . . ."

". . . *'to know the family secrets, and to be feared accordingly'*. Juvenal, I think."

"Something like that echoes in my mind. And I think it was meant to. Whatever Grandison may be he is compounded of the same emotions as all men. No god. Just one among all us other bi-forked mortals, except for a rare habit of thought which makes him delight in uncommon subtleties. I am sure that he said something to me which I was meant to understand and now I don't know what it was. Didn't at the time, except something like a breath of wind stirred the dry summer grasses of my ageing fancy."

"You think the bugger's up to something?"

"Yes. But no more than *yes*."

"So what?"

"Nothing—you cannot make honey without pollen."

*   *   *   *

Going through the small town of Ledbury some time after six o'clock, Grandison made Kerslake stop and they went into a hotel for a drink. Kerslake could have wished it otherwise for he was in some awe of the man and yet—ambition to do well in the service clear in his mind and this a rare opportunity to make some direct standing in the man's favour—he did his best to give a good account of himself when Grandison began to talk to him about his Devonshire days and his ambitions. To his surprise he found himself, after a few minutes, put at his ease and when Grandison discovered that his father had been a pigeon fancier was surprised at the man's knowledge of the birds.

Grandison said, "When I was a young man I kept a loft of birds—blue checkers. In Devon, too. But South Devon on the coast, near Plymouth. The casualty rate on flights was sometimes high for those were the days when the peregrine falcons nested on the cliffs. You know, I would sometimes watch the high stoop of the killer and find so much beauty in it that I could only furnish my heart with a token sorrow for the loss to my loft. Death is a noble thing when it comes from the heavens suddenly . . . like the judgment of God."

Kerslake grinned. "I don't think my old man would have agreed with you there, sir. He loved his birds and hated hawks and falcons. Used to take his gun to them when he could."

"You've killed, haven't you? What would your father have thought of you?"

"Yes, sir. I have killed. And he would have thought nothing of me because, had he known, he would have wiped me from his mind and his heart."

"Yet he would have shot a falcon whose life is as dear in the sight of God as any man's. Faulty logic. To condemn you for what he had done himself. Still, we will not confuse this by no means chance conversation with spiritual considerations. Do you really think I travel with you for minor economic reasons . . . a small saving in our house-keeping money?"

Kerslake smiled. "Frankly, no, sir."

"Have you any idea why?"

"No, sir."

"A guess, perhaps?"

"Oh, that . . . yes, I could make a guess, sir."

"A guess? Is that the full truth?"

"No, sir."

"Then let me have the truth. That bright, shining jewel which all men crave for—until they have it in their hands and find it like any other metaphysical concept a different thing from the treasure that fancy promised."

"Well, sir . . . a little while ago I happened to look in the back mirror. You had your big brief-case open on the seat and I could see right into it."

"And you saw it?"

"I think . . . no, know now that I was meant to see it. You wouldn't carry it for your own use. Not in your position."

"You please me. No. I wouldn't normally carry it and I have never used one. Nor will. It is for you."

"Yes, sir."

"You've used one before?"

"Yes, sir. Shortly after they were first issued. And once since. They——"

"I know the technical details. Quick, silent, and as near instantaneous as the flick of the eyelids of the Angel of Death. When we reach the Dower House you will take it in with you and when Seyton has handed over his package to you you will kill him. There will be no servants in the house. You will then bring his stuff out to me and then drop me at the Hall and go straight back to London. Is that clear?"

"Yes, sir."

"No questions?"

"I obey orders, sir. Not ask questions."

"A discipline becoming rare in other walks of life. So, let us go back to the car for there is no going back to anything else."

They drove out of Ledbury into the fast-growing darkness and in the back seat and because it was Ledbury that had made his memory stir to make an apt connection which pleased him, Grandison recited to himself the words of John Masefield.

> *Man with his burning soul*
> *Has but an hour of breath*
> *To build a ship of truth*
> *In which his soul may sail—*
> *Sail on the sea of death;*
> *For death takes toll*
> *Of beauty, courage, youth,*
> *Of all but truth.*

Kerslake, he knew, would never fail him. His only hope was that others would not fail him. After all, a man could write his own requiem at any time after the age of twelve, or if precocious ten. No, there could be no failure on his part. For others he could not speak . . . though he had spoken and tossed the coloured teasing words like balls in the air. Whether they fell to the ground or were caught by ready hands was almost a matter of indifference to him. No, that was not true. It was a matter of life and death, but the choosing of which . . . well, perhaps he was expecting too much from a few simple words spoken lightly to veil a wish which might never come true. A delightful, deadly game which only a Birdcage mind could invent.

Some time later in London, Warboys rang Quint in his room and said, "I'm glad you are there still. It's been worrying me ever since I left you. This Grandison thing. He took it so well about having to resign . . . and then we chatted, and I've been trying to piece it together. I asked him what he would do when he retired. And just now it came to me—not that it's any help, though I'm sure he was underlining something, some thought or some hope. And now it's just come to me. About his retirement. What would he do? And I suggested he wrote a biography. It's something he's always talked about."

"So?"

"He said . . . well, no. Not right away. He wanted something more immediate . . . something sweeter far than flowing honey. Yes, that's it. You know him. Wrap it up and let you puzzle over it. It's the kind of humour—maybe black—which he would relish at a moment like this. *Something sweeter far than flowing honey*. What does that stir in you?"

"You're rushing me, dear Warboys. Give me a little time. Somewhere it rings a bell."

"So it does with me, but only distantly."

"I shall pour myself a drink and put my thinking cap on."

"I hope to God I'm not chasing straws in the wind. They'll be there by now almost."

"I'll ring back if anything stirs in my mind."

Fifteen minutes later Quint rang back.

He said, "You and I often play a light-hearted game with other people's words. And now, suddenly it's a deadly one. I won't give you the Greek, but it's from the *Iliad* and runs— Revenge is sweeter far than flowing honey."

"Christ! Revenge!"

"Seyton?"

"Of course—he's the cause of his ruin."

"Yes, but there could be more to it than that. I'll come up and talk to you. Though we may be too late. They could be there by now."

*   *   *   *

As they crossed the river and turned right along the valley road which would take them to the Park entrance gates, Grandison said from behind, "Don't stop outside the Dower House. Run up the side road which leads to the private chapel. It's only a short walk back. As I said, there are no servants in the house. That was arranged."

"So I was told, sir."

"And this car? Covered?"

Kerslake nodded, the white-painted open gates of the drive coming up into his headlights. "Yes, sir. Not traceable—those were Mr Warboys' orders."

An owl, like a great white moth, floated through the dipped lights ahead, and there was an indifference in Kerslake which he knew he could never have accepted so evenly when he had first entered the service. But now it was routine. Sometimes they told you why—and sometimes they said nothing. He would walk into the Dower House, empty except for Seyton, would talk and maybe have a drink and then be handed whatever had to be handed to him . . . and then with one small movement of his hand from his pocket, holding the little sophisticated weapon . . . almost a toy, but deadly, looking enough like a packet of cigarettes to lull even a moment's suspicion, and noiseless . . . Well, Seyton would go without time for surprise or protest . . . no change of expression, no wince of pain. He had done it all before. The swift flight of life; and then the body in death standing for a second or two as though it still lived and then slowly collapsing . . . dreams, hopes, animal vigour and appetites switched off like a light. This he would do because it was required of him as part of his duties . . . rare, and never enjoyable, but now easily bearable. And this time:

227

Seyton, who had bedded Georgina, known her body, maybe had her love, or something as near to it as she could ever give—but its being Seyton gave him no joy springing from jealousy. The only joy he knew was in power, not his own, but that delegated to him and to be exercised free—if not from a few wayward considerations of morality as now (Quint had once said that no man ever managed to avoid them, no matter how hard or hardened)—then free from guilt on the soul, though some quirk of the body sometimes arose, like looking at a woman, wanting her, undressing her in imagination but finding that the flesh knew no stir . . . but even that passed with time . . .

Driving on side lights, he avoided the Dower House and went up the back drive and parked a few yards from the lychgate of the chapel and switched off the lights.

Grandison said, "Don't rush things. Get what you have to get, and let him see you to the door. Do it there. When the heart fails he will pass over his own threshold and through a greater. And—if you still have the smallest hankering for the conventional—may God forgive us all."

"Yes, sir."

Kerslake got out of the car and began to walk towards the Dower House.

When he was gone, Grandison left the car and walked up the moss-grown path to the chapel. He went in and taking a small torch from his pocket walked towards the altar and the side transept and stood below the memorial plaque to Sarah Satan. Flicking the light up he read the inscription and smiled. *Quantae sunt tenebrae! vae mihi, vae mihi, vae!* Into the darkness . . . woe is me, woe is me . . . woe . . . Well, the great darkness waited for everyone. No man could tell his own day for going. Though others might be able to. Kerslake walking down now to Seyton . . . One day he might write her biography. It all depended. But one biography could not fill out the span of years left to him. Either they must be filled or shortened . . . Well, he had done all he could, had even spoken a Delphic oracle and made himself a hostage to fortune. He felt no sorrow for Seyton. Revenge was sweet, sometimes bitter sweet . . . or sometimes sweeter far than flowing honey. Those who knew him might or might not be able to read the rune. Did he want that? He could find no answer in himself. He was content to wait and know it.

He went back to the car, lit a cigar and waited. The night was full of soft rain noises and the steadier sound of the river close by rushing through shallows. Kerslake would go far, but never to the top. Pigeons and falcons. He smiled, remembering himself as a boy . . . cycling along the coast road with his birds in a hamper strapped to the carrier. Saw them on the roof of his loft, cock birds with puffed gorges, rainbow coloured, courting the hens . . . could remember the time when he had stolen money from his mother's purse to buy a new bird and braved out with convincing sincerity his lack of guilt when challenged . . . just as he had braved out so many sins thereafter.

He waited, and the rain began to fall heavier, and the car grew cold so that he took his whisky flask and, ignoring the flask top cup, drank from it straight. He drank slowly but continuously until he had emptied the flask. Celebration or consolation? he wondered. The gods would give their answer.

He did not hear Kerslake return until there came the sound of the car boot being opened and the thump of a suitcase being dropped into it. Kerslake came round to the front and opened the driving door. He took off his raincoat, shook the drops from it and tossed it on to the front passenger seat. He got in, closed the door gently, and switched on the dim interior light. He turned and looked at Grandison. In the dim light his face looked drawn and jaundiced.

"Well, is it all done?"

"Yes, sir. Everything that I was ordered. The stuff is all in a suitcase at the back."

"No trouble?"

"No, sir. Everything is as you wanted it to be."

Grandison was silent for a moment or two and then he laughed gently. He said, "My dear Kerslake, what a splendid machine you are. Programmed you work perfectly, not even a shade of emotion when you say 'Everything is as you wanted it to be'. Not even the faintest emphasis on the 'you'. Well, there it is. I may have hoped, but did not expect Warboys to let me down. And neither do I expect you to now."

"I'm sorry, sir."

"Well, a little sorrow does not come amiss. So remember this to tell Warboys . . . *All pains are nothing in respect of this, All sorrows short that gain eternal bliss.* So now, do me the last favour of making it short."

"Yes, sir."

Kerslake's hand came from his pocket and there was the faintest hiss of sound, as brief as a sigh. Grandison sat, unmoved, unchanged, a faint ironical smile engraved on his face. And then he slowly toppled sideways.

Kerslake leaned over his seat and pulled the body to the floor and spread the car rug over it. Then he lit himself a cigarette and drove off, his hands steady on the wheel. He had nearly a five-hour drive before him. Once free of the Park he turned the radio on, found music and let it swamp his thoughts.

* * * *

Sitting at his desk, his back to Warboys, who stood staring out of the gap in the almost drawn curtains at the street and car lights reflected on the rain wet ground, Quint listened as Kerslake's voice came reedily over the telephone. He sat very still, tense and still, not from strain or anticipation, but from the iron fast grip of sadness. Years of deep friendship and loyal service were now ended. Grandison had gone.

He said to Kerslake, "I'm sorry you were landed with it. You did well. Bring him in. We want it to look as though he collapsed here in his office. I'll see you later."

He put the receiver down and turned to Warboys.

"Well?"

"Kerslake was puzzled. Said he was sure that Grandison was expecting it and made no move. He even gave him a message for you and it is word for word. Kerslake forgets nothing. He told the old man what he had to do and Grandison answered, 'Well, a little sorrow does not come amiss. So remember this to tell Warboys . . . *All pains are nothing in respect of this, All sorrows short that gain eternal bliss.*' "

Warboys said nothing immediately. He went to a side table and poured brandies for them both, handed Quint one and then raised his glass. "To Grandison—a man whose trust in us we nearly failed, for he relied on us to do for him what his own Catholic faith forbade him the right to do for himself."

"And if we had failed?"

"He would have accepted the fall of the dice. Had his revenge, sweeter than flowing honey, on Seyton, destroyed the tapes and films and come back here unruffled, knowing we would have no power to deny or denounce him without proof."

"And we?"

Warboys smiled and ran a hand over his thin white hair. "We would have accepted it."

"Eventually, gladly. And we came very close to having to. Kerslake said he was almost at the front door with Seyton showing him out when the hall telephone rang and Seyton, answering it, turned to tell him it was me. Kerslake said his hand was already in his pocket."

" 'Fate's hid ends eyes cannot see'—To the truth of that moment when the telephone bell rang Seyton will never be made privy. A lucky man." He sipped his brandy and smiled thinly. "He owes you much for remembering your Homer."

Quint trimmed his cigar and in between his puffs while lighting it, said, "Every man should have a classical education for in the past resides all knowledge. It saved Seyton. What do we do about him?"

Warboys turned and looking through the break in the curtains at the gold and silver lights which rain and street lamps cast over the night world of moving cars and dark shrub and tree shapes in the Park, said, "That which no man can resist given the chance. Play at being God and give him his heart's desire. Give him back Seyton Hall. With luck he'll keep it till his death, and maybe his son, too . . . but in the end if the world runs true to its present course it will become a National Trust institution or, perhaps, more appropriately, a mental asylum, proud manifestations of democracy." He began to move across the room, but at the door he paused and looking back said, "I hope you will approve of Grandison's obituary in *The Times* when it comes. I wrote it for their library a year ago. They will have little updating to do, except to note that he died of heart failure while working. Some day they will probably ask you to prepare one for me. Be kind but not necessarily strictly honest."

Quint smiled through his cigar smoke. "And who shall write mine?"

Warboys said, "I don't know. But someone, I hope, who loves you enough to abstain from telling the full truth. No man wishes that 'Time shall unfold what plighted cunning holds'."

"Not at Birdcage certainly."

*   *   *   *

When he rang the bell, as he always did, it was some time before he heard steps coming to the door. It opened and a short, grey-haired woman with a broom in her hand confronted him.

"Yes, sir?"

The accent was local and the felt slippers she wore for cleaning had a big toe hole in the right one. In the bungalow a radio was playing pop music so loudly that he had to raise his voice and almost shout, "Is Miss Collet in?"

She shook her head. "No, sir. Not here. She's gone. Went early this morning. I'm just a-cleaning up 'fore I take the keys back. Would you be the one she wrote for?"

"Wrote what?"

"Well, the letter. Said someone might call. A Mr Seyton."

"Yes, that's me." As he spoke he knew that something was dying slowly in him.

"I'll get it."

Leaving the door open she shuffled down the hallway and he followed her as far as the door to the lounge and sunroom and stood looking in. The sunroom was bare of any signs of her drawings or work material.

The woman came back and handed him the letter. He thanked her and gave her a pound and walked hurriedly away from her surprised flow of thanks.

He drove off and turned down a side lane and parked at the side of a small fir plantation. A cock pheasant crossed the road ahead, a chiff-chaff was calling tirelessly from a tree top and a slight breeze shook the delicately coloured bells of the wood anemones in the hedge ditch. He opened the letter and read it.

Dear Richard,

This is the way it must be, for any closer way would weaken me too much to follow good sense and accept the inevitable. I'm a good fighter at most things. But not with this. Though I do know in my mind, if not yet entirely in my emotions, that I am doing the right thing but I can't face a lot of harassing talk about it. So I'm off—like a coward. And so I am.

Oh, darling, don't try to come after me and turn things round. It's all been lovely—a bit of Paradise for a time. Look after yourself. There's nothing the human heart can't get over. No loss, or sorrow. You know that.

God bless you,
Georgina.

P.S. You'll feel bloody after reading this. Go over to Nancy and tell her I'll be sending her father something one day. Be nice to her. She's a dear.

He put the letter in his pocket and drove on, back towards the Hall. But as he came to the turn-off to take the side road which crossed the river to Seyton Hall he changed his mind and carried on along the main road.

Nancy was in but her father was out. She made coffee for him and as he sat drinking it he looked up at her, tall, fair-haired . . . so much part of his life from before Ruth and after.

He handed her the letter without a word and watched her as she read it. He said, "Did you know she was going?"

233

She handed the letter back. "Yes, she phoned me very early this morning. I knew how you would feel. I tried to get her to change her mind."

"You did?"

"Why not? If what you feel for her is the truth then I would want the two of you to be together. Want it—but to be honest—not welcome it."

"I can't understand that."

"I know you can't and never will. For you to want something is all. You just go after it. It works in business, maybe. But not with love, because love often means sacrifice of love. Is that incomprehensible to you?"

He smiled faintly. "I think with an effort I could sort it out."

"Try it sometime."

He sighed. "And I thought this was going to be a great day. I'm getting the Hall back—it'll take a little while. I saw her there."

"An addition to the collection of family possessions?"

"You're a bastard, Nancy."

"Of course. So was the first recorded Seyton. Perhaps that's something you would like to have in the family now. A bastard Nancy? Do you think I'm ready to take the risk that it will work? That I don't have any pride? No jealousy either—if you should meet her in one, two, three, four years' time and the both of you go to bed together?"

"In God's name what do you think I am?"

"I think that's something you must find out for yourself."

He stood up, put his hands on her shoulders, and kissed her and found her lips and body unresponsive. As he stepped back from her she smiled at him and said, "Sorry for that outburst. Understanding is one thing. Thawing out is another. You can't have summer without winter first . . . nor passion, nor love and marriage without first the agonies of doubt and anxiety. If you should ever come round to thinking that you love me and want me . . . you'll have to work at it. I'm giving up the habit of falling flat on my back when you walk into the bedroom . . . of running to you when you call. Damn right, I am! I don't know or want to know now how you have worked the Hall thing. All I know is that if you want me you'd better start on it fast because if you don't I won't be around. So now, I say in the nicest way I can manage, you take yourself off and if you want to—think about it. And don't take too long because you might find I may not be available."

"Jesus—what's happened to you?"

"Something, at least, which you should understand—I've just discovered in the attic of my emotions a fascinating left-over called pride."

He laughed then, and said, "You know, I've just discovered something."

"Important?"

"Not very. Just that I don't want coffee. A stiff drink is more in line." He leaned forward to kiss her on the lips again, but she turned her head so that he kissed her cheek.

She laughed and said, "Don't be put off. Keep trying—you've a long way to go. And you know where the drinks are—help yourself."

*　　*　　*　　*

Quint, peering into his little oven to watch the cheese sauce over the dish of ham and celery hearts turning a golden brown, a glass of Chablis in one hand, said, "You've got what you wanted for your father, done some good work, I gather, in Herefordshire—your drawings I mean. As for the other—and it so happens often that way—you were very little needed. Indeed, it would have gone the right way for us even if you had not been there. But . . . that so often happens."

Perched on a kitchen stool, one leg crossed over the other, and seeing that as Quint turned to her they held his eyes, Georgina said, "I did some good work of my own. I've no grumbles, Quinney, my love. And dear Daddy is happy."

"No regrets, then?"

"If there were, I've left them behind. Bulky things to cart around, aren't they?"

235

"I've always found so. What do sad regrets avail?"

"Damn all. I see your Sir Manfred Grandison has died of heart failure."

"How did you know he was ours? Oh, I see—another of Daddy's indiscretions?"

"Could be. Will it mean you go up the ladder?"

"Step by step."

"And your Mr Kerslake following?"

"Possibly."

"Poor twisted-up man."

"Less so, I imagine, soon. He has been sent on vacation—and, I gather, his secretary, a charming brunette, has also taken her vacation at the same time. And what will you do now?"

"There's no problem. I shall fall on my feet somewhere."

"And occasionally on your back?"

"Oh, Quinney . . . how determined you are to make a whore of me."

He laughed gently. "Well—it's an old profession. Older and more respectable even than mine."